JOURNEY TO CALI BANTU

HIGHMIND BOOK THREE
The Final Reckoning

ROXANNE WARD

GO GO PUBLISHING

COPYRIGHT

OTHER BOOKS

Both series trilogies take place in the same setting of post-apocalyptic Colorado with crossover characters and events, but their stories and perspectives are unique. Check out my website by scanning the QR code on the back cover.

The **From Darkness** series. Set in the wilderness of Colorado, it is an action-packed, page-turner with romance, espionage, escapes, rescues, battles, humor, and so much more.

1: *Sins of Survival*   **2:** *Lion's Creed*   **3:** *Reclamation*

The **Highmind** series tells Connor's story, a genetically enhanced child tasked with decoding the rebel secrets in his memories. This is a clean story with a Christian backstory and is appropriate for all readers. Flesch-Kincaid reading level: middle school and above.

1: *Somewhere Else*   **2:** *New Haven*   **3:** *Journey to Cali Bantu*

DEDICATION

Murl and Kennedy

Whether you turn to the right or to the left,
your ears will hear a voice behind you, saying,
"This is the way; walk in it."
Issah 30:21

PROLOGUE

Good evening, I'm Marcus Miller for the *New Haven Evening News.*

We have a breaking story. Tomorrow morning, twelve of our residents will embark on a mission of introduction and exploration. Their goal is to get to know the Fringers by visiting two of their towns and meeting the citizens. We formed an alliance with the Fringers in the heat of battle, so they are no doubt as curious about us as we are of them. Besides growing our relationship, we hope to establish trade.

Henry Wayther, Haru Abar, AnnDrea Channing, Jillian Takota, and Tanya Jansen are offering their expertise in the areas of civil engineering, spiritual leadership, and health services. The biggest surprise is that a minor child will also accompany them to talk to the Fringer children about school.

Gray Takota will lead the Defenders: Jax Nakano, Sargent Beckett, Axle Takota, Easton Mundy, and Lana Sheldon. Lana is a trained Defender, but she is also a journalist and will document the journey as our town's historian. Our adventures will travel to Eagle and then Glenwood Springs along with the Fringer Commander William Alexander and a team of his Guards.

Many of the roads leading from the territories are blocked to protect us from Corporate invaders. But the team is well prepared to defend itself. Haru will hold a prayer meeting tonight at 8:00p.m. at the high school field after the soccer game. And tomorrow morning at 7:00, everyone is invited to take part in the sendoff. We will line Johnson Street starting at Town Hall, and it will continue on to the West Gate access. We hope to see you at these events.

The report included a brief interview with Lana and went on to say thank you and goodbye to three of our citizens. Dr. AnnDrea Channing was leaving the Rapid Aid Center to take over the medical facility at the Hold. Aniya Peters, the Fringer refugee, was also transferring to the Hold to manage their livestock.

Tanya Jansen and Haru Abar were joining the Friendship Tour to establish a circuit ministry for the Fringers. Tanya had spent her incarceration studying to be a minister. She will work as Haru's outreach assistant while she completes her degree at the Hold, which is now called Fort Sentry. After the Friendship Tour, she will remain, and Haru will return.

I watched the news feed as if it weren't happening to me. It was too surreal to accept, too fantastic to be my life. My little sister, Meshka, looked at me with hero-worship and admiration. Not like a big brother kind of hero, more like a stranger she didn't recognize. My dad patted my back like he would a buddy. But I wasn't his buddy. I was his twelve-year-old son, and I was heading out on a dangerous mission. But no one spoke about that. The only sound that competed with the report was the occasional sniffle from my mom as she held me in a tight embrace.

It was too intense, so I excused myself and went to my room. The real me had been outed. I was a Highmind trained to protect this town, and though my name wasn't released in the report, anyone who knew me would figure it out, and tomorrow morning when we were paraded through the town, everyone would know it was me. All my life, I've had to protect my Highmind status and the secrets critical to the rebellion, but I managed it. My secretive nature and my destiny shaped me into who I was.

My grandad taught me how to maintain a casual façade to avoid attention. When we lived in Denver, it kept me out of the Highmind Camp. In New Haven, it eliminated the awkward division of being a genius. Baseball, school and the activities in New Haven kept me engaged, and I enjoyed the interactions. But ever since we started planning the mission, I have been physically isolated.

I didn't attend school. I ate an early breakfast before going to physical training, and after that, I reported to Rand's office, where I had lunch and spent the rest of my day. Then, I had dinner with my family. Gray made sure I had a couple of hours on Saturday and Sunday to hang out with my friends. But my complete absence from school contributed to the rumor that I had a medical condition or a mental illness. If I were honest with myself, both were kind of true.

Until ten minutes ago, the rumors about me implied I was ill, eccentric, crazy, or all of the above, but this report transformed me into a child soldier. It described the mission as one of exploration, which it was, but it omitted the likelihood of attacks and other dangerous situations. It lacked critical details, like why we were going and what we were after.

The residents were smart enough to know it involved more than an impromptu romp through the perilous wilds outside the sanctuary, but no one said it out loud. I went from a sick, crazy kid to a tragic child being sacrificed to a cause. I'm not sure which image I preferred, but I was about to find out. My tablet started humming with messages, and a crowd of those who guessed I was the child had already gathered in front of our house.

Messages poured into my textbox. I prioritized the people close to me at the top of the growing feed, but I hesitated to read them. They would be shocked and angry I didn't warn them. I decided to start with the texts from people I didn't know well. Their replies included a variety of questions. Such as why does a child need to go when a video would do? When will we be back? What do his parents think? A growing number of people guessed it was me, and they were angry that their baseball hero, their description not mine, was heading into danger.

I didn't want to go outside, and my parents agreed, saying my friends should come here. Within minutes, they arrived carrying overnight gear. I wondered whether it was my mom or they who made that decision, but I was happy to spend time with them. When they greeted my parents and settled their gear in my room, the rapid fire of questions began.

"How long have you known about this?" asked Teke.

"What exactly is this about?" Kato said. "This is about more than a meet and greet, or you wouldn't be going."

"Are you scared?" Hayden probed. I had already spilled my story to him in that concrete pipe at the playground. I shouldn't have, but I was glad he was playing along.

"I've told you guys about my grandad, GD. He taught me things that are needed on the mission," I said.

I told them that a forgotten language had been found written in several places in an area that needed to be translated. It was a language my grandad taught me, and I was the only one who knew it. Though I was told to give that explanation, it stretched the truth and left out everything they would have wanted to know; in other words, it was a lie.

"Why don't they just take pictures and bring them back for you to read? Why do they need to take a kid with them?" Kato retorted. I could feel his ire rising.

It was a good question, and I knew this could go very wrong in a hurry. I had to shut this conversation down.

"If the message is about the surrounding area, they won't know what we needed pictures of. I need to see more than the symbols to translate it accurately," I answered confidently. I didn't want to be viewed as a victim. I was a valuable member of an important mission. "I want to go. They didn't want to take me, but I convinced them they had to."

"Are you crazy?" blurted Kato loudly. "Do you remember what it's like out there? Nothing has changed. What did your parents say?"

"Well, they were heated, for sure, but Gray convinced them I'd be well protected. And yes, I guess I am a little crazy, but I'm excited too," I was trying to temper the mood and answer calmly. But inside, I was a wreck.

"You're being awfully quiet, Hayden," Teke uttered with a tinge of irritation. "Our best friend could be heading towards his death, and you act like," he stopped mid-sentence. "It's almost like... wait. Did you know?"

I interrupted before Hayden could speak. "He only knew I was working on a classified project at Town Hall, and I got in trouble for telling him that." Hayden nodded at my answer. Such a simple gesture, but a lie just the same. Now, my lies trapped him too. Here I am again, tangled in secrets and problems. Will there ever be a time when I'm not?

I shook my down-turned head. "Look, I wish I could spill my guts here. You deserve to know, and I trust you. But I can't. I'm sworn to secrecy. And so are you because I confessed to working on a classified project. Please don't take it personally. And unless you want serious trouble, say nothing but what you read in the reports. You may think everyone here is loyal and honest, but..."

"But what?" Teke demanded.

"Well, look what happened to me in the Hold, and then to Zoey when we first got here. And then Dewy was attacked. People are people, and sometimes they lose it." I was proud of that answer. It was logical, undisputable, and not a lie.

"Okay, but what are you looking for in this old language infested area?" Kato questioned.

"Bros before foes," I said while holding up my hands and shaking my head. They stopped their inquiries immediately. It was the signal we had agreed upon, reminding us we could disagree and end conversations without jeopardizing our friendship. Though it could stop the discussion, it couldn't stop them from conjuring up their own answers as well as worries. "I am leaving in the morning, and I was hoping we could just hang out. I see you guys came ready to spend the night. Let's just have fun." I was on the verge of tears, and Teke put his arm around me.

"You never answered Hayden's question," Kato said. "Are you scared?"

"Honestly, I'm mortified."

Hayden covered his face while leaning on his hands, and Teke and Kato hugged me. This was as intense as telling my parents and just as painful.

Morning came early, and after exchanging our last goodbyes, I watched them fade down the tunnel as they headed to breakfast without me. I packed my new gear bag onto the bus, taking my family to the Town Hall. They led us to the conference room and served us breakfast sandwiches while we waited for the briefing in the Legislative Room. I had eaten little dinner, and the sandwich tasted so good. I wondered what we would eat on the road. Was this my last tasty meal, or perhaps my last?

The briefing included everyone involved in the mission, whether they were going or remaining to provide support. It was a beautiful chamber, and I remember wishing I could be here to see official business being conducted. Well, here I am. Not sure this was what I had in mind. This was more than official business; it was top-secret, life-and-death business. My life or death.

The meeting was a review of all the previous gatherings, laying out the towns we would stop at, the safe areas, as well as everyone's duties. We would follow a prepared route to the Hold and pick up the Guards. The approach to every aspect of this mission had a military drumbeat, and the strict discipline of the team members was palpable. I wondered if I was to be held to the same standard as these trained soldiers.

Jilly and Gray sat on either side of me. In our last meeting, Gray had responded to my condolences about the loss of their unborn child with a frustrated quip, trying to hang on to his control. Understanding, I didn't push further. I hadn't seen Jilly since I learned about her miscarriage. I wanted to reassure her and let her know I cared deeply and grieved with her, but this was neither the time nor the place. I grabbed her hand and tilted my head toward her. She gave me a sad but kind smile, which I returned with a knowing nod. It was more meaningful than any words.

We all gathered on the buses parked in the columned alcove to take us back to the security building. Hundreds of residents filled the streets, cheering and waving signs of support. I saw my three best friends. I could feel their pain because it matched my own. From there, we loaded our gear onto a cargo trailer and drove to the West corridor, passing just as many well-wishers on our way.

Inside a large storage room, the four Mini-Brutes sat waiting. Several rows of Defenders stood at attention, saluting us as we made our way to the vehicles. It was alarmingly similar to the formation they presented at Hannah's funeral.

My mother hugged me in front of the open door of the armored transport. My dad and little sister joined in, and she handed me a thick envelope.

"I've been writing you letters and drawing you pictures ever since I learned you were going on a trip. You can have them with you to look at whenever you want. They will work even if your tablets die." The last word had her swallowing hard and sniffling back a cry. I found myself doing the same.

"You take good care of him," my mother said to Gray and Jilly.

"With my life," Gray answered.

It was a strange hug-fest. My mom was hugging my dad, my dad was hugging Mesh, and all of them were hugging me. I selfishly wanted all those extra hugs. They could hug each other after I left, but I guess they needed each other's support.

"I love you all so much," I said, trying to disguise the quiver in my voice. "I promise I'll come back to you," a promise I had no right to make. "And every day, I'll think of you and know you're thinking of me," I said while holding the envelope and winking at my little sister. My mom gave me a last squeeze, and I got into the vehicle.

Suddenly, my dad jumped into the Brute and took the seat next to me and behind Gray. No one asked him to leave. I was the only one with a surprised expression. I turned to Gray, but he was looking forward and shifting the rig into gear.

CHAPTER 1

"Dad!" I said under my breath. "What are you doing?"

"I'm riding with you to Fort Sentry. They need help setting up their road maintenance program. I've been working on road crews my whole life, and I just finished my civil engineering degree, so I volunteered to come. I thought it would be a good way to spend some time together."

I was surprised, and I wondered how much he knew about our true mission and how much I should discuss. He knew we were looking for a place that would help us defend our home and the homes of the Fringers, but I doubt he knew much more than that.

He was leaning forward to talk with Gray, so I settled my head against the Brute's side and closed my eyes. Though I was tired from staying up with my friends, I wasn't sleepy. But it made people leave me be while I sorted my thoughts.

Looking back over the last two years, I reviewed the wild series of events that turned my life inside out. I lived on the bottom rung of a post-apocalyptic society in the Denver area. Grandad was an architect, and he built his house and underground bunker to survive the meteorite storm that hit the Earth decades ago. My mother grew up in that house, and so did I until last year.

My grandad, GD to me, was my best and only friend since the Corporate run Territory of Colorado allowed no time for friendships. When he died in a work accident, I discovered his world of subterfuge. I was stunned when I stumbled upon his rebellious stash. He was part of a plan to secure a better future, but his involvement ensured certain death if discovered.

Before that, I never thought beyond the current week. We were Dailys, the laborers of society. We were given life one week at a time. Speaking of more could jeopardize our meager allotments. But GD had done more than speak about it. He enrolled our family in a secret program for sanctuary. After he died, my parents were contacted. Initially, we had to move to Fairplay, and then we were brought to a training facility called the Hold and eventually to our home in the free society of New Haven.

New Haven was a dream come true. Tucked safely in the Eisenhower tunnels, it was sealed off from the Corporate rule because of a staged radiation accident. We went from horrid conditions to a world with more than we had imagined. Suddenly, we had so many wonderful things, making life comfortable, fair, and safe. I remember thinking I was finally free—no more hiding, no more secret clues to solve. All I had to do was be a kid.

If someone had told me back then that I would leave my comfortable home, in my beloved free society, to join a military team, to find a secret place, and overthrow the Corporates, I would have thought such a person insane. But here I am, on the road to join the Fringers to search for Cali Bantu.

What is Cali Bantu? No one knows, but most experts think it is a cave that holds a weapon or a cache of weapons. I think back on the long trail of clues that led us on this journey. I was just an infant when my grandad realized I inherited the Highmind traits. He and I spent a lot of time together. He taught me to solve puzzles and memorize historical facts, which were strictly forbidden. I thought it was fun, and keeping secrets gave me a sense of power in a world where I had none. But it turned out not to be all fun and games. Though he expected to carry out the plan himself, he trained me to be his backup in the plot to overthrow the Corporates.

His intensive tutoring and my genetically elevated intellect are the reasons I, a mere twelve-year-old, am required to go on this dangerous trek. It should be my grandad sitting here, but his destiny is now mine. There will be more clues and traps to navigate when we reach the cave, and possibly some on the way too. When I think about it too long, the fear of what we will face clenches my insides into a tangled ball of nerves. Being young does not guarantee me any mercy, and the knowledge I hold guarantees me a horrific fate if I'm captured.

And then there's the Fringers. Four short months ago, I believed these wild tribes were marauders. Stealing goods, children, and even whole families to do the hard work of living on the fringes of the frigid wilderness. Those were the stories I grew up on, and they couldn't have been more wrong.

They used to live in tribes of twenty to thirty, who seasonally traveled within a certain area to avoid Corporate detection. They survived by farming, hunting, and trading with other tribes. But last year, that routine changed.

The Pueblo Territory began kidnapping its women and girls. Even the cruel Corporate Elites did not sanction these attacks, and to keep the peace, William of the Guard, the Fringer military leader, brokered a deal with them. The Fringers wouldn't let the Dailys know about their free lifestyle, emboldening them to join them, and the Corporates would allow the Fringers to establish permanent homes west of the Continental Divide without interference.

It worked out for both sides. Since the tunnel's closure, the region had become difficult to govern, and the Fringers didn't have to live on the run. I am sure there is more to this story because Corporates don't make deals with commoners; they get rid of them. We were told it would be too hard to find all the nomads, but I didn't buy that either. Assembling them into easy targets sounded more like their style. One thing was certain: the

Fringers wouldn't be allowed to have this privilege for long, so defensive preparations were necessary.

Last spring, William of the Guard came across the Hold, the day after our Defenders were attacked. He saw evidence of a battle, causing him to ask, who had won, and were they inside? It was the battle that caused us to abandon the stronghold because we worried it had been discovered. And we knew we could not win a battle against a full regiment of Corporate soldiers.

When William got inside one of the four high-tech buildings, with the help of a dying invader, he found it abandoned. Despite his worries that the victorious owners may come back to claim it, he moved his small team of soldiers in and established the Fringer Guard Army.

Many thought it was deserted because of its overly remote location. Others thought it was because it was on the tunnel side of the mountain range. It was called the Poison Tunnel by the locals. The highly publicized contamination story was sent out by our town founder to keep our sanctuary town safe.

He had been training the Guard soldiers for several months. His tech man, Relic, hacked into the remaining computers and theorized that the Poison Tunnel wasn't deserted. He thought it held a fully resourced, well-armed, advanced community hiding from the Corporate rulers. When the Guard heard that Corporate soldiers were heading toward the old Eisenhower tunnel, William checked out Relic's theory.

There was no evidence the Corporates knew about the hidden town, or they would have sent a much larger army. William concluded they were looking for the missing Dranger team they had sent to investigate this highly camouflaged area.

It was only a matter of time before the Corporates discovered the occupied tunnel and the Fringer's Fort Sentry. The Guard commander knew the Fringers couldn't stand against the Corporates. They needed allies, and he had a gut feeling he might find them inside the mysterious tunnel. He hoped that by helping these unidentified people fight their approaching enemies, that his army and theirs could join forces. His gamble paid off for both his people and ours.

I opened my eyes and saw my dad, watching out the windshield as we drove through the passageway hidden beneath the west yard. Mesmerized by the engineering feat of the excavated escape route, he leaned forward, asking Gray numerous questions about its construction. When we paused briefly to wait for the outer door to open, my dad moved to the front seat, Jilly went to sit with Dr. Channing, and Aniya moved into my dad's spot. My dad and Gray were diving into the logistics of sabotaging connecting routes to protect the town from a large offensive attack. Their conversation morphed into the impressive engineering of New Haven's two tunnels, each and one-third miles long, filled with comfortable, safe, free, and happy residents.

Aniya sat next to me with a book in her hand. After a polite but brief exchange, she immersed herself in her novel. It was a relief to me because I wasn't good at chit-chat. I couldn't think of anything relevant to say to her, or any girl for that matter. I was still recovering from having my heart ripped out of my chest by the Sandra debacle.

I was equally glad my dad was sitting with Gray because I didn't know what to say to him either. We are close about some things, but this inherited destiny has caused me to keep lots of secrets from everyone. For years I've kept everything about who I am, what I know, and this mission from him. I have kept so many secrets that it's a wonder he can trust me, or forgive me, but he does. Well, he says he does.

Finally, we stopped for a pee break at a spot Gray called Maryland Creek. "Hey, G Man," I said, using the nickname I gave him. "My dad wants to talk with me, 'spend some time'," I said with air quotes.

He spoke before I could ask my question. "He is fully aware there are limits to what you can share, and, more than that, he understands it. Remember, our 'purpose'," he used his own air quote notation, "for this trip is to visit the Fringer towns to introduce ourselves. Truth be told, we will do that. We thought about introducing you as our school spokesperson, but we decided it was too risky. The Corporates are very aware that a Highmind offspring will have a role in locating Cali Bantu. They would be highly suspicious of a child traveling with soldiers."

I was suddenly alarmed. "So how is that going to work? Will you lock me away every time we hit a town?" My squeaking voice betrayed my composure.

Gray laughed, "Is your voice changing?"

"You're deflecting, *sir,*" I said with the disdain my ire was building.

"We have a plan we will put into play at Fort Sentry, but before I get into it, I want to get there and ensure the pieces are in place." He completely ignored my jab at his authority.

"So, no hint about how you plan to mess with my life?" Sarcasm radiated from every aspect of me.

"Nope," he said with a sly grin. "But you won't be locked away for long. We'll leave and go on an adventure," he paused before adding with a gleam in his eye, "to the lake!"

I climbed into the back seat with my dad. Jilly asked to be closer to the front windshield to ease her motion sickness. There was an awkward tension between us, so I opened a conversation directly.

"Are you angry with me?" I asked.

"You mean for lying and putting yourself in mortal danger?" My dad could be direct as well.

"Oh, no, not that. I meant for taking the last turkey sandwich," I said with a sarcastic grin. He laughed.

"No, I'm not mad at you. If Deegan were here, I'd have some harsh words for *him,* but I know he had an impossible choice. If your mom had shown Highmind traits, she would have been in your shoes, and I may have never met her or had you. It's hard to know what to wish for."

"I have felt that way for as long as I can remember," I answered, and he turned a warm, but sad smile my way.

"No, I'm not mad, Connor. I'm terrified for you, I'm shocked at all you've dealt with, and I'm extremely proud of you, but no, I'm not angry."

"Did you come because you want to protect me?" I love and regard my father highly, but he is not trained for this kind of duty.

"Well, of course, I'm here for you first. I wouldn't hesitate to throw down everything I had to stand between you and harm, but Gray, Will, and almost everyone else on this mission is better qualified than me to address that. Bannon asked me to assess the road conditions, plan ways to sabotage Corporate access, and develop a repair and maintenance plan. But there's another reason too.

"When I was seventeen, my sister, Diane, got married to a Daily, named Roger. The Corporates don't like family members living near each other. Heaven forbid we should care for and support one another. So, they were assigned jobs and housing in Castle Rock. As you know, Dailys aren't allowed to leave their town, so when we said goodbye, I knew I'd never see her again.

"That was hard enough, but two days after they left, the Neighwah came around asking if we had seen them. After roughing my parents and me up, they concluded we didn't know where they were. They said the only other answer was that the Fringers had kidnapped them.

"We were devastated. We imagined them enslaved or worse. But now that I know more about the Fringers, I asked Will if they could have escaped and joined one of the tribes. He had Nash do some investigating, and there is a couple, around the same age, in Breckenridge named Dilly and Roge. Dilly was the name I used to call her," my dad said with an emotional mood pouring from his face.

"Why didn't you ever tell me that?"

"Well, I guess we all have secrets we protect the people we love from. The good news is, when we head back, and you go on," he paused and gave me a concerned frown, "they are taking me to Breckenridge to see if it's her."

"Those," I said, "are the kind of secrets I wish I had."

"Well, now you do."

We talked for a bit longer before the road and scenery pulled at our attention. My dad started dozing off, which gave me time to contemplate having a living aunt and uncle. Maybe I had cousins too. Then I remembered I would spend time at a lake tomorrow. I had never seen an actual lake before, let alone visit one. I had studied many pictures on my tablet, and several movies had incorporated lakes into their stories, but to see one for myself. Wow, that had my attention. And it kept my attention for several more miles.

We had already driven past a large town named Silverton, which had been abandoned after the tunnel accident was staged. The first inhabited Fringer town we expected to stop at was Eagle, but that would be after our visit to Fort Sentry.

As we stood next to the UTVs, our bag lunches were handed out, and everyone returned to the vehicles. In our vehicle, the Brute, only Gray, Jilly, and I were traveling onward to complete the mission. Dr. AnnDrea Channing, Tanya Jones, and Aniya Peters were moving to Fort Sentry to fill permanent positions. Haru Abar and my father had plans to stay long enough to organize their projects. Then my dad would go to Breckenridge, and Haru would return to New Haven.

That left Gray, Jilly, Lana, Jax, Beckett, Mack, and me going to Cali Bantu. Axle and Easton would join us after we left the Fort. They were on sweep duty, which meant they followed at a distance as covertly as possible to address trouble.

The Brute was bouncing down the road like a discarded can in a rough street game when we came to a sudden stop. A fallen tree blocked our way, but before everyone was fully out of the cab, the Defenders were revving up their chainsaws and working on the problem. I walked away from the road to stretch my legs when I saw Jilly hanging onto a tree. She was getting sick. I went to her.

"Jilly, are you okay?"

"Yeah, it's just motion sickness. The road has been rough, and I'm not used to riding for this long."

"You're probably still weak from ..." I stopped mid-sentence, not meaning to bring up her miscarriage.

"It's okay, Conner. And you're right. My body is still a bit out of whack, but I'm fine, honestly. I'll be right behind you. I just need a minute. Please keep this between us. Gray is already worried sick about me."

I gave her a thumbs up. She was already looking better, so I walked back, but I watched the path, waiting for her to emerge. A few minutes later, I saw her making her way to the Brute, smiling like nothing had happened.

CHAPTER 2

Though I-70 was listed as a well-maintained paved road, it didn't come close to the smooth streets of New Haven. It had many patches, cracks, and places where damage had taken it down one lane. Highway 9 was what they called semi-paved. It was much rougher and, at times, punishing. Considerable potholes littered the remnants of the old thoroughfare, and cracks created rises and falls requiring careful navigation. Its deteriorated patches upon patches left chunks of debris, which made for a lot of swerving.

It was a bumpy ride, but to me, it was tolerable. I looked back at Jilly, who was curled up with her eyes closed, but she didn't look sick. She was asleep. Dr. Channing sat next to her and saw me checking on her. She gave me a smile and a thumbs-up sign.

I had seen several creeks and rivers when my family was driven from Denver to Fairplay, but we didn't pass any lakes. On the last leg of our trip, we came to the Blue River, which used to be the Green Mountain Reservoir. The old water level left a stark line of younger vegetation. We were told the water was up to that line before the dam broke. It must have been quite a sight, but without water, and having never seen a lake, I had to use my imagination and the images I had seen on my tablet.

Suddenly, for no apparent reason, we stopped in the middle of the road. Gray, Jax, Mack, and Beckett got out of their various UTVs. Gray reached into a thick stand of bushes on the side of the road and spoke behind his covered hand. Retracting his hand, he and the other Defenders pushed the bush-covered gates open, revealing a densely forested dirt road. We drove through the opening, while four Defenders stood waiting with brooms and bags of gravel to cover our detour. I tried to remember the drive to the Hold. *Is this the last stop we made before arriving?* We had no windows in the transport that took us there, or in the one that took us to New Haven. With no visible references, I couldn't be sure.

If we thought the roads were rough before, we were now treated to an old gravel road badly in need of gravel. It had gone through several brutal seasons, which could have altered the road I remembered. This one was no more than a packed dirt trail full of deep ruts and sloppy puddles. The caravan of Brutes, true to their name, plowed through each hazard with ease. Gray seemed to enjoy the sport of four-wheeling a bit too much, and Jilly was looking green again.

Dr. Channing was sitting with her in the back, holding a bag in case she lost control. I also felt rattled by the jarring ride. Few of us were used to traveling by vehicle, so many felt its effects. When Gray turned to check on his suddenly quiet passengers, he saw the seats full of pale riders.

Pulling over, he announced, "I think we need a break."

We slowly poured ourselves out and into the beautiful day. The skies were clear blue, and a refreshing breeze wafted around us and into our lungs. Between the chilly air and the still ground beneath my feet, I felt instantaneous relief. Jilly was taking a little longer to regain her composure. She, Dr. Channing, and several others told Gray they would walk ahead and get picked up on the way. Gray traded vehicles with Jax, and after picking up the walkers, we pulled onward to Fort Sentry.

We passed an active lake with a restored dam called Black Creek Reservoir. It was the primary source of electricity for the Hold, now the fort. Jax said it was small as lakes go, but I had never seen one beyond the dried-up formation we had passed earlier. It held a massive amount of water. It made me wonder what standing in front of an ocean would be like. I hoped I would see that someday, which brought me back to the mission and the someday wishes it put at risk. We had a long journey ahead of us with an unfathomable amount of work to accomplish, and a plethora of terrifying unknowns.

"Can we swim in that water?" I asked Jax, remembering Gray's promise to take me to a lake.

Jax turned slightly to answer me. "It's pretty cold, but I bet it would feel refreshing on a hot day."

It wasn't long before we turned onto another minor road and headed up a rise. I remembered the feeling of going up a hill, and I knew we were close. When we got to the top of the rise, Jax stopped to let us see the view. It was breathtaking. I could see the reservoir we passed and another, a much larger lake, further up Black Creek Road. From our perch, I could see everything in miniature. I had never witnessed a view from high ground. It stunned me that all this had been outside of our Hold home, and we never got to see it. I didn't want to get back into the Brute, and I didn't want to get locked up in a building again.

Before relinquishing my outdoor freedom, I turned around, trying to locate the Hold buildings, but all I saw was a tangled forest. It looked... odd and unnatural, making me squint my eyes hoping to get a clearer view. Coming up the trail was a man on a horse. It was the Commander of the Guard. As he approached, it reminded me that as of now, that he and Gray shared command. I wasn't sure how I felt about that.

"Welcome to Fort Sentry," he said in a smooth, deep voice. "It's right over there," he pointed, "but it's camouflaged."

He pointed to the same area I had struggled to see before. I concentrated on the area again, but my eyes couldn't focus correctly. It was thick and blurry, like an impressionistic painting. Everyone was straining to see something in the direction he gestured, but we were all fooled. I thought back to the attack where Hannah lost her life and Dewy was gravely injured. We were told the Drangers who attacked our Defenders had stumbled upon it, and since none of the enemy soldiers survived, it was still a secret. I had doubted that report until now.

As we drove closer to the buildings, I could see the paint shimmer and reflect its environment. Fascinating. We parked in the central area of the buildings. Standing outside, I looked down at the pavement, which did not have the same chameleon effect when viewed up close. I guess that's why I never noticed.

We exited the rigs, and Commander William Alexander jumped down from his horse to shake hands with everyone and gestured them inside. The Alpha building was mostly the same, but the fences around the activity area were gone. Six long container structures stood where the curtain homes had been, and unlike the crowded place I remembered, only four people were in the vast open area. It gave the building a strange, empty vibe. I wondered if they had been sent away because of me. My attention was drawn to two men dressed in civilian clothes walking our way.

"Hi," one civilian said. "My name is Relic." A chorus of greetings chanted from our team.

I remembered that he had been one of the people who came to New Haven to retrieve the injured Guard soldier. He had intensely scrutinized our town, and I wasn't sure about him. The other man held out his hand, and I recognized him too. He was the one with the kind smile.

"I'm Taylor, Will's adopted father."

Before our group could offer any introductions, a soldier approached.

"Commander, the briefing room is prepared."

"Thank you, Nash. This way," the leader of the Guard ordered, and we followed without question.

We were led into what we used to call the DOR (Defender Operations Room) and was now the GOR. Walking past the many desks with computers, view screens, and communication devices, we were led to a small elevator where we were ushered in four at a time. On the second level, it opened into a short hall, and the commander led us into a sizable room housing a large table with a dozen chairs positioned around it. Our team of ten and the six Fringers filed in, and when all were present, we filled every empty chair, leaving several soldiers standing. Commander Alexander sat at the head of the table and reintroduced Relic, seated to his left, and Taylor at the other end, and the soldiers left standing were Rival and Nash. We, in turn, gave our introductions.

Commander Alexander began. "This will be a short briefing. The topic is our youngest team member." On cue, everyone looked at me. "It was reported at New Haven that Connor was chosen for his 'unique abilities'. Though the reporter meant no harm in adding this assumption, if this impression is connected to Connor, the Corporates will believe he is a Highmind. He must be protected at all times.

"It is unlikely the report will escape the secure town of New Haven, but if it does, it will be difficult to contain. Therefore, we must alter our initial plan. We believe the best way to protect him is to change his identity. As far as any of you know, this boy is the son of a Lone Fringer who came here for medical treatment from our new doctor. He will be kept in a secure location until tomorrow morning. A healer woman from McCoy will arrive and walk him in front of the Guards present and into the infirmary. Since he is a stranger, do not interact with him. Are there any questions?"

Jax raised her hand. "Are you worried you have dissidents in your army?"

"I have no reason to doubt my people, but only a fool would dismiss the possibility," he said with a tinge of annoyance. "Traitors have more opportunities outside of a locked-up town to make connections or be compromised. Therefore, we keep much from our troops until they have a need to know."

Haru was next. "What is a Lone Fringer?"

"A Lone Fringer does not belong to a tribe, or a town. We have people from every Fringer tribe in the area. There is little doubt that every child from the towns and tribes would be known by someone here. But few, if any, would know a Lone Fringer's child."

Dr. Channing raised her hand. "Can I assume more information will come my way since he will be my patient?"

"Your patient will arrive with his paperwork completed for you. For tomorrow, all you need to tell anyone is that his condition is not contagious. But you will be briefed on our infirmary policies."

CHAPTER 3

I reflected on my life ever so briefly. I had never been completely honest with anyone since GD. Though I shared much with Hayden, I was a blur to everyone, including myself. It was then I realized I might live this way the rest of my life, which might not be long.

I reluctantly raised my hand but looked down at the table. I did not want this foreboding man using his gaze to tear into my soul, especially since I had only recently discovered I had one. "What's my name?" I asked sincerely.

It wasn't meant as a joke, but everyone began laughing. I gave a weak smile and steeled myself. I felt my lip quiver, threatening to betray my lack of courage in the room filled with talls. I couldn't admit to all these alpha soldiers that I was unfit for the duty before me. The premise of combat is that people get horribly injured and some die. It terrified me. I was restless, and taking flight had more than a passing appeal. I tried to steady my breathing. My dad saw through my armor and grabbed my hand under the table.

Gray gave me a probing, investigative stare. "I'd stay with Connor," he said. "It's what you're used to. Fewer mistakes will be made that way." I rolled my eyes slightly. Remembering was not my problem.

Haru whispered something to Gray, and he nodded.

"You don't have to decide right now," said the Fringer commander. "But we will need to know soon." When no one raised any more questions, he signaled the soldier, Nash, who bent down and responded quietly to his commander's question. Then the leader turned back to us. "Okay, everyone who is not going on the extended portion of our tour will follow the Guard soldiers to your quarters. Your gear has already been taken to your rooms."

Gray looked at me and added, "Connor, you will wait downstairs for a few with Haru, who will go over the details of your assignment for tomorrow's ruse." Although those not joining us on the extended mission didn't know the actual goal, I doubted they were naïve enough to believe all this secrecy was about introducing New Haven citizens to the Fringer towns.

As we left, Nash and Rival sat down, and four more soldiers filed in. I noticed their multilayered uniforms weren't...well, uniform, nor were the weapons they had holstered on their sides. I admired their courage and dedication to the cause, realizing they had scraped together what they had to form an effective army. But I was glad we had brought better weapons and winter gear for them.

Haru, my dad, and I allowed the first group of three to use the elevator. As we waited, I saw the ladder behind a metal gate.

"Can we use the ladder?" I asked. I needed to do something physical to ease my anxiety, and the last thing I wanted was to be trapped in a tiny elevator.

Haru shrugged, and my dad said, "No one said we couldn't." When we were Dailys, my dad was compliant and fearful. But he had become more spirited and confident since we moved to New Haven.

Haru went first, then me, and then my dad. There was only one person in the computer room. His crutches leaned on the desk beside him, and I wondered if he was the soldier who had been treated at our hospital for a serious leg injury.

I watched our group walk by the one-way glass window where Haru, my dad, and I waited for instructions.

"Hi, I'm Hunter," said the soldier, propping himself on his crutches. "I was told to keep Mr. Abar and Connor here. Mr. Wayther, you will go with the group heading to your quarters." My dad waved at us and left to catch up with the group. Then Hunter turned to us and said. "You can sit anywhere you want. It shouldn't be too long."

"Are you the soldier who was treated at New Haven?" I asked.

"Yes," he answered. "I guess it caused a lot of issues."

"Everyone understood you deserved good care, especially since without your troops, we would have lost the battle. People were worried, but not about you personally. New Haven citizens are terrified of two things: being discovered and disease, and you represented both. But I hear you will make a full recovery. That's what matters."

He smiled. I was brimming with nervous energy, and Hunter seemed to notice.

"Hey, come with me. I know you've been rocking down those roads all day. I think I know just what you need. We have a workout room close by."

As he grabbed his crutches, I noticed a scar that ran across his right knuckles. Interesting. He swung his body between the crutches like a pro, leading us out of the command center and into the hall that accessed the infirmary, Haru's old office, and the storage room. My nervousness suddenly morphed into a full-blown panic attack.

"Is he okay?" asked Hunter.

Haru nodded and gestured for Hunter to give us some privacy. The soldier reluctantly started his hobbled plant and swing gait back to his post.

"Connor," Haru was holding my shoulders, "I understand this room holds the memory of being kidnapped, but I think it's one you're ready to face."

"What if I can't face it? What if I can't find this Cali Bantu, access it, and do whatever I'm supposed to do once we're inside?" I could feel my body shaking, and Haru held my shoulders tighter to steady me.

"You are a survivor, not a victim. And you're definitely not a quitter. You are one of the bravest people I know. Look at all you've done. Keeping your grandad's information safe, standing up to the Defenders to save your dog, starting a baseball league, discovering the location of Cali Bantu, and that's a modest summary of your achievements. You are a phenomenon. It's more than anyone, let alone a child, should have to shoulder, but you've accomplished every step and duty with clarity and success. I believe in you. Everyone I've spoken to is amazed by all you've done. They're honored to be a part of this journey. You aren't a tag-along on this mission, Connor. You *are* the mission."

Even I had to admit, my list of accomplishments surpassed any other kid I knew. However, recognizing that only made me glad they didn't have to.

"Take a breath," Haru said, and I did. "How about we just take a look inside? Then, when you're ready, we'll walk in there like we own the place. Okay?" I nodded, straightened my posture, breathed in deeply, and grabbed the door handle with my sweaty palm.

My chest was throbbing with every beat of my heart. Opening my tightly shut eyes, I saw a well-lit room full of exercise equipment encircling a centralized floor mat. Shelves sat along the walls, full of bands, weights, balls, and jump ropes. The creepy, dark storage room that was once crowded with boxes stacked above my head, where I waited in terror, transformed into a gym. It looked a lot like the gym in New Haven. This was a smaller version, but it was familiar.

I walked straight in and climbed onto one of the stationary bikes. Like the bikes at the New Haven gym, the tension was set too high, but I knew how to adjust it. Peddling moderately at first, I quickly rose on the peddles and built up to a furious pace. Haru looked at me like a proud father.

"Oorah!" I yelled while pumping my fist like we did in training.

The timer on my bike read fourteen minutes when a Guard soldier came in and stopped our workout. I noticed he had the same knuckle scar Hunter had. Very interesting. He led us back through the hall to the command center, where we went separate ways. Haru was shown to his quarters, and I was motioned back to the conference room on the second floor. Still pumped with energy, I climbed the ladder. I dreaded going back into that room, knowing that ways to stash me away had been the lion's share of the conversation they had without me.

Fourteen people were sitting or standing around the room. One open seat remained, positioned between the two commanders, William and Gray. The imposing dark soldier had his hands on the table, and I saw the same scar on his knuckles. I quickly scanned the hands of the Guard soldiers and noticed the familiar slashing scar was present on every one of them. It was evidence of some barbaric ritual. Who were these people?

All eyes focused heavily on me as I took my place. It reminded me of a Western movie. There was always that one horse no one wanted to ride, and in walks the new greenhorn, desperate to prove himself. The air crackles with anticipation, and expectations of failure hang like foreboding clouds on the horizon. In the movies, he always succeeds because the script deems it so, but reality has no script. It flows like a cruel river with unknowns around every bend.

The conversation circled the table as the soldiers introduced themselves, sharing details they wanted me to know. The two military leaders agreed to share command, but so far, Commander Alexander had dominated this meeting. He discussed the revised protocols concerning my new status, which didn't involve any big changes for anyone except me. Again, I am going into hiding, both physically and mentally. Yay.

"There is one more person who will join us further down our route. He is a Fringer tracker who is familiar with the area we will travel through." Commander Alexander gestured toward me, and again everyone's attention was on me. It was ironic how quickly I stepped in and out of invisibility. One moment I was isolated, and the next I was everyone's focus. Aside from the danger of dying violently, I had looked forward to this mystery shrouded adventure, but now it crouched, ready to pounce.

"His protection," again all eyes pointed my way, "is paramount to our objective. We must protect him and maintain his cover story. Connor, have you decided on a name?" I looked around the room. Before me were real people with unique personalities, memories, dreams, families, and lives they treasured. The thought of even one of them being harmed or lost defending me was unbearable. Choosing a false name felt like a childish game, and I didn't believe it would fool anyone.

"I ... I'm not sure yet." This day had been difficult, and my nerves were threadbare. I desperately needed to put an end to the pressure weighing down on me. They were all looking at me, waiting for this punk kid to fall apart, so I used that perceived immaturity to gear down the pace. "Not to sound like a kid, but when's dinner?"

The room erupted in laughter, the kind that comes when a moment of brevity releases tension. This crowd didn't know what to make of me. They saw a child, someone to manage and protect, but I was presented as an enigma, a question mark. Giving them what they expected set their world back on its rational tracks, and they were instantly relieved. Gray knew me better than to fall for my ploy, and he mouthed the word *touché.*

Jilly spoke when the noise died down. "I agree. It's late, and this day has dragged on long enough."

I expected to stay at the old Defender barracks, where all Defenders assigned to this building bunked when it was the Hold. But the commander had remodeled that much larger space into a studio apartment for himself. The old commander's office became the on-call duty quarters where I was to stay by myself.

The walls were devoid of décor except for a full-length mirror near the door, with a sign listing dress code requirements. Two sets of oversized bunk beds sat on opposing walls, with a pair of lockers at the foot of each. Directly in front of the door stood a square table with my gear, but no chairs. All the furnishings were the same ones we had in our curtain home, except there were bunk beds instead of cots.

Memories of my stay at the Hold came rushing back to me. I remember feeling unbelievably lucky to discover I could learn, play, and speak freely for the first time in my life. Hiding my grandad's castle and working on my new tablet at a table just like this one brought a smile to my face. It would make a great place to write in my journal. I ran my hand along the edge and made a note to ask for a couple of chairs.

A dinner of wild game steaks, fresh green beans, and buttered bread was delivered to my room. It came with a glass of fresh cow's milk and cookies. My memory flashed to the overly joyful young woman who gave us cookies the day we arrived here. I had never had a cookie before. We had milk at New Haven, but it was a combination of goat's milk and powdered non-fat milk. Cattle need a lot of space and grains, so there must be one or more ranches and farms near here. I took a sip. It was rich and creamy and ice cold. Excellent.

CHAPTER 4

I set my finished dinner tray aside when Haru walked in the open door. We talked about everything but the elephant in the room—the danger before us. But it became hard to ignore later when Commander Alexander and Taylor walked in. Haru stood, so I stood.

"Sit, sit," Commander Alexander said. Everyone sat on the two lower bunks. Though there was a generous distance between the upper bunk and the lower one, Will still had to lean forward with his elbows on his knees.

I decided it was time to address one of the safer issues crowding the room. "I don't know what to call you. Your troops call you Commander, but you introduced yourself as William of the Guard. Which is your preference?"

"What do you think, Haru? I need his trust, but I also need his respect."

"Connor is not like any child I have ever known. He thinks very deeply and intellectually. I believe that if he respects you, it will be because he trusts you. What he calls you will have little effect on him," answered Haru.

"I see. In that case, you can call me Will, but not until we begin our journey. In front of the team, call me sir."

"Yes sir," I said.

"I like you. You're quick. We have a lot in common, you and I," Will said thoughtfully.

"How so?" I asked between bites.

"For one thing, our trust is hard won. We have seen, learned, and possessed things that inspire great caution." He was very direct and to the point, like Gray. He sounded confident and honest, and I might even say sincere. Sincerity has a vulnerable connotation, and to assign such a soft trait to this formidable man conjured a strange combination.

"For another," he continued, "we've been specially trained to carry sensitive information for the rebellion at a young age. And also at a young age, we were both suddenly forced to take up our mentors' goals. That makes for a unique childhood. You experienced the loss of your grandad, and I witnessed...," he looked down before he continued. "I lost both my parents when I was around your age." I could tell it was difficult to share, and the details were obviously painful, if not too gruesome to share with a child.

"Do you think I should change my name?" I was asking this hulk of a man I didn't even know, but suddenly his opinion mattered. "I mean, we are already giving me a new identity of a sick Fringer kid. Is there any reason to believe the Corporates know of me?"

"We can't know," Taylor cut in. "If they suspected Deegan, your grandfather, they may have suspected you, but they made no moves before you disappeared."

"Did you change William's name when you adopted him?" I asked Taylor.

"Yes, I changed his last name to mine. It's hard to say if it helped," Taylor replied honestly.

Will added, "The person who trained me was the daughter of a known rebel who had infiltrated their intelligence agency. After she died, they sent people to watch me. I was just a kid, and it's a miracle the Sanguine Blade wasn't discovered."

"Yeah, I didn't know the castle made by GD, that was my nickname for my grandad, held so many important clues. Not knowing its significance, I showed it to my friend, and I carried it in my tote when we moved to Fairplay."

"I too confided in childhood friends, but destiny doesn't let go of its players so easily." We all chuckled. It was a laugh that recognized the irony more than the humor.

"You know, Connor, you don't have to change your name," said Haru. "That will not be what triggers the enemy to think you're a Highmind; it's your age that will do that. Why else would you accompany us? That's why we created this story. It could delay them from connecting you to Deegan, but they will investigate regardless. But a nickname can redefine you, making a new persona easier to perform."

Will added, "Sometimes people come up with a new name to become more than what they were. It helps them achieve their goals. Take Relic. We call him that, but it's not his given name. I still don't know his real name. Relic reflects the person he chooses to be. Reframing yourself from civilian to soldier is a tough task when you see yourself as Connor, 'a kid who hides'. Drangers choose a name of power after they graduate from training. Mine was Dirk, an assassin's blade."

My shock was evident, and I blurted my response. "You were a Dranger?" I asked with exasperation.

"Yes, I was, and then I became a Neighwah soldier, and now I am a Fringer Commander," he answered proudly. He was defying me to challenge him and expose my preconceived notions.

I was stunned. Quickly reviewing my preconceptions and perhaps prejudices, I concluded they weren't without reason. I again spoke without thinking. "Why should I trust you? Why should any of us? The men in those organizations threatened us, beat us, and killed many others, and you say you were one of them!"

"I like your honesty, Connor," said Taylor. "Will doesn't tell the story very well. Allow me to add some more details. He came to live with me after his parents were killed in front of him. We changed his last name to keep him safe. And yes, he joined the Drangers, but it was the only way to save the life of his friend who had been sold to them. Then Corporates blackmailed him into joining the Neighwah. And again, he served to keep his injured friend and family from being detained, which we all know is just a prelude to execution. He also used his appointments to gather important information while doing his best to maintain his values."

"He really does tell a better story, Will," I said, pointing my thumb toward Taylor. Will smiled at me. "But you are right about trust. It's hard-won."

He nodded. "So, until you are brought in, you'll have to stay out of sight in here. We'll talk about your freedom to roam the building after that. But tomorrow, we have a fun day planned."

"Who is included in *we*?" I asked, remembering I was planning on spending the day at the lake with Gray.

"You, Gray, and I are going fishing."

"I'm jealous," said Haru. "I have a meeting with Taylor and unloading to do."

"I won't be there, but I'll see you on the drone camera," added Taylor.

As Will, Taylor, and Haru stood to leave, I made my request. "May I have a chair for that table?" Will nodded.

"Yes. Is there anything else I can help you with?" he asked, and I shook my head.

"No, thank you," and he left while I was downloading a movie Relic had suggested to me called *War Games*. It wasn't more than five minutes before Nash, one of the Guard soldiers I had met at the meeting, carried in two chairs.

The next morning, after a hasty breakfast, Gray was waiting next to the side door in a mini, and Will was on his horse. It was a quick ride to the lake, and I stepped out and felt the cool breeze blowing off the water. A swath of orange light sparkled and shimmered across the lake with the emerging rays of the sun. The ripples made a soothing, rhythmic sound as they lapped against the shore. It was majestic and mesmerizing.

Gray startled me out of my hypnotic state by handing me a fishing pole. Will settled his horse and walked over to join us. Both Will and Gray went over their personal techniques for casting a line, but it took me quite a few tries to get my line to go where I wanted. Will was the first to hook a fish, and he let me reel it in. This new skill intrigued me. Like baseball, it was fun and challenging. But that it allowed people to feed themselves made it something I wanted to know.

Will and Gray stood by the shore, letting their lines float in wait of a wiggle. They were engaged in a conversation, and by their posture and body language, I could tell their topic was of a serious nature. It was so grave, that both men stood stiffly and were careful not to allow me to read their lips. It could be about any number of subjects. Everything about this mission included danger. I felt I deserved to know more than they shared. They have no problem using me in their adult tasks, but they refuse to treat me with the respect of one, all under the excuse of protection.

Before our adventure was over, we had caught five fish. Gray showed me how to clean them and let me do the last one by myself before we cooked them on a small stove. It was very empowering to take a meal from harvest to table.

Will called me over to his horse. "Connor, meet Little Bet." It was the biggest animal I had ever faced, but I trusted Will, so I petted the horse's neck as Will demonstrated. Will climbed up on his horse and reached his hand down to me. "Come on, Connor, let's ride back."

I took Will's hand not because I wasn't afraid, but because I didn't want to *look* afraid. When I was seated in the saddle, I was very aware of how high off the ground I was. "I gather there's a story behind Little Bet's name," I said to deflect from my nervous demeanor.

"Well, I found this horse when I came upon the Fort. He was stubborn, and I didn't know how to ride. So, I'd made this horse a little bet that I would win his obedience. So, I named him that."

"What would you have given the horse if you had lost?" I asked.

"There is no lose, just keep trying." He clicked the horse into motion. We started out slowly, showing me how to move with the horse. Then he urged Little Bet on faster. Will held the reins with one hand and stood up in the stirrups just slightly over the saddle, and held me up too. I should have been terrified, but he was so strong that the act seemed effortless. I felt the horse lifting off the ground and landing, as if between leaps we were flying. Little Bet heaved powerful breaths as Will maneuvered him through the shortcut. The powerful synergy between man and horse was extraordinary, and the ride was pure exhilaration.

We rode down a wooded dirt road past the turn to Sentry. Will halted his horse when we came to an old truck parked in the middle of the road. Nash and a woman got out of the cab, and Nash walked over to us to help me off Little Bet. Will quickly landed on the ground after me and dashed to the woman. Without regard to me or the soldier, he took her in his arms and kissed her hungrily. She welcomed his greeting with enthusiasm. *Was Will making a quick stop to see his girlfriend, or was she the town healer?* They talked in whispers, and though I could not see what Will was saying, I could read the woman's lips.

"She was getting ready to leave," she said, "when Kory fell violently ill. She told me I was to escort a Lone Fringer child into the Fort to be treated in the medical facility. I am also to hand this to the new doctor." She held out a paper, and Will took it from her and read it. "She was hoping the new doctor could send some medicine for Kory and the town if it spreads."

"Ventura must be beside herself with worry," Will said loud enough for me to hear him.

"She and the kids are worried about losing him, and Tula won't let them near him because she believes he's contagious. That's why she can't come. She's worried about an outbreak, and she's hoping this doctor can help prevent it."

I could see Will was unhappy about the change in plans. No doubt he was worried about another person having a backstage pass to their ruse.

I can't say I was comfortable gambling that this woman was trustworthy. No matter how well Will knew her, she was a fill-in.

"Did she explain this plan?" Will cocked his head, waiting for her answer.

"No, she had quarantined herself in Kory's home to treat him. She sent me a brief note and said you'd fill me in." Will's frustration had me concerned, and the woman looked confused.

"I see," Will said. "Simply put, it's about keeping the rumors at bay. We need to help this Lone Fringer child receive treatment, and then reunite him with his family. I appreciate you filling in."

Will smoothly sold our lie and gave her a wink for good measure. I wondered if he'd explain it better later, or maybe they weren't as close as they appeared. "So, Leita," Will said, "meet Miles. Miles, this is Leita." I instantly knew the change in personnel caused Will to take away my choice of changing my name and replace it with here's your new name.

"Nice to meet you," I said and held out my hand. I watched both Will and Leita stiffen. Evidently, this was not a typical Fringer response. I drilled down on the Fringer files I had studied to prepare myself for this world.

"Okay," Will said, "let's review. I'll ride back while you three wait here for thirty minutes. Nash, when you get to Sentry, pull up to the front entrance of Alpha and walk him to the infirmary entrance. The troops will be there for their briefing on the Friendship Tour. I'll give a brief explanation that the boy is here to see the doctor, but he isn't contagious. Witnessing his arrival will make sure the chatter goes our way."

"Got it," Nash replied.

"Okay," Will said, getting back on his horse. "Let's get this parade going."

CHAPTER 5

I didn't know what to make of this woman. The closeness Will shared with her was obvious, but it was also obvious that this deviation from the original plan crossed a hard line. I knew how to lie; I've had a lifetime of practice. But I was pretty sure she didn't buy my story. I began reviewing my new list of lies. First was my "illness". The story concerned a growth deep under my left arm, which was too deep and suspicious to lance. Dr. Andie was going to diagnose it and decide on a treatment. Next were the details about my life as a Lone Fringer. And last was my return to my imaginary Lone Fringer parents.

Will and I had discussed Lone Fringers, but I was far from an expert. Leita, on the other hand, *was* a Fringer, and I was sure she knew a lot more about them than I did. I could see Leita's mind running through scenarios, trying to figure out what was really going on. She was probably going to attempt to get some answers from me, but I needed information too. She thought I was just a kid, naïve and malleable. This could be fun.

"So, Miles, does your arm hurt?" she asked.

I knew this one. "Sometimes it swells up and gets sore when I do too much. My mom makes me do my little sister's jobs now, and my dad does his and mine." It gave credibility to Lone Fringers trusting a doctor.

Leita and Nash both winced, knowing little sister chores would be an insult to a Fringer boy trying to become a man. "How old are you?" asked Leita.

I figured I didn't have to make this up, so I told them my real age. "I'm twelve."

"Well, this doc will fix you up in no time, so enjoy getting out of chopping wood as long as you can," Nash chuckled nervously.

"What region do you live in?" Leita questioned.

I could tell her friendly questions had turned into an interrogation, and I didn't know the answer to this one, so I played it like I wasn't allowed to tell. "My dad told me not to say. He says privacy means safety." I was proud of my quick thinking on that one, but I decided to feign shyness during the rest of my interaction with her to avoid more missteps.

"I bet that gets lonely for a kid," she answered. "Do you have friends? Someday you will want to find a wife. How will you do that if you never get to interact with anyone?"

"Whoa, Leita. He's still a kid."

I appreciated Nash's attempt to stop this line of questioning, but I knew this answer because I asked Will this very thing when we were fishing. "My parents will arrange it when I am of age."

Leita didn't respond, but I could tell she was as suspicious of me as I was of her. I would have to tell Gray that I bombed my first performance. Secrets I was used to; failure, not so much. I could tell Nash was getting ready to tell her not to ask me any more questions, but I stopped it by saying I needed to use the bathroom. I didn't, but it was getting way too tense. We still had twenty more minutes when I returned, and Nash was waiting with two mitts and a baseball.

"Gray said you might enjoy a game of catch to calm your nerves before you get poked by the doctor," he said with a grin. "Can you catch with your sore arm and throw with your good one?" I nodded.

After a couple of throws, I could feel my shoulders sink into a more relaxed state. I was enjoying the release that the activity gave me, and I wondered if I would get to bring them on the tour. Nash threw me soft pitches, and I surprised him by throwing smokers back. He smiled and shook his head. "Not fair. I have to go easy on your arm." I threw up my hands in a too-bad gesture and laughed. Soon it was time to go.

The soldiers stood lined up in the yard when Nash buzzed us through the front access door. All eyes alerted on me as we emerged from the short entry hall and turned left in front of the Guard Operations Room. I should be used to this by now, but I wasn't. Will highlighted our presence as he explained my visit to his troops.

"Now that we have our own doctor, we will grant clearance to civilian patients requiring advanced medical attention. Be assured that none will have contagious issues. Dr. Channing will also make trips to the Fringer townships to administer medical help and preventative care." Will got his soldiers' attention back on him, and we disappeared through the infirmary door.

Dr. Andie Channing brought me back to the exam room, while Leita waited in the tiny lobby. Just for good measure, she took my vitals.

"So," I asked, "what's wrong with me?"

"You have a suspicious lump under your arm, *Miles,*" Andie said, emphasizing that she knew my pseudonym.

I rolled my eyes in acknowledgment. "I know that. What is it from, and what are you going to do to me?"

"Well, if I were going to actually do something, I would take an MRI and a biopsy. Then, depending on what it was, I'd treat you with medicine or a scalpel. Whatever I decide on, your body will have to physically reflect that treatment," Dr. Andie said with a straight face.

I was leaning away, thinking this ruse had gone far enough when Andie started laughing.

"You should have seen your face," she said.

"That was a rotten joke," I scoffed, wishing I had a retaliatory response.

"The good news is that I am diagnosing it as an infection, so I'm prescribing a round of antibiotics which you won't actually take. It will also allow you to travel immediately without worrying about stitches ripping or getting infected. I printed an MRI film this morning from a textbook example, which will go into the file under your new name."

"Do I have a last name?"

"Good question. We'll have to ask William." She was looking at the incomplete chart.

Later that afternoon, Gray and Will sat with me in my room. They said we needed to "discuss the additional measures required for my protection," which was just a kind way of saying we needed a new plan because I had failed my cover story. If I had been a few years older, this conversation would have gone much differently, and though I don't like being scolded, I wasn't sure I preferred this version either.

Will took his usual seat on the bottom bunk and leaned forward to fit in the space. Gray and I waited until Will was settled, and we sat at our usual places, the two table chairs. I found it amusing that this huge man made a habit of sitting there when one of the chairs would accommodate him so much better. We had already had so many of these talks, and I guess we had established our territories. I don't know which is weirder—that people behave this way, or that I am overly interested in it.

"When you are in public," Will explained, "you will wear these thin gloves. Leita read through our ruse in seconds, starting with your hands not being those of a hard-working Fringer."

"I noticed," I said. "She and Nash kept looking at me curiously when I answered their questions. I realized I had totally bombed my cover, so I just stopped talking. I should have prepared better, sorry."

"That is our fault," Gray sighed. "We didn't prepare you to be a Fringer because this plan developed so suddenly."

"Well, the good news is," Will answered, "Leita is someone I trust completely, and she has been a Fringer for almost twenty years. She has agreed to work with you and escort you around the Fort."

"Now, by trust completely doesn't mean she knows what the Reclamation Mission is about, so stick with the Friendship Tour story," Gray added.

"You know, after I was told I would be presented as a Lone Fringer kid, I asked myself. Why would skittish people trust fancy medicine? It has a Corporate feel to it. But if a kid was sick, especially with an illness the parents had seen go badly, his mom would risk the danger to save her child; in fact, she would insist. And then there's the lonely, restless, adventure seeking kid who overhears their conversations. He'd be so excited to go to town, he'd pester his poor parents, and maybe threaten to go on his own. Then his mom would freak, and his dad would relent. Moms, dads, and kids are like that," I said.

Will and Gray looked at each other and smiled. "He's right. Hell, I was that kid," said Will.

"Yeah, me too," Gray grinned.

"Nicely done, Connor. That is a vast improvement and completely believable," Will said.

The two men reminisced about the trouble they caused their parents with unashamed glee. Gray wanted to try coffee, so he stole an Upper's cup. His dad had a devil of a time sneaking it back to the site. Will snuck past the barrier after curfew to hike and spend the night in the woods alone at ten years old. Taylor was beside himself with worry. Gray stopped mid-story about his sneaking off, and I could tell that tale and more would be finished later without me.

"Okay, it's agreed. We'll leak the willful kid story and say his parents dropped him off at McCoy."

"I like it," agreed Will. "Well done, Connor, well done."

Yes, well done indeed! I thought. Now I wanted to hear more stories of willful disobedience. A voice in the back of my head said this mission was not the time or place for carelessness, but I successfully turned off that nagging noise.

The next day, Leita brought me to the Gamma building to see the new ranch and greenhouse section. She said she wanted to get to know me better before we dove into my Fringer lessons. Plus, a look at the new farm and ranch offered us the chance to talk privately. The dedicated section encompassed more than a third of the building, with an additional barn and corral extension, giving the animals plenty of space and us time.

When we were at the Hold, all four buildings housed animal husbandry and indoor crop farms. The point of the Hold was to keep people and other living things separated until the vetting process was complete. Diseases affecting people, livestock, and crops could be quarantined and treated as needed without exposing all the residents and our entire food supply. There were two four-week sessions at the Hold, and within our groups of forty to fifty per building, we received education and job training.

Though the only building I had seen before now was Alpha, the structures were similar. But this was no longer a stop-off for people and animals waiting to be settled. This was a military base, and each building was assigned different objectives and equipped accordingly.

Copper, Will's dog, met me at the entrance with great excitement and bound after me as I toured the building. The building's main area was dedicated to maintenance along with the living quarters for the men and women who worked here. Leita met with a few of the people she knew as we walked across the mechanic shop area to the animal hold. I was fascinated by the machinery inside the open casings and the work being done. I looked up and saw her watching me, and I hoped I hadn't made another Fringer error.

Chickens, geese, pigs, and goats roamed about as Aniya and two teenage boys cleaned, groomed, and fed the active animals. She walked over to greet us. "It's been crazy here. This place is a mess. I've got a lot of work to do," she smiled. "There's a greenhouse through those doors, but I've barely started on it."

"I thought I'd see Commander Will's horse," I said before I could catch myself. Aniya nodded and led the way as Leita gave me a look. I realized that if I had only just arrived here, I should not know Commander Alexander or his horse. My memory would not be enough to pull this off. I needed training.

I thought the door led to the outside, but it opened up to another immense area for larger livestock. Seeing the outer walls of the original building, I knew that this was a new addition. It was noticeably colder in the stable area, but not frigid. Rows of stalls held cattle and a couple of horses, and on the far wall was a large sliding barn door. After lunch, Leita took me back to the Alpha building and what used to be the animal hold, which was being transformed into the new ministry office. Leita said this would be the safest place to begin my Fringer lessons.

"This morning was more than a walk around. It was my assessment of what you are like, so I can properly train you."

"What did you learn?" I asked.

"Well, for one, you're smarter than most kids, a lot smarter, I'd say. But if I can see it, so can others. Are you ready to get to work?" I nodded. This woman was smart too, and I was glad she was on our side. At least I believed she was.

CHAPTER 6

The ministry section contained an office with ample storage, a small chapel, and Tanya's sleeping quarters. Haru and Tanya were busy sorting items to be taken to their labeled locations. Leita and I were unpacking the boxes and putting the supplies on the assigned shelves. I set up the podium and the chairs for the small service area, and set a bible on each seat. It was the same bible Haru gave me when I came to the Hold. I thought of the scriptures we had highlighted together at every service, and I wished I had brought my copy with me. But it seemed like one more thing that could get us in trouble on the outside. I wondered how Haru planned to navigate the people's fear of the laws that forbid religion.

During our industrious efforts, Haru and Tanya asked me questions, and Leita guided me through the believable answers. I learned about the old and new Harfest traditions, what it took to live in the woods, and how they used to move twice a year to keep off the Dranger and Neighwah radar. I learned many Fringers had escaped their lives as Dailys and Drangers, and even Neighwah and Uppers. Fringers helped many of them get past the territory borders, hence the rumors of them being kidnappers. Where they lived was densely forested, and the tribes' resources were so few that the Corporates decided they weren't worth going to battle with. The Corporates also knew if they attacked them, their free lifestyle would be discovered, causing people to realize they didn't need overlords.

I learned Will was the one who united the tribes and helped them establish permanent homes in the old cities. When I asked how they stayed off the Corporate radar now, Leita said he blackmailed them with something so bad that they promised to leave the Fringers alone.

"What in the world would scare them like that?" I asked her.

"Only a few people know, but if the Corporates break the agreement, it will come out."

"Did it break the agreement to attack the tunnel?"

"No," she said. "Your town wasn't on the contract. But if they ask us why we helped, we are to say we thought they were coming for us."

"What happens if the Fringers break the agreement?" I was afraid to hear the answer.

"I don't know for sure, but I imagine they would annihilate our towns, and that would cause the information to be released anyway. Neither side wants a war."

"Neither side may want it, but it's coming. We're just in the shaky peace stage," I stated.

"Very shaky," Haru mumbled as he passed with a stack of Bibles.

"This puts a new spin on the dangers and repercussions of our Friendship Tour," I said, raising my eyebrows.

"Yes, our fate spins a jagged cloth," Leita said with a mix of determination and dread in her eyes. I'd have to sort her metaphor out, but I liked it.

I felt good about my Fringer background, and with my shy Daily persona, I regained my confidence. I wasn't even worried about what I didn't know because I could blame it on the ignorance of childhood. At dinner, which was my actual debut, I conversed smoothly and without hesitation. I even spoke with genuine emotion about how much I missed my family, making Gray nervous and Will amused.

After dinner was done and the conversations died down, the soldiers folded up the bench style tables and rolled them to the side. Breaking into two teams, they prepared to play a game of basketball. With the old fences down and the curtain area decreased, the open space was big enough for a full-sized court. I watched the lines form under the clear floor coating. I vividly remember how amazed I was when it happened during our class activity.

The scoreboard listed the teams as "Skins" and "Shirts" and half the players pulled off their t-shirts. Gray and Will were on separate teams, and they eyed each other with competitive smiles. I wasn't sure who I should place my mental bet on. Both were toned, but Will was taller, and in basketball, that can make a big difference.

The contest was fierce, and more like a battle than a playful game. This was how they prepared for the fight. I thought back to Alex, from the NH museum, who said all competitive games have a warrior aspect to them. Each fought and functioned together to control that ball. It occurred to me that both sides had a destiny. That concerned me.

It meant that there was more than one destiny. Not the romanticized version of providence, but the reality of it. I imagined higher conscious beings battling simultaneously to ensure their objectives. Were we just pawns on a greater plane? I identified with that ball as it was tossed, grabbed, and used to gain an advantage. It was the ultimate key, the essential tool, and whoever controlled it would prevail. I couldn't decide whether the ball represented me or the weapon. The weapon would not ponder its destiny; it was not sentient, but I was. That, however, didn't ensure I would get to choose who used me, or who got to win. An alarming reality.

"I'm a mess," I said softly under the noise of the game. "Leave it to me to turn a game into a philosophical prophecy."

I was sitting at the one table still set up near the trailers when Haru sat down next to me.

"I see you've placed the world back on your shoulders," he said.

I laughed. "It must belong there because it keeps finding its way back."

"You know what's funny? Every person on this mission bears the same weight. Think about that. The burden feels heavy because you think you carry it alone. It's like the game we just watched. It takes all of us doing our job. Your only job is to decipher information, report anomalies, and follow orders. It isn't your job to keep everyone safe or evaluate command decisions. You don't even get to decide what we are fed. If you try to take on all the jobs, you won't accomplish yours. Trust is difficult; our tasks are difficult; but Connor, the *only* way we'll succeed is to work as a team."

"Thanks, Haru," I sighed. "You always knock me off that high horse of mine."

He laughed. "High horses make for a long fall."

"Yeah, but you make the landing hard enough to learn, but soft enough to carry on." He smiled and handed me a book, *Recruited by the FBI* by . The cover said it was a Christian adventure story, cool.

The next morning, we would be back on the road, so my dad snuck into my room to watch a show with me. I found an old series called *Numbers*, which both my dad and I liked. My dad had impressive math skills. I mean, as a civil engineer, he would have taken a lot of math, but he was more than proficient. He was clever.

The show was about an agent who investigated high-level crimes with the help of his math genius brother. The theories weren't explained in detail, but I recognized many of them, and we both enjoyed seeing their practical applications.

That night as we watched the show, the final items were being loaded, and last-minute preparations were addressed. The utility vehicles lined up like railway cars inside the courtyard, surrounded by the four buildings as gentle snow fell upon them.

When we walked outside, the snow was several inches deep. Usually, the snow was more established in this area by now, but it was late this year. Though such weather could be treacherous, it was a sight I hadn't seen since we moved to New Haven, and its beauty overrode its threats.

Eighteen people climbed into their respective rigs with choreographed efficiency. Leita was my mentor, so it was logical for her to ride in the truck with me, Haru, Tanya, Henry, and Will. Since everyone in the truck knew who I was, we engaged in unfettered conversation. I noticed Will watching Haru and Leita laugh and talk. I wondered if it bothered him. I didn't see the normal ring or twin bracelets that signified two people were pledged, but they kissed like they were.

Slowly, the rigs made their way down the sloppy, frozen road. The flakes grew in number, and soon the world was flocked in white. It outlined the lake as the frozen edges reached for the center to claim it completely. Soon the beautiful winter landscape became a wall of white as the benign snow grew into a storm.

"It's nothing to worry about," assured Will. "We can get through this. We have snowplow crews along the road. Besides, it's excellent cover because snooping drones can't fly in this stuff."

Though the Brute handled the road with ease, it took longer to navigate the drive on their way out. Once they came off the ridge and onto a flatter path, the ride was steadier and quieter on the snow-covered road.

When we reached the gate at the end of Black Creek Road, it had already been shoveled and opened. After pulling through, we got out to stretch and took a break before heading down Highway 9. It was a semi-paved road, and our speed was dictated by the issues riddling it. Will said the Guard had the personnel to repair it, but its poor condition gave the impression it was not used, which helped hide the Fort. But now the Corporates knew about it, which is why my dad came to evaluate the road conditions and develop the plans for repair.

The closer we got to Silverthorn, the better the roads became. We rolled past the outer boundary of the town, which had been a bustling city before the radioactive rumors sent its residents back to the eastern side of the tunnel. No Fringers settled here, although it looked well maintained. I asked Will about that, and he said they found that lots of the buildings had traps and bombs in them. But now that the radiation lie had been exposed, they may be worth defusing.

As we got within a couple of miles of I-70, Will got verification from Gray that several Corporate drones were hovering over the junction. They did little to conceal their presence or their interest in where the large group was heading. Gray and Will hoped the information regarding the "Friendship Tour" would leak out naturally, and their direction and activities over the next few days would reinforce their cover story. No one believed the Corporates would buy it completely, but as they continued to investigate, we would get further down the road.

The road conditions improved immensely as we passed through Silverthorn. We reached I-70 and proceeded to the meeting place where Axle and Easton were waiting to join the caravan as the sweep. It was too early for lunch, but we stopped and got our lunch sacks to eat when we wished. The Corporates had upgraded I-70 in anticipation of the twin tunnels' repair, so the worst of our drive was behind us, at least for the next four days.

The road stretching before was freshly plowed, and we proceeded down the best road we had traveled so far toward the town of Eagle. We passed ponds of various sizes that the weather had reduced to flat white sheets. Edging the road were the remnants of abandoned lives, scattered under a layer of winter white silence. As we traveled further away from the tunnel, signs of life emerged. Hand-built sleds and wagons, used for hauling, leaned against recently patched houses and smoking chimneys.

The manmade structures were regularly interrupted with picturesque sections of evergreen forest and rugged canyon walls impressively contrasted by the new-fallen snow. Chimneys smoking in the distance proved many had settled outside of the city centers, where the excited Fringers greeted us as we passed. The beefy tracks of the Brutes plowed on in eerily silence over the snow-packed pavement. The whole experience amazed me.

I was developing a wanderlust, and I wished I *had* been raised a Lone Fringer traveling through Colorado's Wild West. Blackbirds flew above, and I envied them too. I knew many experiences had been chiseled from our lives, but I didn't realize how it diminished me. We were born in wonder and forbidden to notice. It made the thought of being sealed back in my tunnel town much less appealing, but being a Fringer had its downsides too.

Last year the Fringers lived a nomadic existence in small tribes because constantly changing locations made attacking them a logistical nightmare. But now they lived in permanent dwellings, and their only protection was some risky blackmail scheme. It was a precarious peace indeed, and maybe that was the way of peace, always preparing to fight for it.

CHAPTER 7

Will announced that we were almost at Eagle. The sweep team of two minis and three soldiers would set up a camp in the woods outside of town. Their vehicles were covered in high-tech camouflage, so they wouldn't be pursued by the drones that accompanied us on our journey.

We, however, would be tracked, and as alarming as that should be, it was part of our "in plain sight" cover. We would spend two nights in Eagle to participate in the Harfest activities. The night before we were to move out, the sweep team would drive past the town, wait for us to pass, and follow us to Glenwood Springs. That would be the end of the Friendship Tour, where our caravan would split up. Some would head back to the fort and eventually to New Haven. I was curious how we would justify heading past the last town into the wilderness in the thick of winter.

The town of Eagle was smaller than Silverthorn, but it bustled with busy people. A dilapidated electric truck pulled in front of our caravan and led us to a parking lot. When we came to a stop, the town's people descended upon us with excited enthusiasm. As cold as it was, I wasn't the only one in gloves; however, very few had a facemask like I did. It was another annoying last-minute protection, not from the cold, mind you, to hide my identity.

"Welcome to Eagle. I'm Warren," said a tall, slightly rounded man. Sporting a neatly trimmed beard, he had no need of a facemask. I envied him. "This is Town Center. It used to be a middle school," as he gestured toward a large one-story building with many branches sprouting from its center. "It houses everything needed to run a town. There are shops, offices, services, the dining hall, storage, and the justice hall. It's where we hold the Harfest celebration." I couldn't help but notice he never used a possessive pronoun. He used "*a town*" to describe "*his town*," odd.

I learned from Leita that Fringers prepared all year for the annual Harfest celebration. All the nomadic tribes got together during their migration to their winter grounds to trade goods and information. But the highlight was the couples' meet. All the eligible men and women over nineteen gathered in set apart areas to hear live music, dance, and meet each other. This was their only chance to court, fall in love, and make a pledge because pledging within one's tribe was frowned upon. Then the couple would decide which tribe to join for their year-long courting period. At the next Harfest, they could get married in the joining ceremony, renew their pledge, or go their separate ways.

Now that the Fringers were settled into permanent towns and not hiding in the forest, the Harfest celebration would be different. Their workloads were less, and their dwellings offered better protection from the elements. And though they worried about the Corporates knowing where they were, they couldn't hide if their enemy wanted to find them. The hardest adjustment involved relinquishing their tribal sovereignty. Their lives now included a much larger, diverse population of numerous tribes, all with different mindsets. As Leita put it, they had a lot of scrapping to get through.

But they had more hands to meet their needs. Gardens and livestock were corralled and fenced in, and barns and greenhouses, though in need of repair, were available year-round. The Fringers could visit and send communications between the towns with little trouble. But going to Harfest now meant leaving their permanent homes at the mercy of marauders. The compromise was that there would be two Harfests. One at Eagle and the other at Glenwood Springs. Though they gave up the annual party, they were uniting into a larger community that maintained regular contact and looked out for each other.

While the crew got together unpacking the items New Haven brought as gifts and trade, I went on a tour of Town Center. Leita and Nash joined me on my exploration, but I have a feeling their presence had more to do with assessing security and watching me. It reminded me of a story I had recently read about a young prince who was tired of his constant guards hovering around him. He ditched them for a weekend of fun, posing as an unknown peasant. I fully understood why I was under scrutiny, but ditching my detail was appealing.

There were several halls, each leading to a row of classrooms. Signs above the hall entrances designated the type of services housed there. They read *Municipalities, Shops,* and *Residential.* I was told single adults lived in the *Residential* section to conserve the energy and resources required to maintain dwellings. Unless the town held a gathering, families cooked and ate at their homes, but the singles took turns cooking in the large cafeteria kitchen. There were restrooms in their hall, and they used the gym for showers.

We turned down *Municipal Hall* first. The Town Hall and the Justice Center took up one whole side of the hall. I was informed that it included a jail, and I wondered if anyone was being held there. Maintenance Service shops lined the other side of the hall, sectioned into various specialties.

The last hall held the shops. In New Haven, we had a monthly market, but we didn't have stores. These stores weren't open all the time, but most were available a couple of times a week. Not even the Territories had a place for choosing and buying goods. The Uppers ordered many luxuries, but there were no walk-in stores allowing browsing and sampling. I had passed vacant, dilapidated shops on walks, but I had never seen a functioning store. This town had created storefronts facing the hall, so buyers could see the goods inside.

One mercantile displayed handmade soaps, lotions, hair products, and other hygiene items. The next store offered household décor, kitchenware, and furniture. Another store had clothing items, toys, and crafts. All the items were reclaimed or handmade, and the craftmanship was impressive. The last store sold tools and hardware items. They had not lived here long enough to establish themselves yet, so their inventories were small.

I knew the trailer full of crates of unused goods would cause a lot of excitement when we unpacked them. I imagined their faces when they saw all we had to trade and gift to them. Down the hall from the established stores were the rooms we were assigned for the New Haven merchant stores, and beyond that was the library. I wondered if I could borrow a few books.

It was assumed that our whole group would return to our homes after we finished in Glenwood Springs. Some of us would journey further, but we couldn't reveal that. I wasn't sure if I should, in good conscience, borrow books I may not be able to return.

The next five rooms held guest quarters, and the one at the end was used for storage. The construction and furnishing of the guest quarters impressed me. They were divided into ten rooms, and the closed off hall was made into a large common area with a comfy couch, a bench style table, and a bathroom with four stalls and three showers. The furnishings were in surprisingly good condition. I was informed that after the tunnel accident, the Corporates hastily left all the large household items, like beds and furniture, giving Eagle's new residents ample choices to fill their town's accommodations.

I found my room by the names, Miles and Haru, written on the whiteboard affixed to the door. Nash unlocked the door with a metal key and checked it out before letting me into the windowless room. There was a hint of pine coming from the fresh boughs decorating the dresser and shelf combo, accompanied by two ceramic cups and a pitcher of water. I poured myself a glass and sat at the end of the bed with my gear on it. Setting my cup on the nightstand, I lay back on the mattress, finding it free of lumps and worn-out low spots. Sitting back up, I turned to Leita.

"Does Haru know I am his roommate?"

"Probably," she answered. "We're heading to the Ministry room next. So, you can ask him."

"You know," I said as I set my cup back on the nightstand between the two beds and flopped back down. "I'm getting tired of everyone except me knowing what the plan is. You'd think something as harmless as who I share a room with would be information I could be *trusted* with," I emphasized the word with air quotes. "No one tells me anything until I'm in the thick of it." It wasn't her fault. Gray and Will were the targets of my frustration, but they weren't here, so she and Nash would have to do.

"I know it feels oppressive," Nash answered, "but we have orders to secure you 24/7, and I ain't about to cross Will."

"Yeah, but they're going overboard with my protection. People are more likely to notice *that* than me." I said, looking directly at him. I released a noisy breath, showing my frustration. Then I flopped down again. This bed really was comfortable, at least as good as mine back home. "I thought you guys grew up together. Are you afraid of him?" I asked more to poke at him than to answer my fears.

"Dude, it's not fear, it's knowledge," he chuckled.

I sat up again. "How about you, Leita? Are you afraid of him?"

"I'm not under his orders. Oh, well, I guess I am now. Huh," she said as if she had just thought that through. "I guess I wouldn't cross him on purpose if that's what you're asking. He doesn't do things for no reason." I could see her still thinking through her sudden realization, and concern flickered across her face.

"Great," I said under my breath and pushed myself off the bed. At least I could look forward to a good night's sleep, maybe read a book.

I was in the Ministry room hanging signs, placing handouts and sched-ules on the table, and arranging chairs in front of a foldout podium seated on top of a student desk. I was almost finished when Gray walked in. He had been securing the vehicles and our mission gear where it wouldn't be messed with. Where that was would never be revealed to me. That was understandable; everything else was not. I planned on having it out with him because I didn't think Will would feel the need to discuss the validity of his orders. And though I hadn't seen him angry, his soldiers suggested he had a temper.

"Gray, I—" a call on his radio interrupted me.

"Got it. I'm heading there now. Miles," he winked, "Will is on his way. Stay with Nash and Leita until he gets here." And with that, he made a quick get-away to meet the caller.

That night, the whole town gathered in the gym to share the evening meal together and begin the Harfest celebration.

The mayor of the town raised a glass. "We welcome our honored guests from the town of New Haven. We look forward to new friends and great trades."

"Salute," came the loud response.

Jilly sat next to me, but I was quiet and still stewing over my feelings of imprisonment. "So, Miles," she said, addressing me by my pseudonym, "how has your journey been so far? And how is your arm doing?"

I moved my arm with the fake aliment adding a slight wince for show. "The swelling in my arm is going down, and my range of motion is much better. As far as the drive, it's faster riding in a vehicle, and I like that, but sitting so long makes me feel restless."

"I know what you mean," said Will on his other side. "I'd rather be on my horse."

I smiled. It was time to push the boundaries. "I like horses too. We have one."

Gray eyed me at my improvisation. "I didn't know that," he said with a slight warning look.

"Only my dad rides it, but he said he'd teach me when my arm works better," I said to correct the liberty I'd taken, but I was tired of being managed with lie upon lie. Even though I understood not being identified was critical, I enjoyed grabbing back some control and seeing my watchers squirm.

Will smiled at me. It was a genuine smile that glowed with understanding. I wasn't sure what he understood, but he seemed to see my defiance as a sign of courage. He had told me he knew what it was like to lie and hide year after year, but unlike others who sympathized with my plight, he never responded with pity or coddling. He believed in me and pushed me further, like he did when he hauled me onto Little Bet. He may be a formidable man, but he also had a sense of humor.

"I am sure your father is very proud to have a son like you," Will said. I thought Gray would choke on his slice of bread. Will gave Gray a huge grin. It took everything I had to hold back my laughter.

Leita sat on the other side of Will, but her attention was devoted to Haru, who sat opposite her at the long table. I hoped Will wasn't a jealous man because Haru was no match for Will, and he was quite bold to push himself into this alpha's territory.

The next morning, Gray, Jilly, and I came down to breakfast late. The halls were already filling up with shoppers. We stopped at the candle store to buy my mom a gift. The room was bathed in wondrous fragrances of vanilla, honey, sandalwood, and some I didn't know. I found a candle with a rosemary scent that smelled heavenly to me. Suddenly I realized my credits wouldn't work here. Gray smiled and pulled a couple of trade coins out of his pocket and paid for my purchase.

The shopkeeper was excited to get the currency that allowed him to trade with the New Haven stores, and she said so.

"When did we get those?" I asked quietly as we made our way to the door.

"You can't be seen with New Haven coins," Gray whispered in my ear. "No problem, Miles. It's a gift from me to show all Fringers they are welcome into our alliance," he said a tad louder than necessary. My ire picked up again.

"Hey, Miles, Gray," Henry said, coming up behind the son he was not allowed to recognize. "Did you buy someone a present?" he asked, pointing to the item weighing down my tote.

"It's soap for my mom," I answered and pulled it out for his inspection.

He smelled it and nodded with approval. "I'm getting this for my daughter." I knew he was letting me know I didn't need to buy Meshka a present too. "Hey Gray, Warren was looking for you by the tool shop. He said it was urgent."

CHAPTER 8

We stopped at the medical room where Gray left, and Will came in to shadow me. Dr. Andie and Jilly were treating a line of customers, but they brought me behind the screen for a quick check of my vitals. I felt more like a prized pet than a sentient person, and I was trying not to lose my cool. But remembering Leita and Nash's reaction to opposing Will kept me in check.

I asked to go to the library, and Will nodded. I quickly found five books I wanted to read. Literature seemed more appealing when it was in a tangible form. Something I could hold and thumb through with ease. It reminded me of reading with GD in front of that boarded up front room window. I know he hated the board, but it was fun to imagine the world beyond that wooden wall rather than see the reality through it. While I was promising the librarian that I'd return the books, someone called Will.

"We have to go," he said calmly, but I could tell he wasn't. He put a hand on my back and led me down the hall at a quick pace. I tried to ask what was happening, but he silenced me. Terror thrummed through me.

We went through the hall with a chain and sign that read *No Admittance!* It was swinging back and forth as if recently disturbed by someone else who ignored it. I crawled under it, and Will stepped over it. My heart was pounding, but I followed him. He was a Dranger, a Neighwah, a Fringer, a military commander, and for some reason contrary to logic, I was following him instead of running away.

We ran down the hall to a room where Jedi and Nash were standing guard. They let us in and locked the door behind us. Visions of my kidnapping at the Hold once again ran through my mind. Like that room, this room was a storage closet, lined with shelves with backpacks, thick coats, and weapons. It was a one-stop get-out-of-town-quick room.

I stood in a state of shock as Will ripped a bundle of gear from the shelf. It was smaller than the rest, and when he removed the binding straps, it bloomed on the table, revealing a full pack, a child-sized coat, and a small pistol.

"This is the Go Room," Will said sternly. I had figured that out myself, but he said nothing about why we had to go. He handed me the pack and coat, saying, "Put this on."

"But I already have a coat on," I answered in half a whisper. I could see the intensity of Will's manner, and my hackles were bristling. In the Hold, I thought I was in trouble when the Defender locked me in the storage room. I was feeling like that again.

"Quickly, Connor, we need to move."

I think he saw the terror growing in my eyes. He took my shoulders and squared me to face him. "Unsafe people are in town. I can protect you, Connor, but you have to trust me and do exactly as I say."

I nodded, set my books on the table, and took off my lightweight jacket to don the oversized, heavy coat and saddled the backpack over my bulky outer layer. Will was also gearing up. He had a large caliber handgun and a compound bow he strapped under his thick coat. He turned to me and put a warm headscarf over my head, topped it with a straw hat, and tied it below my chin.

He checked the safety and tucked the 22 caliber pistol and a small box of bullets into my jacket's left side pocket. I tried to console myself that I had been trained to use a handgun at New Haven, but being trained was not the same as being ready.

I watched his efficiency during this whole ram-rod preparation for what I still didn't know. I could see the plan had been fine-tuned and practiced. But I hadn't been invited into this loop either. I was supposed to behave like the gear on these shelves and let myself be stowed and grabbed with no forewarning, with no say.

When we left the Go Room, Jedi and Nash were joined by Mack, all standing armed and ready to help us escape. They secured each hall with lethal proficiency and rushed us to an equipment garage.

I expected a fast vehicle at the ready, but what we got was a well-used buck-board wagon hitched up to two gigantic horses. With tall sideboards and a driver on the perch, it was hiding between two old school buses and the remnants of a utility truck, all of which would have been faster than that wagon and two plodding horses. But there they were, poised to go in front of the large shop door.

Three Fringers and a load of supplies were already seated and waiting to move out. If fitting in was the objective, they accomplished it. It looked like every other cart traveling in and out of the Harfest celebration. I just hope we don't have to outrun anyone. It was then that I felt the weight of the weapon in my pocket, and I said a prayer for safe travels.

Will secured our packs behind the passenger seat while I climbed up to sit in the middle section of the bench. I stopped when I noticed the odd shape of the seat next to me. The seat and floor were lower than the rest of the bench. I thought about Will's height and smiled at their attention to covert detail. Will sat in the height-shortening seat and smeared his face with light-skinned makeup. Wiping his hands on a towel, he handed the jar and towel to someone standing by, pulled on a pair of gloves, and tucked his hair under a forest green beanie.

The garage rolled open, and the driver grabbed the reins, clicking at the horses to move. We joined the innocuous traffic of Harfest goers on a rural street leading to Highway 6, since I-70 was only for motorized traffic during the festival. We headed west as Relic tipped his hat, heading over to talk with Gray, who was watching the strangers head for the school building.

Though everyone else in the cart engaged in conversations about the festival, I was afraid to speak, let alone ask questions, but I had plenty. I wondered if Gray or my father knew where I was or what was happening. I hated worrying them. They had done enough of that on my account. Though I assumed the other people in the cart were trustworthy, none of them were speaking candidly about our hasty retreat. Maybe hasty was an overstatement since the horses were sauntering at a very relaxed pace. Where they were slow walking us to, I did not know, but I hoped at some point Will would share the plan with me.

I was so in my head that I had ignored my surroundings. Being aware and what to watch for had been part of my training at New Haven. Being scared and confused wasn't an excuse to tune out. They were reasons to be extra vigilant. I wasn't aware I had been looking downward until I looked up and saw Will studying me. He gave me a slight smile and turned to survey the surroundings. I followed his model and began searching the trees and abandoned buildings, watching and listening for activity, flashes of surveillance gear, or sudden movements by the wildlife.

The ride in vehicles down the poorly patched roads had been bumpy at best, but a horse-pulled cart with solid wheels gave me a new experience in rough riding. Every deviation in the road was met with the bouncing of the noisy cart springs.

We had been traveling for the better part of three hours without a break, so I was happy to pause our slow escape. The driver pulled into a parking lot of a plain building in a horrible state, as most uninhabited buildings were. But this one was definitely a church, because there was a sign, and "*Church*" was the only word left.

Passengers lumbered out of the wagon, rolling shoulders and adjusting the abused parts of their bodies, while struggling to stand up straight. It was a brutal ride. Then they scattered to find privacy to relieve themselves before they got back into the wagon.

Will and I walked to a grove of trees where two people were hiding under a camouflaged tarp. The small woman and the tall man were of our height and build. Their coats were camo-colored and of much better quality than our roughly worn ones. As expected, we traded coats and headgear. Then Will and I took their places under the tarp. Our imitations left the shelter of the trees and got in the wagon. I watched it leave.

"Will ..." I said in an anxious whisper, but I was cut off by a single gesture. I didn't know how long we waited under the tarp, sheltered by that group of trees, but my limbs became stiff from the cold before Will snuck us into the church building. I was shocked to see a horse, not Little Bet, standing in the lobby beneath a suspended tarp and munching on hay.

"We can talk now. I don't detect any drones," Will whispered.

"Then why are you still whispering, and what's with all the tarps?" I asked.

"The tarps shield us from infrared detectors. And though I can detect drones that are actively flying, I can't tell if they have landed to observe the area and listen for voices. We'll wait until it gets dark and then move on. Since we'll be traveling through the night, I suggest you get some sleep.

"Look, Connor, I'm sorry I whisked you out of there without an explanation. I know what that feels like. I was about your age when my dad did that to me."

"So, what exactly caused the sudden escape?" I was nowhere near calm enough to take a nap.

"Strangers were spotted in town, and they turned out to be two Neigh-wah agents with a hostage," he said the word hostage a little too mat-ter-of-factly.

"A hostage?!" I loudly whispered. "Who?"

"A girl about your age," he said with a worried look.

"Why? Why would they kidnap a girl?"

"If they hadn't been discovered, I'm sure they would have used her to get to you, maybe lure you out so they could grab you."

"That wouldn't have worked," I said with confidence.

"Gray said she was beautiful and terrified," Will said, tilting his head.

That might have worked, I said to myself. "Did they save her?"

Will shrugged his shoulder and said, "I'm sure they will try. It depends on the soldiers' insurance plan."

"Like other soldiers hurting someone else if they didn't come back?" I said, remembering my defensive training. "We were told not to give in to blackmail."

"That's easier said than done," he said. "Three times I gave up my freedom to keep people I cared about safe."

"I know about the time you were forced to join the Drangers and then the Neighwah, but when was the third time?" I asked.

"Well, about three years ago, I was on a mission to make a hostage trade for my dad, but it was a setup by the Robinhooders to help me escape. My dad and stepmom died when I was eleven. But there were rumors he was alive, rumors even I believed. You see, my stepmom was the daughter of a legendary rebel spy. She and her father tried to escape, but he died in the attempt. The Corporates tortured and abused her to find out what she knew, but the Robinhooders broke her out of the Highmind camp, and my dad found her in the woods."

"So, Robinhooders are the rebel faction?" I asked, and he nodded.

"I believe your grandad was pretty involved with them because he participated in the Highmind experiment," Will said.

"I was supposed to go to the Highmind camp, but my grandad helped me avoid the test by teaching me to act simple-minded. It's ironic that at two years old, I was intelligent enough to realize I was in danger and act accordingly. He was afraid that they would make me get tested."

"If they had tested you, they would have discovered your secret. It's easy to detect the Highmind gene. You may have been able to fool your neighbors, but the Neighwah use brain scans to determine one's abilities. Then they would have taken you to their camp."

"How do you know that?" I asked, not really wanting to know he had taken part in exposing Highmind children. He lowered his eyes and gave me a 'you know the answer to this' look. I decided to change the subject.

"Did they try to find your stepmom?"

"Yes, and when they started searching for her in our community, we ran. There was a group of workers trying to cross into the Colorado Springs Territory. After an avalanche killed two dozen workers at a Colorado Springs lumber camp, Pueblo agreed to sell them replacement workers. Though the three Colorado Territories work together, they rarely give up their workers, but they had an ulterior motive.

"They knew my stepmother would be among them and wanted to retrieve her. When we met up with the rest of the group waiting at the border, my parents told everyone that I was an orphaned child they were delivering to a relative. I think they suspected there could be soldiers waiting for them and wanted to protect me."

"Wouldn't the Pueblo soldiers know you were their son?"

"Pueblo was notorious for its poor record keeping, and I had all but disappeared because I shadowed my stepmom to work on the farms. As a good worker, I increased crop yield without being counted in the worker allotment, so the Upper in charge hid me. And an eleven-year-old kid just wasn't on their radar.

"Tianna had taught me the rebel secrets, which I thought were just fanciful stories, until that day. We were surrounded, and my mother refused to be recaptured. She made my father..." he paused, and I could see this was a heartbreaking memory. "She made my father kill her. He shot her as she awaited capture. Then, he detonated a bomb, taking out many of the approaching soldiers. I lost them both in that field. I was so distraught that Taylor's son, Pierce, drugged me and threw me over his shoulder. He ran with me and caught up with the cart before it got to the border."

I wanted to express my compassion and horror at what he had to witness, but he was a warrior, and in no way did he look like the sensitive type. "That must be an excruciating memory," I said.

He let out a long breath, tilted his head slightly, and moved on unceremoniously. "I got my dark skin from my mother, so no one knew my dad or Tianna were my parents. Taylor registered me as his adopted son. When I woke up. I was no longer William Alexander. I had a new name and a new reality. "

"I don't know Pierce, but I like Taylor. I'm glad you had him."

"I gave him a rough time. I was an angry, messed-up teen, but they kept me safe and allowed me to grow up. I was with the Drangers for almost a year before the Corporates figured out who I was. That's why they trapped me into joining the Neighwah. They thought they could spy on me and get me to help them find the Sanguine Blade. They told me that my dad escaped the blast, and he was still alive. I had fed them the story that I wanted to kill him because he killed Tianna. They thought I would reveal something if they paraded a man who resembled my dad in front of me."

"So, are you looking for your dad?"

"No, the RH, Robinhooders, confirmed that was a Corporate trick to get me to cooperate with them. Before they could use their decoy on me, the RH ambushed them, kidnapped me and Rival, and helped me escape into the woods. I was living off the land for the better part of a year before I joined the Fringers."

I imagined witnessing my family being killed and my dad being a part of it. It was inconceivable. It would be a life-changing moment for the most grounded person, but a child would be profoundly altered. I wish I had the right words to convince him that the boy he was and the pain he suffered mattered. But I said nothing. There were no such words for William of the Guard. He wasn't that vulnerable young boy anymore. He was a warrior.

"Get some sleep. We leave at sunset." And just like that, Will was back in commander mode. Despite the horrific details, I valued the exchange.

I thought back to a few weeks ago when I questioned traveling with this frightening Fringer. For him to share that story showed he trusted me and respected me. And my respect for him had grown exponentially.

CHAPTER 9

Will seemed to ease into sleep easily, me not so much. I needed to reason out the girl hostage, the events that made Will into William of the Guard, and where the heck this warrior extraordinaire was taking me. I grabbed my pack to find a place to rest in what was left of the church. Though the roof seemed to be intact, the place had been gutted. Only the front few pews remained, and Will was stretched out on the back one.

As I walked to the second pew row, a ray of light came through a top window. The dust particles swimming in its beam mesmerized me as it highlighted a space between two pews. I recalled the story of the two Greek scientists seeing such a scene and theorizing the existence of atoms, and that it happened now in this place of God made it spiritual and surreal. I felt a sense of comfort that my prayers for a sign of divine providence had been fulfilled. As I bowed my head, something glinted in the holy ray. Scooting my way across the bench, I lay on the weathered seat and retrieved the object, and shook off the decades of dust it had accumulated.

It was a small silver cross on a broken chain. It made me wonder who had left it. Was it lost while making a travel stop or during the disaster? I held it in my hand. It was small and broken, but it still had meaning, and that mattered. Before I sat back up, directly in front of me, in the pew pocket, was a book also layered in dust. I shook it off, suppressing a cough, so I wouldn't disturb Will.

It was a songbook with scriptures at the back, arranged by topics and events. Though old, the pages were of good quality and didn't crumble like some books. I read the musical notes, and I recognized some of the melodies from Haru's services.

A blue ribbon hung down, so I opened the book to the page it marked. At the top of the page was a verse from Deuteronomy 31:6: "Be strong and courageous. Do not be afraid or terrified because of them, for the Lord your God goes with you; he will never leave you nor forsake you."

They were the perfect words of encouragement, but how to be strong and courageous baffled me. Yet, they resonated and sang like a chorus in my head. This faith and the hope it offered had a powerful effect on me. I could see why the Corporates saw it as a threat. I looked at the items and considered leaving them. Just having them was enough to get me severely punished by the Corporates, but the hope they offered outweighed the threat.

I put the book in my breast front pocket. I smiled, remembering the movies where characters were saved by hiding in stick-built structures. In my training, I learned bullets could go through walls, and though words can't stop bullets either, maybe these items would bring me luck—another Hollywood fable.

I put the cross in my left pocket, so I could hold it when I needed courage and strength, and I laid my head on my pack. I was sleepier than I thought. I was gone as soon as I closed my eyes. Will woke me by shaking me.

It's common to struggle to slough off sleepiness when one first wakes up, but this was more than sleepiness. I felt awful. "Is it time to go?" I asked wearily.

Will gave me a worried look and put the back of his hand on my forehead. "You're burning up, Connor. How do you feel?"

"Not so good. My head hurts, and I'm cold."

"Well, you're going to get colder," he said as he took my jacket off me. He opened his pack and took out a med-kit. I watched him plow through it while I shivered. When he found what he was looking for, he sat me up. Nausea and dizziness rolled through me, causing my head to reel. "I think I'm sick, Will."

"I see that. Here," he said, handing me a small white pill. "This will take care of the fever. We still have a way to go to get to Glenwood. Don't worry, there are medicine people there, and the docs will be there tomorrow."

I took the pill with the water from my canteen. The water felt good on my throat, but Will didn't let me drink too much at once. "Don't they know that's where we were headed?" I didn't want to disrupt the plans, but I was sure the Corporates would follow our caravan there, and it was probably the last place we should go.

"Plans change. There are several secret places we can hide in until you recover."

"Okay, I'm getting up. I'll be fine."

Will shook his head. "Lay down and let the meds kick in, then we'll leave." I wanted to push through like he would, but I just nodded and lay back down. In my mind, I hoped this new destination was closer than he made it seem, but safe was good too.

Will woke me again, and I felt better, not great, but better. He had already loaded our packs and saddled the large horse still inside the church lobby. Walking the horse and us outside, he climbed up and effortlessly lifted me in front of him. I was glad he was that strong because I was weak and struggling. Will draped the infra-blocker tarp over us and put on a set of goggles to help him see in the dark. We began trotting the horse he called Ranger down a side trail that paralleled the road.

I'm not sure how I could fall asleep while riding a horse, but I did. It was pitch black, making the ride unnerving, but I tried to relax, knowing Will was in charge. After a time, we climbed down and took a quick break. My fever had calmed down, and my headache was reduced to a dull throb.

I felt a nudge as Will woke me up again. He handed me some banana chips, which I struggled to eat. But he was insistent that I drink the electrolyte juice.

He climbed onto the horse, and I set my foot in the stirrup, but I had no strength to lift myself. But he did so effortlessly. When we were settled, he pressed the horse's sides, saying, "Let's go, Ranger." I felt the familiar sway of the horse and realized I was sore from the previous ride. Or perhaps the ache of fever was creeping back.

We continued down the night-black trail where a river rushed below us, making traveling in the darkness more than a little frightening. I wanted to stay awake to get my bearings, but my attention drifted to the patches of shimmering snow illuminated by the crescent moon. Soon, the sway of the horse and the powerful arms securing me allowed me to fade in and out of a restless sleep.

I desperately needed to lie down, but I didn't want to sound whiny in front of Warrior Will. I thought about the scars slashed across the knuckles of all the Guard soldiers and remembered Hunter said it was from a blood-brother ritual. It must have hurt, and I wondered if I was brave enough to have my hand cut open like that. But I could appreciate it as a test of bravery and an enduring mark of loyalty.

"How much further?" I asked as Will paused our progress. I was shivering again, and I could see Will's concern return, and I shared it.

"About an hour to town, but we aren't going there. We're stopping by Bayley's. I'm looking for the hidden route to his cabin. He lives outside of town, and we need him to tell us if the town is safe. Plus, you need to get some horizontal rest in a warm house."

He took out the paper and flashed his dull light on the clues, and I eyed the handwritten document.

"What does emanon mean?" I asked weakly. "See the note at the bottom, 'find emanon'."

"It's written in some kind of code, I think," Will said, deep in thought.

"Well, emanon spells no name backwards. Not much of a—"

Will interrupted. "Of course, No Name Creek. There's a trail called Jessie Weaver that follows it. We're close." With that, Will led Ranger at a slightly quicker pace.

My fever was back when we got to Bayley's rustic cabin. But it was warm, and Will carried me to the spare bedroom where I was quarantined. Then he put another tablet under my tongue. I had never felt so sick.

"Will, am I going to die?"

"No, Bayley already went to get a healer. I know you feel bad, but you'll feel better in the morning. I've seen this before." Will answered, but I could tell he was worried too.

"Blood brother," I said weakly. "Hunter, he told me about the soldiers being blood brothers. Before I get worse, can I be a blood brother, so I can die with honor?"

"You're not going to die, Connor. But I had every intention of making you a blood brother. I just wanted to get permission from your dad and wait until we were on the mission trail. But if you want, we'll do it now." That confirmed that he was more than a little worried.

I watched Will go to his pack and get out a knife. Not any knife, THE knife.

"Is that—"

"Yes, this is the knife Tianna gave me on that day."

It was beautifully made, with a handle of deep mahogany highlighted with a magnificent grain pattern. The grip had a finger-hold shape, with carved markings I was too weak to analyze.

"I recognize this," I said, "means balance... of...," I moaned and rolled my head, beaded with sweat. "Can't think. Sorry."

Will pulled out the double-sided blade with a jagged ridge running along the top. As weak as I was, I tried not to focus on the mysterious relic, and I hoped he didn't have to use the jagged side. The blade had a burnt reddish hue as if it were permanently stained by the violent prophecy it was destined to set in motion. A silver lightning bolt shot down the blade, flashing through the bloody pigment.

Will heated the blade in the small fireplace, running it through the fire several times. I tried to put the impending pain out of my head as I rethought my request. I was glad he didn't give me the option to back out. He went straight to the business of it

"Repeat after me. 'I pledge to fight at your side for the glory and allegiance that brings a better fate to all'. Say it and ball up your fighting hand into a fist."

I made a fist with my left hand and repeated the pledge while keeping an eye on the formidable weapon he was about to slice me with. I knew it would burn, but I couldn't look away like a coward. I wondered how much blood was required for the ritual, yet I remained silent with eyes open. I could feel my nails digging into my palm with nervousness, but I still held it out to him.

"Look at me, not your hand," he said. "Don't overthink it."

He took a cleansing breath, and he slashed across the existing scars on his balled-up fist. Then he took my wrist, so small compared to his own, and before my doubt got the better of me, he sliced across the top of my four fingers and smashed our bloody fists together. At first, I felt nothing; then it burned like nothing I had ever felt.

My eyes watered as an intense sensation of pain burned on my hand and spread throughout my body. I didn't cry out, but I wanted to. My vision blurred, and I was swirling down into a thick, dark world that consumed me. I must have collapsed because it was hours later that I woke up to an old woman bending over me. I looked at the woman and around the unfamiliar room with concern until I located Will leaning against the doorjamb.

"Are you the healer?" I asked, hearing the roughness in my voice.

"Yes, I'm Freida. My grandmother trained me. Tell me how you are feeling, Miles."

Though my mind was foggy, I remembered the name Will had given me to protect my identity. "My throat hurts some, but my headache is gone. I feel better than I did when I got here. But I have this weird tingly sensation all over me. It isn't painful, but it's ... odd."

"Rest is what you need, and the short nap you got is the reason you feel better. The tingling is probably due to the rash you have. Open your mouth so I can see your throat." I obeyed.

"It's red and swollen, but not too bad. It's your fever that concerns me. How did you hurt your hand?"

Will interrupted, "He was delirious and tried to swing at me while I had my knife out."

"Odd that it matches the wound so many in your charge have. Please tell me you don't believe in bloodletting," she said with a knowing glare sent Will's way.

"No, nothing like that," Will let her insult go. "It's a long story," he said, and then quickly changed the subject. "I didn't know he had a rash. Maybe I didn't notice it because I kept him bundled up as we rode here. Can you make him well?"

Will was leaning in the doorway, and Freida leaned close, whispering, "Do you feel safe with him?"

"I don't feel safe without him," I whispered back. "He has taken good care of me."

She sat back up and addressed Will. "He needs rest, liquids, and easy food. He seems to have improved already, if the report that brought me here was accurate. Use these herbs in a tea to ease the skin rash and the fever. Let me know if you need me to come back," she said. She sighed heavily and leaned on the mattress to slowly rise into a bent state. Will walked over, took the herb bag, and handed Freida her intricate wooden cane.

"Thank you, Freida," he said over his shoulder, and she nodded. Then he came over to the bed and asked, "Let me see your arm."

I bared my arm from under the blankets. It was covered with red spots.

CHAPTER 10

I woke up feeling disoriented, but I quickly sorted out the events of the last day. I tried to sit up but thought better of it halfway up, flopping back down. Again, I sat up, and most of the dizziness from moments ago was gone. Will must have heard me because he came in with a bowl of soup and bread. The more awake I became, the better I felt. I was even hungry, so I slurped down the whole bowl and wolfishly devoured the bread.

I lay there for some time, and though still feeling weak, boredom was kicking in. I forced myself up and made my way out to the main room. The short walk had me hanging onto a chair back, and the next thing I knew, Bayley was carrying me back to my bed. I heard him say that my fever was spiking again. I felt the tablet melting under my tongue, and sleep pulled me back into its foggy depths of a dream.

Though the cave was cast in shadows, I could still make out the beautiful six-armed woman with a pair of swords poised to strike. She swayed her body and waved the weapons in a violent dance, smiling as she approached me.

In my hand was an ancient sword. It was large and heavy, but I easily wielded it, causing it to gleam and shimmer in the gloomy arena. I faced her, my body positioned to match her blow for blow. She stepped forward, and I tried to bring my sword down on her shoulder, but she countered. Each contact sends sparks flying from our enchanted swords. Thrust, parry, thrust, parry, again and again with no blood to satisfy our thirst for the other's demise.

A whimpering sound came from the dark, where Jilly was huddled in a corner. She was using her body to shield something. My distraction had undone me, and I watched in slow motion as her sword made a mortal swing toward me.

I awoke with such a start that I almost fell out of bed. My breath was rapid. My heart was pounding. I closed my eyes and practiced the calming meditation GD taught. Breathing in and out slowly and methodically while tapping my fingers to match my pulse, slowing the pace until I estimated my rate was under 70 beats per minute. I swung my legs to the floor and got out of bed. Though my body felt better, the dream left me disturbed.

I walked out to two grown men pointing me back to my room.

"Look, I'm better," I said, doing a silly jig to prove my condition.

"I need you well enough to travel tomorrow, and it will be a grueling trek," Will said, contemplating his steaming mug.

"Well, do you have any books around here? If I'm going to be grounded to this room, at least give me something to do," I argued.

What I really wanted to do was decipher the code on the Sanguine Blade, but that was another thing Bayley needed protection from. "Here is my box of library books. I get a new batch each month. They're probably too hard for you, but you can have at 'em, Miles," said Bayley, and he closed the door to my room.

I smiled, realizing Will had told him nothing about who I was. Dumping the books on the bed, I sat cross-legged, rifling through them like a pirate inventorying his treasures. I could hear Will and Bayley mumbling purposefully beyond the closed door as I went through the books. If I had been back to my zealous investigative self, I might have listened at the door, but an interesting book had grabbed my attention. *Dancing with the Lion* by Jeanne Reames was a semi-fictional look at Alexander the Great as a child. I had noticed several books about this ancient king on the shelf in

Will's studio room at the fort. I opened the book and settled in: *Chapter One, Runaway*.

I must have fallen asleep again because it was high noon when I woke up. My rash and fever were gone, and I felt cured. Discovering Bayley had left for town to lead some of the team members back allowed Will and me to speak privately.

"Can I look at the symbols on your knife?"

"Well, good afternoon to you too. Yes, you are welcome for the care you received, and I'm so glad you feel better."

I froze. I hoped I hadn't damaged the respect I had gained with Will. "I'm sorry. I appreciate how you took care of me. Thank you—"

Will laughed, "Stop. I was just poking at you. I know you are a good kid, and I also know when you are obsessing over something, like your inability to decode the symbols on my knife. Your fever was pretty high. I wouldn't be too hard on yourself."

"Well, I've never had my brain betray me so completely, but I would like the opportunity to prove it was that and not my lack of skills. So, before Bayley comes back, can I take a look?" Will was already opening his pack and digging deeply into some hidden chamber to retrieve it. He handed it to me.

I looked at the rich auburn mahogany and the symbols etched into it. I analyzed the metal sheath, which was masterfully etched and highlighted in black. It displayed a rugged cliff with a river edging past it.

"Well, I'll need to confer with Relic, but it could be a clue to the entrance. There are no photos of the range after the meteorites, so I'm not sure how we can confirm it. But this side," I said as I turned the knife over, "looks like a Celtic cross, so the letters are probably Celtic too. The Celtic cross symbolizes health. The twisting serpents represent how physical and mental states are entwined and require balance for complete health."

"I don't see how that is possible in war," said Will.

"Yeah, I get it, but maybe it's the most important time to try," I said while deep in concentration.

Will agreed and watched me slide the knife out. He froze when he saw that it still had the remnants of our mingled blood. It did not startle me. It was proof that it was real, and the stain signified the intensity of the act.

"Thank you for making me a blood brother. I know I am not worthy, and I'm sure the tall people will harass you for it. Sorry about that, but thank you."

"Tall people? You mean adults?" he asked, and I nodded. Will laughed a deep laugh, a genuine laugh, the kind one shares with good friends. He gestured for the blade, poured some water from my water glass onto his shirt, and wiped the blade clean. He handed the blade back to me, saying, "You are worthy, Connor. You are much braver and more honorable than you take credit for."

He wasn't the kind to give fluffy compliments or undeserved praise, and it filled me with pride that we were brothers. I had earned his respect, and he had my pledged loyalty. I gave him a silent smile that spoke of all the tough decisions he and I had endured. Will understood.

"This lightning bolt boldly striking down the business end of this weapon is a symbol common to most cultures of power, strength, and energy. It has also been interpreted as a sign of divine intervention. Hmm," I turned the knife back and forth. Something about divine intervention. I couldn't remember, and I remember everything. It must be from deep in my childhood. Think, think, but I couldn't.

"What are you looking for?" asked Will.

"Devine intervention," I answered. "Do you have a magnifying glass?"

Before Will could respond, we heard Bayley's voice entering the cabin. Will stealthily tucked the knife under the sweater he wore, and I sprinted to the bedroom. Only Gray was with him, no Jilly. They came in with an urgent tension that swirled through the room.

"We've got spies everywhere in town," Gray said with an undercurrent of urgency. "I imagine they're in these woods too. How's Connor? Can he travel?"

"Yeah," I said, coming out of the bedroom. Gray instantly directed his attention to the bandage on my hand and looked at Will.

"Will tell me that was an accident and not an inflicted wound," Gray said with an alarmed expression.

Will looked away from Gray and adjusted his guilty posture to defiance.

"I asked him to make me a blood brother. I... I thought I might die," I said in Will's defense. But I detected Gray's expression wasn't all anger. He was... frightened. I convinced myself his fear was about explaining it to my dad. Or maybe he worried my dad would pull me? Would they let him do that? Could they stop him?

"I say we stop bellyaching over things that are done. Let's get out of here. Connor go pack. Bayley, is there a hidden trail out of here?"

"No, this ravine is pretty steep. Where do you want to go?" he asked.

"Warren told me they have an underground bomb shelter we could bring him to. It's under the Holy Cross Power Plant. There's an access tunnel at the horseshoe turn near the end of Red Canyon Road," Gray said.

Bayley nodded, saying, "I can draw a map to avoid town, but it will take a long time to get there by horseback. First, you have to cross the Colorado River, and—"

"I have another idea," Gray interjected. "We smuggle Connor in the mini's undercarriage, and Will can track us through this ravine to keep the Corporates troops from stopping us. If we need to, we can find a safe transfer site to unload Connor. It's cold enough for kids to be wrapped up, so a trusted Fringer could get him to the power plant."

"It's risky," Will said, shaking his head. "But so is traveling with him for the better part of a day through treacherous terrain. Are you afraid of tight spaces, Connor?"

"Did you just call me a wimp, *blood-brother*? Is this where I call you out? Rather unfair advantage, but if it's required to save my reputation as a—"

"Oh, crap," Gray said, pointing at me. "I think he just became a teenager. That's the first symptom, reckless defiance." All the talls began laughing.

"Oh, you're funny, you are," I retorted, but it took everything I had to hide my amusement and relief that Will didn't accept my challenge to give me a life lesson moment.

Gray was still chuckling as he motioned Will outside for a sidebar conversation. I was pretty sure it was about my hand and the details of our escape plan. I tried to make my way near the door, hoping to hear the plan, but Bayley herded me into my room to finish packing.

"Can I take this book with me?" I asked.

He sighed and looked at me. "Yeah, go ahead, but when you give it back to me, don't go spilling the tale and spoiling it for me." He was trying to show he believed I would be back, but not quite pulling it off.

I smiled, trying to convince him I believed it too, but I couldn't pull it off either.

I came outside, feeling the uneasy tension like static. Will and Gray didn't seem at odds with each other, but something threatened their cohesiveness, and I was at the center of it. I looked at Will and Gray, and they relaxed. Gray patted me on the shoulder, and Will took my pack to secure it behind the saddle.

"Are you feeling up to this?" Gray asked, looking at me.

"I feel great. When I first got here two days ago, I was afraid I might not... um, get better, but now I could climb that tree," I said, pointing to a particularly tall pine. It didn't relieve Gray to hear my report, so I tried to double down on my restored condition.

"I'm not lying to be brave or anything Gray, I feel as well as I ever have, maybe better. You don't need to worry." He smiled, but the worry lines on his forehead deepened. If he was worried about my mental well-being, this was the time he would have offered one of his platitudes of encouragement, but he said nothing. Interesting.

Will and I said our goodbyes, and he headed into the woods.

Gray handed me earbuds so I could hear them talking, and he helped me into the mini smuggler's hold. But I sat back up, holding the earbud I had yet to put in. I had to know about Will. "It would be tight, but there's plenty of room for two. Why can't Will come too?"

"First, there is not enough room for Will. But more importantly, there are soldiers positioned in this ravine. Some are ours, some are not, but they are aware of each other, and we can't get caught in the crossfire. We need an advantage, and Will is the best bowman around. He can eliminate trouble without a sound."

They didn't need to explain to me what eliminating trouble meant. I looked at the scar across my hand, the mark that said I belonged to the soldier world. This was the ugly part of that world.

CHAPTER II

"How does Will get to the power plant?" I asked.

"He'll get there," Gray said.

And then they enclosed me in this hiding place. The width of the space was roomy, but the ceiling was just inches from my face. With the blanket and my thick jacket, I wasn't cold, but I wasn't warm either. Normally, moving around could warm me up, but I didn't dare move when I heard the rumble of a vehicle. When it stopped, I heard two doors open and close. It could only be the enemy soldiers. They were here.

I couldn't hear all of what they were saying because the listening device wouldn't come on until the mini was powered up. But I heard enough to know it was small talk. No doubt they were biding their time to eye every inch of the area and probably recording it with a hidden camera. Their voices became louder and clearer as they moved over to the vehicle. I held my breath in fear. Then I regained my composure and let my breath out slowly. I was told they wouldn't be able to hear my breathing in the undercarriage. I wasn't panicking, but I was fighting the urge.

"Nice ride here," a stranger's voice said. "Mind if I check it out?"

"Actually," Gray said calmly, "I do. What are you after? Why don't you get to the point and leave?"

"I'm looking for a fugitive, William Alexander. It seems he has kidnapped a child in addition to his other crimes."

"What does he look like?" asked Bayley.

"Dark skin, tall, battle scars and tattoos on his forearms," said the voice.

"What'd he do?" asked Bayley.

"Ask him," he said, gesturing to Gray. "He knows."

"What I know is that you broke the treaty signed by your top general when you invaded Fringer territory. He caught you attacking our town, and he assisted in our defense."

"The tunnel was never recognized as part of Fringer Territory," the stranger countered.

"Actually, it is within the boundaries of the negotiated area," Gray said smugly.

"There's more. For starters, he deserted the Neighwah and sabotaged an operation. If we had known he survived... I know you know something, so is he here, and if not, where is he?" the man was yelling now, and every word was clear.

"Relax," said Gray. "It's no secret. He was with us, but he left days ago to return a kid to his family. Where he is now, who knows? Probably taking some long nature route back to his fort. He's a bit of a loner."

Why would Gray tell them about the fort, let alone send them there? It must be part of the plan because Gray would never betray an ally.

"Is he in that cabin?" the voice asked.

"Come see for yourself, but leave your camera-infested jacket out here. That's my house, and I don't have to let you inside. This is Fringer Territory, and your rights here are limited," said Bayley.

I heard the door squeak, and then it was quiet for what seemed like forever. The next thing I heard was the shuffling of feet on the wooden porch and the slamming of a door. The blustery man grumbled as he passed the mini.

"I will find him, and if I think you've been helping him, I'll drag both of you back to headquarters."

The vehicle started back up, and I heard its motor head away. Gray and Bayley got in the mini and started it up. After a minute to warm it up, Gray tapped three times on the floor, and I tapped three back, meaning I was okay.

Now that the vehicle was running, my earbuds worked, so I could hear every word between Bayley and Gray. I just couldn't join in. I'm sure Gray will tease me about how nice that arrangement was.

We hadn't traveled very far when Gray said, "Stay still, slugger. We've got company." Then the mini stopped. Gray whispered something to Bayley that he didn't want me to hear, not a good sign. There was a commotion outside, though I never heard the doors open, so I knew it wasn't Gray and Bayley.

"Keep 'em up unless you want to have a couple of holes added to your person," said someone outside. "We got the road covered, sir. You can continue."

"Nice work, thanks," said Gray. And the mini started moving again. I knew Will was out there perched on the hill clearing the road for us, but this wasn't him. In fact, this voice didn't belong to anyone on our team. Will must have employed some of his Reserve Guards to secure our way.

"Did you know my road was crawling with soldiers?" Bayley asked with exasperation.

"Arranged it, well, the ones on our side, anyway." I could imagine Gray smiling as he poked fun at his new friend.

"Uh-huh," Bayley huffed, probably feeling both happy and unhappy about the plan. "Guess I should be grateful, but can't say I like that kind of company. And how did you know Will was with me?"

Gray dismissed Bayley's complaints but addressed the question about their mutual friend.

"Will didn't leave word about where he would go, but we had set up several places when we came up with the escape plan. Your cabin was one of them."

"Thanks for askin'." Bayley huffed, but it was just his way. I knew he was happy to help.

"With all the attention we had at Eagle, we concluded that your place was his most logical choice. Then the medicine woman, Freida, told us about being sent for to treat a sick child there. We knew that a team of Garrison soldiers would pay you a visit, so we lined the trail."

"Garrison? Sounds like some kind of combat troop ready for war."

"You aren't wrong, but they aren't massing for that kind of operation. Not yet anyway. It's just what the Corporates call their teams when they contain both Neighwah and Dranger soldiers."

"I've never heard that term before," Bayley responded.

"Yeah, I just recently learned it myself. I don't think they employ those two armies together very often, but lately it has become a standard," answered Gray.

I was feeling panicky. Maybe it was because the conversation above had turned more threatening, or maybe I was just sick of feeling like I was buried alive. I said a prayer. "Please, Jesus, get me out of here."

"So, what is it about this kid that makes him so important?" Bayley asked. "I mean, the fact that you brought him is evidence enough, so don't deny it." I tapped vigorously on the lid. It's not that I thought Gray would tell him about me, but I was feeling more trapped by the minute.

"You okay, Connor?" asked Gray. I tapped three times in response.

Gray opened the small door to allow me to talk. I took a breath, and seeing daylight gave me the relief I needed.

"How much longer?" I asked, trying not to sound anxious.

"Ten minutes, fifteen at the most. Can you do that?" asked Gray.

"Yeah, but I don't want to do this again. And Gray," I said with a pleading tone, "please drive faster."

"You got it, bud," and I felt the motor rev up and the bouncing increase. Their conversation had ended, making the small space feel more ominous.

Even though the conversation had turned dangerous, it was comforting to hear.

"So, back to—"

"Hey, grab your gear, here's your stop," Gray said, and I felt the mini swerve and stop. "Enjoyed getting to know you. If I'm ever in Glenwood, I'd love to stop over," Gray said, dismissing the conversation Bayley wished to continue.

Bayley huffed a chuckle, and I heard the door open. "Anytime."

I was beyond relieved when they slid me out of that tray. I looked around and saw we were in a garage with four soldiers standing guard. I was shivering, and Jilly greeted me with a warm blanket. We were led by one of the soldiers to a closet where he tapped in a code, and a false door slid open. Jilly and I were led down a ladder into a dimly lit tunnel. The three-foot wide tunnel felt overly small after my recent ordeal. It snaked back and forth for at least fifty yards before a door came into view.

Through the door was a hallway with three doors, one on both sides and one at the end. We went through the end door, which opened up to a small medical facility.

"How are you doing, Connor? I see you had a rough ride to town," Jilly finally spoke as she directed me to a patient bed and began putting a blood pressure cuff on my arm. She smiled, recording my results, which she said were understandably elevated but within healthy limits.

I didn't feel cold anymore, but I was still shaking. Jilly said I was probably in shock, but nothing bad had happened, so why was I so rattled? I finally answered her, trying to sound like it was just another day as a soldier.

"It wasn't fun, but I'm okay," I gave a nervous chuckle, adding, "I think that was the point." I would have been better off if I had just stopped there, but Jilly and I were too good of friends for me not to tell her what happened.

"It wasn't bad until we were stopped. I heard Gray talking with the soldiers who stopped us, but they turned out to be ours, so we kept going.

But it was hard to be trapped like that." Jilly saw my bottom lip quiver, and she brought me into a hug.

It undid my attempt at having a soldier's resolve. I was full-on crying as she held me. "You're okay now, Connor. We've got you. They got you here safely, and they will keep you safe."

"Look," I sobbed, and I pulled off my bandages to show her my slashed knuckles, still raw from the trauma. "This is the mark of a brave soldier. I made a pledge, and here I am crying like a baby," bringing on a fresh round of sobs.

"Seriously?" said Jilly. "I've seen plenty of soldiers cry. I've seen Gray cry."

"Gray?" I said, heaving a shuddered sigh.

"I bet Will has cried too. It's cathartic. It is an honest way to express grief and acknowledge your emotional pain. Being brave is about staying the course when choices are hard and times get difficult. It's about caring enough to go through hardships to accomplish an honorable goal. It's not about being an uncaring robot." The whole time she was examining me, she became more relieved with every healthy reading.

"She's right," came Gray's voice from where he stood leaning on the door frame. "Soldiers may keep their emotions in check during a battle, but it's normal to break down after. I would be worried if they didn't. If Will were here, he'd agree." Gray winked at his wife, and she smiled in return. "Just to be clear, Connor. No one is questioning your bravery. In fact, I am more than impressed." With that, he left to go to the lab where Relic was.

Jilly was about to put antibiotics on my hand wound, but I drew it back. "I want it to scar," I said, and Jilly rolled her eyes.

Just then, Relic came through the lab door and gestured for Jilly to join him. After a few minutes, she came back. "I need a few drops of blood to see if we can figure out why you were so sick."

I stuck out my hand, and she pricked my finger, squeezing out several drops into a vial. After bandaging me up and taking the vial to the lab room, she led me to a small cafeteria. She put a pan of water on the stove and set a soup packet on the counter with crackers and dried apples.

"Can you watch this?" she asked, pointing to the stove. "I need to tell Gray something."

"Yeah, I got it," I said, and I started opening cabinets and drawers to find bowls, cups, and spoons. It had been a long time since I had cooked. I used to take care of all the cooking for my family when I was a Daily back in Denver. I kind of missed it, cooking that is.

CHAPTER 12

It was less than ten minutes when Jilly came through the door. She looked pale. Without a word, she stirred the pan of bubbling chicken noodle soup. Within a few minutes, we were taking our bowls to the table and grabbing at the plate of crackers and dried apples.

"Wow, Jilly," I mused, "this trip sure has roused your appetite. I used to wonder how you survived on the mouse-sized helpings you ate, but ..." I paused. When Jilly told me she was pregnant, I researched the symptoms and risks that she may endure. Learning is my way of managing the worries her condition generated. It also avoided having to ask private questions. I also researched miscarriages, and her recent symptoms didn't add up to one recovering from a miscarriage; they indicated quite plainly she was still pregnant.

"Jilly," I said carefully, "are you still pregnant?"

She laughed out loud, almost choking on her soup. "Leave it to a child to figure it out." She was still laughing, but it was a troubled laugh.

"I seriously doubt it, but I have to ask. Does Gray know?" Jilly got up and closed the door.

"No, but I never meant to hide it from him. I had a suspicion a day or two before we left, but I dismissed it. The likelihood of losing one child while keeping another is quite rare. I really didn't know for sure until Andie made me take a test that I was sure.

"The Fringers and the Guard need Andie, and this mission needs me. I also thought to myself, do I want to sit home alone worrying about Gray, and whether this world we have fought for is at an end, or do I want to be with the man I love and fight for what I believe in?"

"Well, sounds like you have all your justifications in line," I said, knowing it was not a supportive response.

"I know. I'm risking the baby, lying to my husband about his own child, and jeopardizing the mission if something goes wrong. I've hashed these things out a million times. But I keep coming back to a couple of undeniable truths. I can't bear to raise this child as a Daily. That is if any of us are allowed to survive a Corporate victory. And just as importantly, I am the only medical person trained for this position."

"I get all those reasons for you wanting to come on the mission, but I think you should tell Gray. At some point, he's going to guess, like I did, and that won't go well."

"I don't know if he has the time to guess. He's up to his neck in problems. Every time I think about telling him, some new nightmare gets dumped on him. I just overheard the latest one, and no, I'm not telling you. You already have a secret about me." She had a troubled look that went beyond duty and loyalty. It reeked of the secrets Daily used to have to keep. What has she discovered?

We sat there looking at our empty bowls when Gray walked in with Relic. Jilly stiffened slightly, and I knew instantly the latest nightmare came from the conversation they had and Jilly had eavesdropped on. So, Gray and Relic were keeping secrets too. Why was she not allowed to hear it? She was drowning in guilt for all the lies she had to manage. I've been there, and though I don't need to lie anymore, I am hidden away while everyone around me lies.

I felt that familiar knock, the one that compels me and begs me to find the dark truths I'm stuck in the thick of.

The mood changed immediately as Gray and Relic came for lunch, attacking the task as they would a mission duty. I watched as Jilly gave a convincing performance of normalcy, holding my expression in check. When I snickered, Jilly bristled.

I smiled because I knew how to play the talk about everything else game too. "I was just thinking about being worried that I wouldn't feel safe outside of the tunnel. But when I got outside, my fear evaporated. I found the open sky and crisp air invigorating and realized how much I missed it. The next thing I know, I'm being smuggled by horses to abandoned churches and shoved into cramped dark places. And now, I'm back to living underground. The tide of irony is staggering. Hey, you, Destiny," I shouted to the ceiling, "give me a rudder, or at least an anchor."

We all laughed, but none as loud as Jilly and me.

"When we get on the road to our next destination, you won't be hiding in mini holds or in underground facilities." Although Gray was trying to assure me, he didn't know. What he should know is that those assurances may work on innocent children, but I am beyond that.

"You mean when the Friendship Tour ends and we begin looking for something to destroy the Corporates with. Yeah, now I'm afraid of the outdoors all over again. More irony," I added with an eye roll.

Gray gave me a thoughtful look, nodded, and patted me on the back. He was already done with his meal. He was a fast eater. Always on the ready, he said, on duty soldiers weren't given much time to eat. Relic and Gray left while Jilly and I cleaned up the lunch dishes, rekindling our laughter at my ruse. Then Jilly led me to the staff bunkroom.

"You'll sleep here, but you can wander about. There's a small physical therapy room where you can work out and a screen room that offers lots of movies and TV series. There will be a Defender or a Guard here at all times to protect you. They know where everything is, so they can help you with the TV and—"

I tipped my head and rolled my eyes. "I think I can handle turning on a movie. But I have a request. Before we leave, could you get me a couple of books from this town's library? Maybe some adventure stories or a couple of science fiction stories about space travel."

"I'll try," she said, "but we are leaving tomorrow, so I'll have to hurry."

I was almost finished with the book I borrowed from Bayley, and I had my tablet, but I like physical books. The memories they offer of me and GD comfort me. Though I was an accomplished reader by age three, I loved hearing him read the stories, and it is his voice I hear when I read.

After a day of hiding in the bunker, reading, writing, and watching movies, I was bored. I was thankful that I wasn't wrestling with life challenging issues, but I had no one to hang with. I finished the book I borrowed from Bayley and wrote several entries in my journal. My tablet had lots of reading material to choose from, but nothing called to me. Lying on my bunk with my hands behind my head, I ran through the mysteries they were keeping from me and tried to connect them to the secrets I knew. I had heard enough chatter to know the Fringers had some information they were holding over the Corporates'. It was the reason they weren't being overtly aggressive. It must be horrific. I couldn't think of anything that would shock the Dailys or the Uppers when it came to the actions of the Corporates.

And something else was going on with the mission plans, probably a medical issue because it involved the med lab. Jilly referred to it as 'the next nightmare'. I hoped we weren't in the middle of an epidemic. Dr. Andie had openly talked about a virus a couple of Fringers were being treated for. But the patients were responding well, or that was the last time I heard about it.

I tried to list the resource options available to me for investigating mysteries, but my list was blank. In the tunnel, GD had left clues for me to find, and, being connected to our network, I could access tiny pieces of information, which I could assemble into a bigger picture. I could ask directly, but I was sure that would only cause them to protect me from it. My only option was my lip-reading skills. I took a deep breath and let out a sigh. Gray, Will, and Relic would not make that easy.

I set my thoughts on the mystery I knew about. I wondered how and when Jilly would tell Gray the truth about his impending fatherhood. I almost envied Gray for being blissfully unaware of his newest circumstances, but when he found out, he'd be very unhappy, and that would go badly for everyone. I was sure Jilly was waiting until he couldn't send her back, which is exactly what he'd do. I chuckled at the thought of Jilly holding back her appetite and sneaking food when Gray wasn't looking.

The mind exercises didn't take nearly enough time or effort to settle my restlessness. Though it was way too early for dinner, pondering Jilly's eating habits was making me hungry.

I waited as long as I could before I found my dinner of rice and pork stir-fry in the fridge. The microwave was quick and easy, but I missed cooking. It was the one thing about the tunnel I wasn't fond of. At first, the idea of not preparing three meals a day or cleaning up sounded like a dream come true, but I liked cooking. I enjoyed planning meals and putting ingredients together. The supplies we were issued as Dailys were below substandard, but I dreamed of cooking with the groceries available to me now. The other benefit of taking time to cook was that it was something to do. I am a loner at heart, but this solitary existence was killing me.

I was in the screen room watching a series called *Supernaturals* when I heard a familiar voice. It was my father. I ran out and came in fast for a hug, almost knocking him over. Our eyes grew watery, threatening to spill, but we steeled ourselves against it. I wondered if this was a sign of growing up or becoming hard-hearted.

"I've missed you so much," Dad said, squeezing me closer to him. "I can stay for a bit, but they're smuggling me out of here tonight. This mission is getting more risky by the day," he said, and I nodded. "You know," he said slowly, "Gray said if you wanted to go home with me, you could."

I stepped away from him. "You know I can't do that, Dad. There are clues and answers inside me that are needed for us to succeed, to win. I don't even know what to expect, so I can't just tell someone how to do this."

"I know. If I drag you home, all of us could lose everything. If I leave you here, I may lose you. You can't know how impossible this is," Henry sat with his head in his hands. I put my arm around him as he let the tears come. I watched my father sit with his head in his hands and saw his shoulders shudder slightly as he let out a shaky breath. I put my hand on his back. I could understand what he felt, but I couldn't imagine the depth. I envisioned children of prehistoric tribes being taken from their parents to be sacrificed to some pagan god while their parents watched in agony. Maybe that was a little overly dramatic, but it wasn't too far from the truth.

"I'll come back, Dad," I said with all the determination I could muster.

It was sometime later that Relic came in. "Henry, I'm glad you could come. I can't tell you how amazing this boy of yours is. You should be incredibly proud."

"Honestly, at this moment, I wish some other father was proud, and I was counting on someone else to do this job."

I laughed. "Remember when I said that? We were hiding art, moving around, leaving all our stuff at every place we landed, and I was so frustrated you wouldn't tell me why."

Henry chuckled. "Yeah, you said, 'How will we get somewhere else sometime soon to live in whatever they give us for the work thing? I guess the answer to that is somehow'. Now we should add 'for someone to do something' to answer why."

We laughed hard, belly laughs. It was restorative, and we basked in its reprieve. But too soon, the veracity of our duty snapped us back to reality and the deadly dedication that loomed before us both.

"Dad," I said, "can we talk about baseball instead?" Henry smiled, and Relic went back to his lab.

We discussed old games and victories and dreamed of future games in fully restored fields with crowds of citizens attending, cheering, and living free and happy lives, which brought us back to the challenges before us and our precarious prospects.

We only had an hour together before they called him to the garage. It was time for him to go. He told me he was going to spend some of the trip in the smuggler's hold and the rest in the larger storage area of the Brute. I said a prayer in my head, knowing firsthand how miserable that ride would be. My dad kissed my forehead and said goodnight and goodbye for now.

I heard his footsteps pad down the hall as tears rolled onto my pillow. I miss him already. I miss my mom, my sister, my friends, my dog, and my life. "My life," I said sarcastically under my breath, and let out a mocking laugh. I can't remember a time when my life wasn't complicated or brimming over with tragic irony.

CHAPTER 13

I tried to remember one of GD's platitudes. They didn't make the world better or change what I was going through, but they occupied my mind with logic and reason. I found it often pushed my woes aside. The only one that I could bring to mind was, "Fate is a cruel creature who assigns benefits and malice without rationale, but it is also she that gave birth to kindness." It wasn't helping. It felt like this creature was cruel or stupid. Her cruelty consumed whatever kindness she gave.

As I lay there, Haru's words echoed in my head. "You are never alone, Connor. Just bow your head and focus on what you are feeling and needing." So, I prayed. It wasn't magic, and I wasn't going to wake up in a perfect world, but I wasn't alone. Most importantly, I couldn't lose because I believed.

I don't remember falling asleep, but I woke up to a shuffling sound in the hall. My security detail softly mumbled, and the next shift soldier mumbled back. I lay back down, assuming it was a shift change. Then I heard it. His laugh was unmistakable. He was back! I bounded out of bed, shocking the Defender standing guard outside the bunk room.

"Will!" I cried and rushed into his arms. "I thought, I was worried that..."

"Dude, I'm hurt that you have so little faith in me," he chuckled.

Relic came out at that moment and slapped Will on the shoulder. "Good to see you. When you're done catching up, come and see me." Will looked at him with concern. "No worries, I just need a small blood sample. I don't want anyone spreading any viruses. Get some sleep. It can wait," Relic said and turned to go back to the lab. Could it be that the medical issue and all the blood samples are just a preventive measure?

"Does that guy ever sleep?" I asked.

"Yeah, I've seen it once or twice," Will smiled.

"Will, tell me about your adventure. And by the way, am I ever going to get out of this dungeon? And will I then just go to the next? I know I can't be seen by the enemy, but I'm kind of done with being moled up in this place and that."

"Whoa, you are talking at light speed, and I've been up too long to keep up. Long story short, I hung out on the freezing ridges, and I didn't get captured, wounded, or worse."

I nodded. Hey, I finished this book about Alexander the Great as a kid. You should read it." I looked at his casual clothing and assumed he had been here long enough to shed his soldier's gear.

"I long for the day I have that kind of time and live in a well lit, warm place. Maybe someday," Will said, and he stretched out on one of the beds. "Let me sleep, little man. I'm beat."

I slept soundly until I heard Will get up and go down the hall. I heard mumbling about getting ready to leave in a hurry. I sat up.

"Good, you're awake," said Will. "Pack your gear. We're heading out."

"To Aspen?" I asked.

"That's the plan." The way he said it made it seem like there were other options on the table. Where else would we go? Aspen is the closest outpost near Pyramid Peak, which is where we believe Cali Bantu is located. Why does everyone have to talk in riddles?

I was led out of the hospital hideaway and back into the garage. Gear was still sitting on the garage floor. It made me wonder why I was being hurried out, and I worried they were going to hide me with the gear. But my shocked look had Will smiling.

"The real gear is already loaded. The gear lying around was a decoy to fool the Corporate watchers, who were now unconscious or worse at the edges of the building. The team members emerged from behind boxes and doors and quickly popped into the seats of the vehicles, silently warming up in stealth mode. Will and I were secured under blankets in the Brute. When the team was in place, the Brute and the minis left the garage. It was the middle of the day, and the sun peppered through the blankets covering me. I imagined the stunned faces of our enemies as they watched our team roll by.

"It won't take long for them to follow us, but the sweep team will block their progress with fallen trees and snow berms," I heard Gray say.

"Those men lying on the garage floor," asked Jilly, "were they…"

"No, we just put them out for a bit. Same with the ones slumped in their vehicles outside. Of course, we also messed with their vehicles a bit," Gray said. "We're not trying to start a war by killing Corporate soldiers. Not yet, anyway."

We were moving. I wondered how long I would have to sit on the floor and hide under the blanket. But it was a vast improvement over the smuggler's hold, but I missed seeing where I was going, even if it was behind a window.

Within five minutes, Will and I came out from under our blankets. The snowy road before us was already worn with the tracks of the minis in front of us. We were warned that we should be prepared to go back under the blankets because there may be enemy soldiers camped along the road.

"Do they know where we are going?" I asked.

"There are several roads leading away from this town. This way is the least maintained, but I assume they are prepared to cover this road. We identified fifteen spies in town, though I know there are more," Gray answered.

"I located two camps, one with three troops and one with four. I flagged them with a beacon, but they may have moved. That being said, they're on foot," Jedi said.

"They knew we were leaving, but we are well ahead of the scheduled time we let leak out. There are several roads leading away from this town. But the only town that still exists along this road is Aspen, so I assume they know we are headed there.

"We identified fifteen people who no one knew, so we assumed they were spies, but there could be more. The Fringers were our best eyes and ears because they pointed out the unfamiliar people. Even the Loners have someone they know in the towns. But the Corporates likely had some people dressed as locals hanging around the edges, and then there are the Fringers they've turned with funds or blackmail. I believe that number is relatively few, but to answer your question, yes, we expect trouble," Gray answered.

I was dutifully watching my assigned window when we heard gunfire up ahead. Gray stopped the Brute and grabbed at the dash to engage the heat detector and a button labeled G-Gun, for Gatling gun. I knew from my training there was a huge belt of large bullets that fed it, and it could shoot them in rapid succession.

Gray handed Jilly and me our handguns and said, "Jilly, Connor, stay low. Jax, man the Gatling gun." With that, Gray and Will hopped out with weapons in hand.

I went through my training, and with my memory, every tidbit was voiced inside my head. I recalled the feel of the gun in my hand as I fired at the targets, and what I did that delivered the best results. I had the knowledge. I could do this. I had to because I wasn't just protecting myself, but my friends, and most importantly, Jilly and her baby.

Jax climbed into the driver's seat, watching the four views on the split screen. On the forward screen, I saw the outline of a body, but it had a green X on it, and on our left was another green X body. She let them pass. I assumed it was Will and Gray, and the green X's defined them as friendlies. It was silent; the gunfire had stopped. I looked at Jax, still actively searching our perimeter for heat signatures.

The silence and darkness made me more edgy than the popping of weapons' fire. I was sitting on the floor, holding my weapon. I knew not to fire at the bulletproof windows, but if they got in, we'd need to use our guns.

I felt the Brute moving, and I wondered how long I would have to huddle on the floor under a blanket. It was unsettling to travel without seeing the landscape, and the bullets sent the whole experience over the top, even if it was from behind a bulletproof window.

Within minutes, it was over. We stared deeply into the dense woods, watching for the enemy presence to spring back into action.

Jilly whispered, "Breathe, Connor. With Jax on the Gatling gun, bullet-proof windows, and a dozen soldiers securing us, we're going to be fine."

"Unless they have drillmos. That's what killed Hannah. Those bullets can drill through just about anything," I said. I instantly regretted scaring Jilly and added, "But you're right, they have a lot to get through, and it's doubtful there are very many of them."

Just then, something rocked the vehicle. Shocked yelps came from several passengers, and one of them was me. The enemy had rolled a rock against our side door. Jax steered the G.gun that way, but before she did, the back of the Brute was struck again. I turned to see, but all that was left was a red smear.

Gunfire erupted, only this time it was all around us, not up the road. A bullet struck the side window, fusing itself into the clear panel. The men not fighting rushed to free the Brute from the large boulder impeding its escape. Strained voices yelled, "GO!"

Jax floored the rig, and it lurched forward, but then was stopped again. She regeared the vehicle and punched it again. Were we on our own? Where were our leads and sweeps? My question was answered quickly when two wounded men were being helped toward the rig. Jedi tried to open the crushed side door, but it didn't work.

"What the heck happened to the door?" asked a Guard named Nash.

He set his man down and climbed onto the roof. Jax climbed back and released the locking mechanism, and a panel was removed. It was instantly cold as the warm air rushed out the top of the rig. The men were passed inside, and the latch reclosed. The passenger seating room was completely commandeered as the seats were transformed into thin beds.

Relic stood in the small aisle assisting Jilly with the injured while I sat on the console between Lana and Jax. The other men went to their mini and signaled them to follow.

Jilly got to work with Relic assisting her. The big Brute's lights illuminated the red stained snow, and the three bodies littering the sides of the road. One had a shoulder wound and a long gash on his leg. She asked for help to hold the man down. He screamed and fought as she inserted a thick syringe filled with spongy material into the hole left by the bullet. He passed out, making addressing his minor leg wound less traumatic, but it didn't allow her to ask him about her husband or the others. She turned stitching the laceration over to Relic.

The other soldier was a woman named Tommie. She was groggy, with a cracked helmet. Jilly checked her vitals, scanned her eyes, asked her questions, and tested her abilities and reflexes. When her patients were stabilized, she made her way to the front of the vehicle.

"How will our guys get back?" she asked Jax.

"There are four minis, two sweeps and two leads. One of the leads is in front of us now. So, between the three left, one will be assigned to follow us, and the other two will be along eventually, depending on how things went back there."

What if one of the minis is undrivable?" Jilly asked. "Is there enough room for all of them?"

"I didn't see anything wrong with the mini we passed on the side of the road," said Jax. "But even if one of the rigs is damaged, they'll fix it or tow it with another. If the battle was still ongoing, I would have heard it on my headgear. They're just doing cleanup. When we get to Aspen, we'll assess our situation."

"Are there any facilities in Aspen?" Jilly asked.

"It isn't considered inhabited, but a small group of people live there. We are picking up our tracker there, so there might be some place they hold up for winter. Aspen was struck pretty hard by a meteorite. Not much is left of the main town. How are our injured doing?" Jax asked.

"They should make it if we don't have to travel too far. This road is rough and may reopen their wounds," Jilly answered while adjusting the IVs swinging from the roof hooks.

"It could take a while. We've not covered half of our journey yet," Jax sighed. "Keep me apprised of their condition. There may be one place we could stop."

"No matter what, these two are out of the fight for some time," Jilly said while using straps to secure her patients from falling off their beds as the Brute rocked over the deep snow.

CHAPTER 14

Jilly's patients were stable despite traveling at a hurried pace over rugged roads. The light was fading, but she resolved not to let the darkness compromise their care. The tinted windows made it darker inside, but they kept outsiders from seeing in. Using the overhead lights would make her job much simpler, yet even a small amount of light would turn them into a beacon and an easy target.

Due to our limited seating, I was sitting on top of the compartment between the two front seats of the Brute when we came upon a long, straight stretch in the road. I was watching Jilly straining forward to look into the rear-view mirror, searching for Gray as if her determined focus could conjure him. They were like entangled particles, and no amount of distance could break their connection. But fulfilling her wish for headlights came with the threat of those beams belonging to the enemy.

The lead mini was stopped in front of us. Both Nash and Jedi were out of the vehicle, and Nash was pounding something into a tree. Jax slowed down and redeployed the G gun. The only signatures were the friendlies checking out their suspicions, so she waited for the team to call on their direct line.

"I saw a flash of movement," Jedi said into his shoulder mic. "But whomever or whatever it was is gone now. Nash marked the area with a beacon to alert the sweeps, over."

"Copy that. We'll keep a lookout too," Jax responded.

Rocking back down the snowy path, we followed the tracks of the lead team before us. One of the wounded soldiers moaned and tried to sit up, but he quickly lay back down. Jilly said something calming, and he relaxed into the makeshift bed. The mountains made for short days, and night was rapidly closing in. She strapped a monitoring bracelet onto each of her arms. It would be hard to see her patients soon, but the monitors would track their vitals.

When we got to another straight passage, we saw lights bouncing behind us. It had to be the sweep team, and soon a radio call confirmed it. Jilly seemed to sink into her tiny jump seat when Gray's voice rose over the speaker.

Another hour went by with no enemy threats, but the condition of the road was grueling, and the injured soldiers were in danger of more than just the suffering it caused. I could see Jilly was also feeling bad because she was cautiously nibbling on a protein bar. I could do nothing to help her.

"Jax, can we stop for a minute?" Jilly asked. "I really need to pee."

"Me too," I replied, hoping my support would increase her odds.

"Yeah, I think we all need a break," Jax said, as she signaled Lana, riding shotgun, to contact the lead and sweep minis.

Lana grabbed the radio mic from the dash. "Lead, this is Main, come in, Lead."

"Lead here, go ahead, Main."

"Need a short break, over?"

"Rodger, that." The lead vehicle stopped while Lana repeated the message to the sweep.

Jilly opened the door and stepped outside. She held onto the side of the Brute momentarily. I stepped outside just as the sweep car pulled up, with Gray quickly charging out of the mini upon seeing Jilly hanging on to it. Before he could reach her, Jax helped her stand up.

"She's just a little carsick. I'll walk her a bit," I heard Jax say to Gray.

"I can take her," Gray said, holding his wife on the other side.

"Well, we both have to pee, so it makes sense I go with her."

"Okay, but stay on the road. You both can pee behind our rig." He pointed to the mini parked behind the Brute.

I watched Jax walk Jilly to the back of the sweep rig. She staggered and began to heave. Jax looked at the crew talking outside. They were all looking away from them, so she walked Jilly into the woods along the road. I immediately turned to see if Gray saw them go where he had just warned them not to.

We were being hailed to load up, and I saw Gray walk toward his rig and stand ready to respond to any signs of trouble. He must have heard them because his head spun toward the side of the road where they had exited. He went for his weapon and stopped, putting his hands on his hips in obvious irritation. It was a bad idea to disobey him and a dangerous one to surprise him. Husband or not, he was their commanding officer, and they wandered off without notifying him. When they stepped back onto the road, they came upon Gray with his arms crossed and waiting.

I hung back at the corner of the Brute. Eavesdropping is wrong, and I'm not sure how I could help her, but she was my friend. I couldn't leave her at this moment. She froze at the sight of Gray's challenging stance. I could only imagine what was going through her head. She had no more reasons to keep him in the dark. She had secured her place on the mission. He couldn't send her back now. She had to tell him. Jax came to where I was standing and tugged on my jacket, pulling me into the Brute.

The passengers were watching the exchange at the meeting taking place in the middle of the road. It was a short meeting because within minutes, Jilly climbed into the Brute. She couldn't have told him. That conversation would have exploded, and Gray wouldn't have cared who heard his reaction.

No one spoke for miles until we came upon a mountain of large trees lying across the road, frozen in the snow. I'm not an engineer, but even I knew this was a formidable blockade. Looking up at the origin of the mammoth trees, I could see they fell naturally, with one toppling the other.

The four ranking officers got out and discussed the situation with gestures and head shakes. Gray and Will seemed to have decided, and we waited for the inevitable back-breaking orders.

Gray leaned on the Brute with his head looking down. "Set up the shelters; we'll have to wait until morning to resolve this." Gray's voice boomed over the intercom of every vehicle.

We all poured out of the five different rigs, grabbing gear to perform our assigned camp tasks. It was quite cold, and I was happy for the physical work, taking my mind off the brutal temps after lounging in the cozy cab.

My job was being the gofer for those assembling the shelters. The fold-out pieces reminded me of a construction game I found on the borrowing shelf at the Hold. Like the game, the hinged pieces attached in various ways, but these locked into place with surprising stability. It took only fifteen minutes to create the shell of a large open dwelling that attached to the Brute through the side door opening. When the walls were in place, the insulated floor was laid down. Rolls of insulation hooked to the top of the walls unfurled, and we attached them to the floor.

As the other workers were arranging the beds, heater, and cooking station, we went to build the next shelter. It sat in the middle of the four minis, and it was also attached, giving access to the equipment in the cabs. I marveled at how sturdy and versatile the design was. The quick connect clasps allowed for speedy set-ups and teardowns. The driver's cab became the duty station for monitoring the instruments and manning the weapons while remaining within the bulletproof environment.

Soon two large shelters were constructed, settled, and warm. The heat felt good after being in the icy breeze outside. The two shelters housed the fifteen team members, who were all inside now. Darkness came quickly, as the mountains had their own timeline for nightfall. The campers sat on their beds, where their cold weather gear sat in heaps behind them. It was a cozy scene with bowls of steaming stew and sliced bread.

Dinner wasn't the only thing that was simmering when Gray motioned for Jilly to follow him outside. They re-donned their winter gear, and the cold air crept past the door curtain as they made their way back outside. Maybe the chill would help keep his temper to a minimum, probably not. She shivered outside, and without a second thought, he drew her close to him.

The windows of the shelter had fold-down panels, but they all were open now. Though the couple outside had little privacy, the soldiers knew better than to look directly at their angry commander. Gray would never hurt Jilly physically, but when he found out what she had been hiding from him, he'd be enraged, and words could deliver dire wounds.

I could see Jilly was holding her emotions in check as they made their way back into the shelter. We focused on our stew and bread, not daring to look Gray in the eye. Jilly wormed through the cramped quarters to sit on a bedroll next to Jax. Gray eyed the way she and Jax exchanged whispers and bristled. Jilly had pulled Jax into her deception, and Gray was no doubt ticking up a list of extra details she would be punished with. Then he called for everyone's attention.

"It has come to my attention that Jilly has a medical condition you all need to be aware of. She is pregnant." His disciplined troops listened without reacting. "Therefore, she, along with Connor, require around-the-clock protection. Jax, set up a schedule and send it to me. Don't forget to check the guard duty roster I will soon send to your bands. I have the first watch, but first I'm going to brief the other shelter." Then he left abruptly. I got that he left without kissing her; he was in the company of his soldiers. But not sending her his typical smile—that was all about being furious.

We tried not to stare at Jilly, but the news created a vacuum. And that vacuum was pulling at every one of us to give a response. My heart went out to her, but I didn't want to hint that I knew by not playing up being shocked by the news. Jilly went to her patients hoping to busy herself through the uncomfortable hush that filled the cramped space and held us captive.

Finally, Jedi said, "Wow, a baby," and a round of congratulations broke the awkward silence. She gave a half laugh, more like a nervous release. I wondered how long I should wait before I offered Gray congratulations. It was a complicated situation. Jax handed Jilly a bowl of stew and a slice of bread. She ate hungrily while she gave a shortened version of the story I was quite familiar with. Before she finished her tale, the meal was cleaned up, and we settled down for lights out.

I realized that the life of a soldier was probably not a good fit for me. True, I had to be one now, but yesterday did me in. After being shot at, we spent the rest of the day waiting to be shot at again, and then working in the night chill to create our shelter, hoping we wouldn't be shot at during our setup or while we slept. It's a lot, and we are not out of the woods yet. I looked out a window and chuckled, mumbling, "We are literally in the woods."

Gray was rolling the window coverings up as a warning to get up on one's own, or get rousted out. Putting on my bundle of gear, I left the shelter, leaving Lana, Jilly, and Dom still slumbering. They had pulled guard or medic night duty, earning the right to sleep in. A breakfast of oatmeal, dried fruit, and hot caffeinated tea was being served in the other shelter. I got hot chocolate.

We brought enough hot chocolate packets for me, but then we shared some with Fringers, and I shared them with Jilly. These two cups were the last. After today, we had to drink the herbal teas we got from the Fringers. They were good, but not rich and sweet like chocolate. That was an easy sacrifice, but it made me wonder how rough it would get. I knew what hunger and living in a cold house felt like, but I didn't like it. Yep, I'm a terrible soldier.

I remember the first warm shower I had in my life was at the Hold. It was so relaxing and soothing that I washed up quickly, and then I just stood in the heat turning back and forth until my water allotment ran out. After yesterday, I needed that. I longed for the soothing reprieve of warm water cascading over me. I wondered what Aspen would be like and whether things like beds and showers were available. Our intel assured us there were people living there, but not many, and the accommodations were uncertain.

Bringing myself back to the current issue, I looked at the chore before us. The trees across the road were massive, which is why we would build a way over them. Relic showed us the steps on his tablet. Numerous logs were needed for several structural aspects of the design.

The slope had to be just so to keep the vehicles from stalling or rolling; the gaps between the trees and the ramp leading to the hill's apex needed to be filled with snow and compacted enough to support the heavy rigs. When Relic was done, Gray and Will assigned the crews. It seemed like a huge undertaking, and I hoped we wouldn't need to spend another night allowing the enemy to catch up.

CHAPTER 15

My job was to gather the brush cut off the trees and pile it for the soldiers to stuff into the small gaps where logs wouldn't fit. I was working as hard as I could, trying to do my part to get us out of here and keep us safe. But when I started to shiver from sweating, Will sent me inside. I felt useless, but I wasn't ignorant of the wisdom. Tommie was on light duty, packing up the shelter bedrolls and cooking stations. The shelter structures would remain as a place for warming up and to prepare for the unfortunate possibility that we didn't finish before nightfall.

With Dom's shoulder and leg wounds, he was relegated to surveillance type duties. So, I sat down in the passenger seat to talk with him.

"How long do you think this plan is going to take?" I asked.

"We are making good progress. I think we'll be on the road in a couple of hours." He went on to describe what the project entailed and ended with, "I mean, unless the whole thing gives way," he said, and then added, "But don't worry, kid, that won't happen."

I am halfway through an engineering degree, but he didn't know that. All he saw was a child confused by the adults' plan. My body and social skills were twelve, but my brain wasn't. It was hard to sit through explanations that I understood better than he did, but it could have been worse. He could have said I was too young to understand.

"I get the plan," I said respectfully, "but I don't know how fast the work can be accomplished."

He chuckled. "True that. Every construction project I've ever been on takes longer than the estimate. Unexpected issues are always to be expected." He laughed at his own joke, so I joined in.

"It won't be good if we have to stay another night," I said. "The corporate soldiers will get here before morning."

"Don't you worry about that. I believe we'll get done, and if not, we'll blast those bas—bad guys back to … their bad place." He gave an oops grin for his language, and I laughed. I'd tell him not to worry about it, but Gray would punish them if he caught them swearing near me.

I left the cab to go back to work, and I waved to Will and Gray to let them know I was back outside. They were on the chainsaws trimming the fallen trees, while others were assembling the make-shift crane. I stood next to Relic to watch the amazing process. Nash flew a drone to an enormous branch, where the drone landed and crawled along the tree to snap a ring of rollers around it. Then he brought the drone back and attached a rope to it, and flew it back up to secure it on the rollers. When the drone returned with the rope, four men grabbed it and pulled the heavy cable over. The time to create this block and tackle would be more than recouped by its efficiency. I watched the test run with a small log before I resumed my brush removal. This time I would pace myself.

I needed a break, and I went over to Jilly, who was emerging from the shelter. She was listing off the team quietly to herself to memorize their names and faces. I thought about how others struggle to recall things. That had happened to me once when I was feverish at Bayley's cabin, and even through my feverish state, I remembered how it felt to forget. If it had ever happened before, I couldn't recall, which made me chuckle out loud at the irony.

Jilly turned and smiled at me. "I guess everyone let the preggo lady sleep in. I woke up and everyone was in full work mode. Did I miss the briefing where I would have received my assignment?"

"Yeah, but everyone who did duty last night was allowed to sleep. I guess you could ask Gray about the duty roster," I said tentatively.

"He'd probably sit me down with some knitting needles," she said sarcastically.

"Well, maybe you should start knitting some stuff. I mean, who knows when we'll get home?" I was sorry I said it out loud, but she wasn't unaware of our circumstances.

"Ugh, Connor. Not you too." I gave her a wink, and we both laughed. It was good to see her laugh. It had been a long time. Maybe humor was just the help I could give her. "I guess I'll see if I can help Lana with whatever she's doing." She looked up where Axle was securing the drone back in its case and shouted, "Hey Axle. Where is Lana?"

"She's writing," he yelled and pointed. "Other shelter, where breakfast is being served."

She waved as she went toward the mini shelter, and I went back to brush duty.

Progress moved at a hard and steady pace, and it was time to fill the overpass with snow. The mini with the plow was detached from the shelter while crews used logs with spiked handles to pound the snow down into the cracks. Slowly, the evidence of logs disappeared under a white blanket of packed snow. The shelters were broken down, and the camp was fully packed.

Everyone gathered to see the ramp's test run. Axle and Easton won the honor. Everyone watched as the mini tugged over the hill. It sank a little here and there, but the stability was better than expected considering the smile on Relic's face. One by one, the minis would cross over to pack the elevated road down before the Big Brute would be driven across.

Just as our cheers of triumph broke out for the successful first try, the surveillance crew came barreling into camp.

"Take cover!" yelled Jedi. "They're coming on foot!"

With the camp completely broken down, Gray sent Jedi and Leo over the ramp in the mini, followed by the Brute carrying Jilly, Relic, Dom, Tommie, and me. Before the other two minis could approach the ramp, shots came from the wooded roadsides.

I couldn't see over the hill, and before I got my bearings, Tommie quickly secured me on the floor of the Brute. Though the vehicle was well protected from weapons' fire, it was not soundproof. Hearing the pop, pop, pop of gunfire, the constant rat-tat-tat of the Gatling guns, and even the occasional grenade boom was not new to me. I had spent many hours at target practice exposed to many weapons, and yesterday I experienced live fire. I hunkered down in fear, but now I was in a state of panic. I wanted to run, which I knew was irrational, but the voice saying it pounded in my head.

I knew nine of our team members had made it to this side of the hill, and I imagined the other six were tucked behind the two mini barricades. From my training, I knew that the space between the vehicles and the shields was cramped, and it could withstand quite a bit of firepower, but it was not a place to get trapped in for the long haul.

A rapid succession of grenade explosions rocked the slight lull in gunfire, followed by another mini barreling over the hill. It was mere seconds before the volley of gunfire began again. Then quiet. I waited for it to end, but it didn't. I had been praying for an end to the pounding of weapons' fire, but when it came, it gave me no relief. It meant someone had won, but I didn't know who. I tucked down harder into the already cramped space. Plans of escape and the methods of resistance to the enemy's horrific methods to break me were racing through my head.

Then someone knocked on the Brute window. It was Jedi. "You can sit up now, but stay in the vehicle."

Was he saying we had won this battle, or wanting me to get ready for a retreat? My thoughts centered on the welfare of our team. The number of deadly projectiles I heard whizzing about must have had an impact. I desperately needed to exit the vehicle and see for myself. And when no one was paying attention, I quietly opened the door.

I know I am a valuable asset, and I was not commissioned for combat, but these were my friends. The need to check on them was overwhelming. I walked out and saw a row of soldiers reclining near the top of the ramp. The soles of their boots lined the slope in an orderly row. I jumped when a single shot splintered a tree trunk to my left, and I realized the enemy wasn't finished. I heard two distant shots from what appeared to be a single shooter.

Our soldiers sent a volley of 50 caliber bullets as their bodies jerked with the recoil. I quickly went to return to the mini when I heard a single rifle shot from the side of the hill. Then silence. Then cheers. I turned toward the area where the single shot came and saw Jilly. She was standing on the hilltop in the firing zone.

Again, I leaped out of the mini, but this time Easton caught me. Besides me, he was the youngest member of the team.

"What is happening?" My plea was desperate enough that he softened, but he pointed me to sit in the closest mini. I complied, but not completely. My legs dangled out of the open door. "What's going on?" I shouted.

"Jilly just took out the lone sniper that was aiming at Commander Takota," Easton said proudly. "But the commander's hurt. Don't know how bad yet. They're bringing him over. I gotta go. Stay in the mini!" he ended with a demanding tone and ran to assist.

I still hadn't closed the door, so I overheard the chatter. The last mini came to a stop after bounding up the ramp with Gray inside. The damaged vehicle had a crack in the door and who knows what else since it sustained a sticky bomb hit. I had learned about those. They permanently adhered to whatever surface they hit, causing more damage than a proximity bomb.

I watched as a limp Gray was removed from the damaged mini. A belt was around his thigh, and blood covered his pants. I knew that a wound to the femoral artery was often fatal. I collapsed back into the seat of the mini desperately praying he wouldn't die. I couldn't lose him like I had lost Hannah. They brought him into the Brute, where Jilly was setting up the med-bed.

Will looked up at the feat of engineering that we had labored so hard on. I knew he was thinking about destroying it. It was logical, considering the Garrison soldiers were after us, but it was our only way home. All the roads west of the Continental Divide had been sabotaged to protect the Fringers and the tunnel. If this barricade were destroyed, it would be tough for the enemy or us to untangle it before spring.

We needed time to find the entrance and access it. If they caught up, all they'd have to do is follow us and take the treasure we unveiled. Then the mission would fail, and we'd be at their mercy, which they had none of. Jilly was pregnant; Gray was mortally wounded, and though he was the most critical, he wasn't the only one.

Then I heard it, like the slamming of a door. "Blow it up!" Will yelled, followed by, "Move out". All but one mini got in the line of vehicles ready to head down the road. The enemy was on the other side of the mound, but no one doubted they would try again. The last mini with the demo crew had very little time to set the explosives and destroy the bridge.

Beckett and Mack were chosen to demolish the ramp we had all just worked so hard to build. It was their area of expertise, and they had all the supplies they required in their mini. It was a dangerous job, for more reasons than just the lurking adversaries.

Once again, I was relegated to sitting on the console of the Brute and. They told me to face forward, but I was concerned about Gray. So, I turned around, dangling my feet into the passenger area. The talls were too busy to correct me. Jilly was working frantically to stop Gray's bleeding. She was pumping plasma through his veins, but it wasn't enough. He needed blood. I remembered from studying the team profiles that only one person had the same O-negative blood as Gray—Will.

"Can we pull over? I need to..." Jilly said, letting out a soft sob. "Will, please stop the Brute."

Will was driving, and I knew he'd be happy to donate his blood, but something else was going on. Instead of getting to the task with urgency, she acted like it involved an unbearable choice. Maybe Will had the virus Relic was checking for. If he was infected with something, I could have it too. I looked at my fist scar. Maybe his entire army had it. That could be disastrous.

CHAPTER 16

"He needs a blood transfusion. The plasma gives him fluid, but without red blood cells, he can't oxygenate. I know you're injured too, but..."

"My wound is minor," he answered. "Take what he needs."

"Will, come outside for a few," Relic said solemnly. "I need to talk to you."

"Now?" Will asked, incensed. "What could be more important than Gray's ebbing life?"

"Yes, now." Will looked at him suspiciously as they exited the Brute. They stood with their backs to me, which was a shame because this was a conversation I would have definitely eavesdropped on.

Will came back into the Brute and looked at Jilly. "Relic filled me in. What do you want to do?" he asked her. I wanted to shout my questions that I had a right to know, but Gray's life was on the line. My questions could wait.

Jilly stripped Gray's arm. "As his doctor, I get to decide for him when he's unable. The thing is, he'll die if we don't do this, but he's going to be fighting mad when we tell him."

"Well, I'll fight that battle when he recovers. Jax, get us back on the road as soon as we are hooked up. I don't want to get stuck out here in this snowstorm," Will said. Jax was already making her way to the driver's seat. Now I was even more intrigued. Whatever it was that made Will's blood questionable would not interfere with Gray's recovery. I think my virus theory just took a nosedive.

From my studies of field hospitals, I knew that blood transfusions were risky, but patient-to-patient transfusions ran the additional threat of not being able to know how much blood was being transferred. But we weren't set up for anything else. She took Will's blood pressure and did some calculations on her tablet to estimate how much time she should allow between checking Gray's levels.

Will sat back in the seat close to Gray, and Jilly opened the valve, allowing Will's heart to feed his blood into Gray's limp body. I wondered what Gray was being fed as the red snake edged through the tube. I wasn't worried about Gray forgiving anyone; I just wanted this to work.

The Brute rolled forward at a slow speed as Jilly monitored Gray for fever and signs of rejection. Letting out a long breath, she remembered Jax and Relic had worked on several other patients, and she did not know their status.

"Tell me about the injuries you and Relic treated while I was busy with Gray," Jilly said, collapsing onto a small jump seat she had folded out from the wall. She looked exhausted, and she let her head fall back against a cushion she had propped on the window. Jax gave her a list of the minor wounds they had treated.

"Connor was kept safe in the Brute. A bullet grazed Jedi on his left thigh, requiring eight stitches. Tommie is fine, and she's driving Jedi. Dom's leg is stable enough, so he's driving Easton, who had some shrapnel and glass wounds requiring many stitches, but none of the wounds were threatening. Nash and Lana are uninjured and riding Lead.

"Relic tripped while diving for cover and landed on his wrist. I secured it, and I think it's just sprained. Axle took a round in the butt. It's deep, but it's not bleeding anymore. I believe it's all muscle damage, no bones or spinal issues, but it will have to be surgically removed. I started him on oral antibiotics. That's everyone but Mack and Beckett demoing the ramp."

Jilly looked over at me. I had moved myself to the floor behind the compartment and was tucked into a ball. Upon seeing me, she moved me into the jump seat beside Will.

"You look like someone stole your lunch money," he said to me.

"My what?" I asked, and Will laughed.

"What's going on in that big brain of yours?" he asked me.

"What did you and Relic talk about?" I asked straight out. Will wasn't someone you engaged in small talk with.

"That's classified," he answered matter-of-factly.

"Does it have to do with your blood? Is there something about Gray I should know?" I was whispering now, not that the passengers slumped in sleep cared. But he had my attention when he said the word classified.

"I'm fine, and there's nothing wrong with my blood. Gray will be fine. Stop worrying." He said it calmly, but there was a stern undertone to his voice.

I was near his ear now, making sure no one heard my words. "We shared blood, so did all of your soldiers. I want to know. I think I have a right to know."

"Not today, but if your need-to-know changes, I'll tell you." I could tell he was done holding back his commander side, so I changed the subject.

"Okay, I will trust you. Next issue. It seems we've blown up our only way out of here unless we want to drive through all three territories and knock on the east gate."

"That we did. That's what we call a compelling motive to find that weapon or whatever it is and use it. Don't worry, Connor. You and I have a destiny, and she's not going to let us off the hook that easily."

"That is not very comforting, but I agree. We can't fail. I can't fail."

"I prefer to say, we *won't* fail. There is an old saying that failure isn't an option, but lots of people choose it whether or not they mean to. Every plan has roadblocks; just keep a steady eye on your goals and pursue them vigorously until, well, just try harder than you ever have."

I knew what he wanted to say. The sentence should have ended with "until the day you die," but I was a kid, so he held back. The garbled static on the intercom distracted him, ending the conversation. Jax turned up the volume to hear the message.

"...pha Gho... It's Delta G... - Mack ... urge... om in Al...," the message skipped and crackled over the intercom.

"Delta Ghost, this is Alpha Ghost, please repeat."

"Beckett... help..."

"Jax, what's going on?" asked Will, hearing the chatter between the minis. Jilly stopped the flow of blood and checked Gray's counts. She signaled a little more with her thumb and pointing finger. Will gave a thumbs up.

"It's Delta, sir. I think they're in trouble," said Jedi over the intercom from a mini.

"Okay, let's stop. Sounds like Beckett might be hurt. They can't be that far back."

Pulling over, Jax picked up another call from Delta, which came in better and clarified the situation. With absolute efficiency, Jilly began getting ready for another mortally wounded soldier. Axle was painfully moved to the passenger seat, leaning on his good side.

By the time they brought Beckett in, she had untethered Will from Gray, put out the other bed, and laid Beckett on his right side. To focus on something besides our trauma ridden space, I watched her work and eyed the equipment readouts.

Beckett's vitals were sketchy, but not life-threatening. He was in a lot of pain, so she administered a painkiller. As it was kicking in, she examined his wound with the mini ultrasound device. It was not the ideal tool, but it was good enough to show the pool of blood around his kidney. When the bleeding stopped, she concluded that most of the blood was from a minor artery. She started him on antibiotics and let him rest.

Gray was stable but still unconscious. Axle curled up on his side in the front seat. His pain was increasing, so she gave him additional pain relief. Beckett was resting comfortably. She leaned back and watched the snow blow toward us in the headlights. The flakes were growing thicker, making the trip slow.

Will suggested Jilly move to the back seats that weren't converted into beds, so she could get some sleep. She settled into the soft seat with its headrest and closed her eyes. I too found a place to close my eyes. Our naps were cut short when we stopped. In front of us was an enormous building with a sign that read Aspen/Pitkin County Airport. We had arrived.

Our headlights shone on the faded label, *Hangar 3,* where four heavily cloaked residents were exerting a significant amount of energy to slide open the tall door of the metal building. They ushered us inside and rolled the doors back to their closed position. Though we got out of the Brute, we all clung near the vehicles.

We were out of the wind, but the below-freezing temperatures inside the hangar made it clear we would be setting up the shelters. Jedi and Will walked up to the strangers and were gestured toward an enclosed section that spanned the length of the building. A soft light shone through the curtained windows, but they did little to illuminate the dark expanse of the hangar. The covered windows hid the accommodations within the enclosed area spanning the edge of the extensive open structure.

When the door to the enclosed area opened, I saw the warm glow of a wood stove, and though I understood their caution, I hoped they'd invite us inside. Jilly was pacing, waiting for the reception committee to return to find out how her patients would be housed. She still needed to extract a bullet from Axle; Beckett's injury could take a turn; Gray was still in critical condition and needed an artery repair, and infection threatened all those suffering wounds. These needs went beyond what the vehicle shelters could provide.

Another glow appeared on the far side of the hangar, where two heavily dressed people stood in front of a second fiery porthole. They added more wood to the stove and swung the door shut. My eyes were getting accustomed to the dark, and I could see them holding their hands to the heat. We assumed Will knew and trusted these people, and they him. But they were wasting a lot of time when our wounded needed help.

Suddenly, four people burst through the enclosed space, approaching with the clank of rolling wheels. It was hard to make them out being silhouetted by the now opened curtains behind them, but I easily identified Will by his height. The shadowed items took the form of three gurneys and a square cart hurrying toward us with great urgency. Thankfully, there was a place inside the long office for our three injured men. Hopefully, there'd be room for us too.

The faceless stranger, who appeared to be in charge, called those hovering around the stove on the far edge of the hangar to help. Quickly they settled the patients on the gurneys, as others helped Jilly grab her medical gear. Axle and Beckett were moaning but awake, but Gray lay silent and motionless. The rest of us began loading the gear we needed into the cart.

Jedi and Mack stayed to secure the vehicles while the rest of us made our way to the office. I went from understanding their cautious nature to feeling my own. The warm lounge area inside the door wafted with the heavenly smell of cooked food.

With all that had happened, I had forgotten about lunch and dinner, but I was soundly reminded now by a growling midsection. Venison steak with carrots and potatoes was graciously prepared in anticipation of our arrival. The food and hospitality melted our apprehension. Those kinds of things should make me worry about who else knows we are here, but I didn't care. I forgot about the threat and dug into my meal, delighting in every bite.

Everyone was relaxing on the couches, which were old but incredibly ornate. In fact, all the furniture in the lounge was luxurious, but none of it matched. We were told that Aspen used to be a fancy tourist town full of wealthy people. After the disaster, most survivors gathered up what they could carry and left the area. Their priceless items, too large for transport, got left behind and claimed by the remaining residents.

Jilly didn't stop in the lounge. She raced through without even a glance, following her patients. When she finally came in, she carried an empty tray with her. Jax had brought her dinner while she helped get the injured settled, which included her boyfriend, Axle.

As Jilly laid her tray near the others, they fired the same round of introductions her way. Lana scooted over, creating a space for Jilly to sit down. She sank into the soft, cushioned seat with an audible sigh. Etcher, a young woman with curly dark hair and steel-grey eyes, approached her.

"Do you like tea?" she asked.

"Yes, thank you. It smells heavenly. I'm Jilly."

"I'm Gretchen, but everyone calls me Etcher. Do you want a drop of honey?"

"Wow, honey. Extravagant," Jilly said and nodded with a gleeful expression.

I watched Jilly clutch the warm mug between her cupped hands and inhale the herbal blend. She took a careful sip of the steaming cup, and her eyes rolled in delight.

"This is excellent tea. Is it blended here?" asked Jilly.

"Yes, it's my favorite," Etcher answered. "I have traveled all over this side of the divide with my father, and I know all the places where the best herbs grow."

"Oh, are you our guide?" Jilly asked.

"Yeah, I know the area you are going to inside and out. I grew up in that playground," she said confidently.

"She'll take you there alright. I raised her on the trail. She's taken over my tracking business since I busted my leg in several places. No one knows the Elk Mountains better than my daughter, Etcher," said a grizzled man with a cane leaning next to his easy chair.

"I'm glad we have an expert because these parts are unknown to me," said Jedi. "That said, I'm off to bed. Not sure what is on the docket tomorrow, but there's always somethin'." Everyone agreed, setting a row of empty mugs on the already crowded counter with dishes needing attention.

Etcher started rounding them up, and Jilly went to help. I wanted to help, but I wasn't even sure I could drum up the energy to make it to my bed in the bunkroom.

"Jilly, I was told you were pregnant, and I heard you've had a hard day caring for your husband and the other injured. Please have a seat, finish your tea, and then turn in. It's been awfully slow around here, so I'm good. I got this." Etcher smiled as she held the tray full of cups and plates. I guessed her age at around twenty. She had a friendly smile and genuine kindness.

"Thank you, Etcher. It *has* been a long day," Jilly sighed into her cup.

CHAPTER 17

Relic helped Etcher clear the mound of dishes. Though still dealing with the wrist injury he received during the attack at the ramp, he held the tray while Etcher filled it. After filling her own tray, they headed to the kitchen. I wanted to talk to Jilly, but she was still enjoying her tea. I stayed in the room with her, doing my best not to fall asleep.

"Are you okay?" I asked her. It was the first time I talked to her since this whole crazy day began. I realized my question encompassed a plethora of topics, but I figured I'd let her choose.

"I'm tired, but I am monitoring my health, so don't worry. I won't jeopardize this mission's lead medical member or my child. And as far as my patients, which is the other question I know you have, they are all stable for now. Jax and Relic are on night check duty, so I can get some sleep. What they need is time to heal. If they get that, I believe they will all recover nicely."

"Time is a tall order. The enemy knows where we are, and they will come. But I think we all need a day to get our strength back. Everyone looks like their reserves are running on empty."

She nodded, and we both got up to turn in. She went to her room within the little clinic where her patients were, and I went to the bunk room I shared with Will, Relic, and Jedi. Having both Jedi and Will in my room proved how guarded I was. The testosterone in that room was pulsing with the ready warriors. I didn't know whom to feel sorrier for, me or Relic.

There were four rooms set up for our team, with two sets of bunk beds in each, but with four people in the medical room, we only needed three. The rooms were like other places I had stayed in, and the beds were pretty good. Although Jilly was allocated power for her needed medical equipment, this town was serious about energy conservation. This may have been an affluent town at one time, but the current residents used the dwindling resources carefully.

The next morning, Jilly called me to the med room. She wanted to take a blood sample from me. I asked her why. She said it was a routine procedure, but I didn't buy it and gave her a look that said so. She had plenty to do, and taking routine blood samples seemed pointless. Her face showed the strain she was under, and her eyes were puffy from crying, lack of sleep, or both. She couldn't have had much sleep last night. It made me wonder if her patients had taken a turn in the night.

"How are Gray, Axle, and Beckett today?" I asked.

"They're all stable. Axle had a bit of trouble last night, but I think we've got him back on track." She could tell I was questioning her answer. "I'm not just saying that, Connor. But the good news is, Will assured me they don't have to be moved right away."

"I just wanted to say that I'm feeling good since my illness. You don't have to worry about my health when you have so many things to do," I said.

"Well, thank you for thinking of me, Connor. But your health, especially on this mission, is top priority business," and she smiled. She had a smile that was hard to argue with. I let her take her sample and turned to leave.

"Okay, I'll see you later. And Jilly, please get some sleep. You look worn out."

"Will do, Doc," she winked.

I discovered Will left early this morning in the two undamaged minis with Easton, Jedi, and Etcher to plow and clear the Maroon Bells Road. They were expected back at dusk. Relic assured me it was unlikely the

Garrison troops could get through the tangled mess left by the explosion at our constructed bridge. It was also reported that they lost a good number of soldiers in the explosion, which caught many of them as they attempted to breach the structure. However, we didn't have much of an army left either, and I had only seen six other people here so far, and one needed a cane. I hoped they had more than that if the Corporates came storming down the road.

Gray had told me several times that it would be difficult for Corporate to send more troops because we had sabotaged the access roads. Translation: It will take them time to repair the roads, but they are coming, and the more frightening thought was, we're trapped between the sabotaged roads. He forgets I was on the team that mapped our way here.

But I focused on the more exciting news. We are close to Cali Bantu. I don't believe the Corporates know where it is, or they would have beaten us there. Either that, or they need me or Will's blade to enter, and following us was part of their plan. Regardless, I believe it is a fortress with significant protection. I more than believe it. I'm counting on it.

The original plan had the whole team traveling and clearing the road today, but with three of our band badly injured and several of our rigs damaged, those plans got revised. It was highly improbable that we would be ready to move out tomorrow, or even the next day. But that did not include the three men in the infirmary. And two of those injured included half of the upper echelon, which left a disconcerting gap in our leadership.

The Aspen locals were being very generous with their limited power, recharging all of our rig's batteries on a charging schedule to ensure we would have plenty of power to reach the site. Few knew where that was, but I did. I helped locate it. But not even I knew what would happen after that. And no one was silly enough to fully believe that what Cali Bantu was hiding would instantly solve all our problems. What we needed was this weapon, or whatever it was, to give us a fighting chance against the Corporate tsunami plodding ever closer.

I woke up to a rowdy commotion. Gray had regained consciousness, and believing himself captured, he was undoing his lifesaving tethers. I crept down the hall to check on them and walked up on a conversation between Jilly and Relic.

"We were up a lot of the night giving Axle ice baths to lower his fever. Then this morning, Gray's monitor alarms went off, showing Gray's vitals went flatline. I rushed in here only to find he was tearing them off. He thought he'd been captured. I gave him a mild sedative so he could rest, but when he wakes up, we have to tell him what we did."

"This whole concept is amazing, and as far as we know, beneficial. The blood samples you sent me show Connor's levels are decreasing, meaning he's fully recovered. Now the only patient I am worried about is Axle," said Relic.

"Don't get ahead of yourself, Relic," Jilly scolded. "We aren't going to start infecting everyone who gets a scraped knee."

"Well, I agree with not rushing to expose anyone else, but Axle has more than a scraped knee. It may come to that. You stay here with Gray. I'll go check on Axle," Relic said, and then he moved, so I made a quick exit.

What is in Will's blood? My blood? Half our team's blood? That's the secret Jilly found out. There is more to uncover, but the knuckle scar on me and Will's entire army took on a whole new meaning.

I stirred my oatmeal and raisin breakfast between bites as my head tried to wrap my head around what I'd heard. This was something I had to keep to myself. There were a lot of questions to research before I let them know I was on to their secret. In truth, the only thing I knew was that they had a secret, and it had to do with Will's blood, Gray's recovery, and perhaps me and the Guard soldiers. I wonder if they knew? Maybe I could start there. No, I couldn't question them. This was obviously top secret.

I pulled on my warm gear and walked into the hangar. The soldiers left behind, assigned to assess the damaged vehicles, toiled busily dismantling the damaged sections. Tommie, Dom, and Relic were discussing how to repair the hole in the side of the damaged mini. The crew that rode in it yesterday had minor cases of hypothermia, so sealing it from the winter cold was about more than comfort.

"If there are aircraft panels, we could use them to cover this area," said Tommie.

"That would be perfect," Relic nodded. "Are there aircraft here?"

"Yeah," Theo answered. "There are a couple of planes in the other hangars that may work. Grab some tools, and we'll drive over there."

"Can I go?" I was bored hanging around with nothing to do. I was tired of following rules that limited my freedom, so I could fight for everyone else's. And I was still simmering over being kept in the dark. Since I would have soldiers with me, I shouldn't even have to ask, but I would leave a note. Not the same ask getting permission, but my mood emboldened me. That made me smile.

"Run in and let someone know. Better hurry, we need to get going on this," said Dom.

Jilly was busy checking on Axle, and Gray was asleep. Knowing Gray had regained consciousness and would wake up, I left a note in Gray's room. I knew I was sneaking around a possible 'no', but I didn't care. Not today.

Two other soldiers were working on the damaged Brute and checking the batteries on the trickle chargers. Though none of the ED (energy dense) batteries were completely depleted, it took a lot of power to charge them. Our hosts' generators were already taxed by the demands of winter, extra guests, and the medical room. It was proof of their loyalty to the cause.

I came upon Tommie and Dom discussing how to repair the hole in the side of the damaged mini. I gave them a thumbs up for my tag along, and they nodded.

"We'll drive my truck over there, so we can put what we find in the bed," Theo said.

Theo gave us a quick tour of the airport. The original passenger area was reduced to charred stones, but the pictures hanging in the lounge showed it was once a rustic but welcoming place to arrive and depart from. Only the buildings on the northern side survived the meteorite disaster. Inside the hangar were small propeller planes Theo called cessanas.

"Have you guys ever tried to run the engines?" asked Dom.

"No, I mean I know a little about how they work, but none of us knows how to pilot them, and where would we go? Not to mention, it would put us on the Corporate radar. But a mechanic who used to work here taught my uncle, an engineer, about planes. He and my uncle repaired a jet engine and turned it into a generator. They siphoned the fuel from all the planes, so they wouldn't leak or blow up. When we used up that fuel, we pumped some out of the underground tanks. It was pretty contaminated stuff, but we made a filtering system," Theo answered.

"And it still works?" Tommie asked.

"Yeah, but it breaks down sometimes. When it does, I cannibalize parts to fix it. My uncle taught me how to work on all the things we've made from these planes. Hey, come on. I saved the best for last," Theo said excitedly.

The next hangar was much larger than the one we had just visited. It held a mean-looking jet with weapon racks under the wings. On the sides, it had a star in a circle of blue with stripes coming off the sides. There were missing panels and dangling lines marking the chunks that had been pillaged from its sleek body.

Theo rolled the portable stairs up to the cockpit and waved us up. The instrumentation was impressive, and we were all intrigued, but none as much as Tommie.

"Are there books on this stuff? I mean, this is an airport, surely they had technical manuals here," she said hopefully.

"Yeah, there's a library in the office over there. On one of the shelves, there are tons of binders. I think they are about maintenance, but in the tower, they have flight instruction manuals. At least, I think that's what they are. It seemed a waste of time to me, so I never really checked it out," said Theo.

"Can we get into the tower?" she asked.

"I don't have clearance. I'd have to get permission. We do surveillance there, so it's a 'need to know' place."

I left them to their conversation, and Dom and Tommie to their work on the pieces we grabbed from the previous hangar. I wandered around to a plane on the far side of the hangar. It was a small jet with a single jet engine. It appeared untouched by the scavengers.

"What would it be like to fly above the ground and see so much of it at once?" I questioned out loud.

I saw someone from under the plane approaching me, and it wasn't Dom or Tommie. It was Theo. I felt the hairs on the back of my neck stand on end.

CHAPTER 18

His voice fractured the solitude I thought I had secured, and I was on high alert..

"I imagine it would look like the images you see on the drone footage, but with a full panoramic view," Theo came around the plane and toward me. "We could probably repair these machines or build our own, but there's no place to go. The runways are in horrible shape. How would we get away with it? The Corporates would instantly detect and destroy a plane like this with their dozens of drones." He had come around the plane and was in full sight now.

"We think they have all the power, but they don't. I'm tired of being afraid of them," I said, but Theo was moving closer, and the hairs on my neck tingled with danger.

"They have all the power, and we can't hide from them forever," he said as he continued to move ever closer. I couldn't let him get close enough to lunge at me.

It triggered the events with Relic this morning. I was upset after overhearing Relic and Jilly talking. I wandered outside to get some fresh air and time to think by myself. Relic followed me outside, examining me with a weird look in his eyes.

"Let's say I was a spy who was waiting for this very perfect moment," he said eerily. "There's a mini outside with full batteries, and I could drive you back to the bridge before anyone could catch us. How lucky for me you childishly escaped those protecting you from this very thing happening, so you could go outside and play." Before I could react, Relic grabbed me and covered my mouth. Shocked and trapped, I panicked, unable to make a sound, not that anyone inside the hangar would hear me.

And then, just as quickly, Relic turned me loose and spun me around. His hostile expression was replaced by one of concern.

"Connor," he said with sincerity, "the enemy sees you as a commodity they desperately need, like the last crust of bread in a room of feral rats. I don't want you to be afraid all the time, but I want you to be careful *all the time*. Bravery is best left for moments of necessity, not reckless impulses. Let us do our job by you doing yours."

He didn't just lecture me; he scared me. But watching Theo moving in on me, I saw the potential trouble I was in, and I dashed under the plane and ran to where Dom and Tommie were working. Theo followed a few minutes later.

I was seeing monsters everywhere, and I sat near the door, next to Tommie on the drive back. When we returned, we were happy to hear Axle's fever had broke. I went into the patient area, telling Jilly I needed to report to Gray. He was talking over the partition to Axle, who was softly moaning words that made no sense. He sounded so groggy and weak. Soon his breathing deepened into a sleepy rhythm. I came into Gray's area. He was sitting up, and he crossed his arms against his chest when he saw me.

"There you are. Can't say I appreciated the way you snuck off." I hung my head.

"I know. I'm sorry. You have no idea how sorry. I was trying to keep my emotions in check, but he could see I was upset.

"What happened?"

I told him everything. About Relic and Theo. When I finished, he had that thinking, fuming, protective; I told you so expression, which I deserved and couldn't disagree with.

"I'm not sure I am completely on board with Relic's method, but it sounds like it was effective."

"Maybe too effective. Now I'm seeing ghosts everywhere."

"Well, if you keep to the rules of security, you don't have to worry about ghosts. That's our job. Yours is to figure out how to access this place. You probably need to talk to Relic about what happened. Clear the air, so to speak. But Connor, I want you to stay away from Theo. I'm not sure what his intentions were, but let's play it safe. If you got a bad vibe, I'd say pay attention." I nodded in agreement, looking down at my hand on his bedrail.

"Don't worry, Gray. This day has been fraught with hard-way lessons that I don't care to repeat. I'll go talk with Relic."

He tipped his head and looked at me. "Dude, what else is bugging you?" I wanted to ask him about Will's blood, but he had only regained consciousness this morning. Maybe he didn't even know yet, so I shared the other complaint on my mind.

"Although I understand the security protocols, they don't allow for much fun. All I get to do is work. Figure out this, analyze that, and plan the impossible. It's too much thinking. I miss hanging out with my friends. I miss staying in one place for a while. And I miss my family. I miss my dog."

"Missions are lonely business. It's hard on us 'talls'. It's got to be twice so for you. So, what do you do to take a break?" Gray asked, adjusting his bandaged leg and scratching the surrounding area.

"I read and watch shows, but what else is there?" I asked. "What do you do to take a break?"

"Well, lately I've been stuck in here. But even in here, I have a team to manage, and I have a wife, which takes more time than I have." He was smiling while rolling his eyes. I thought about all the difficulties his team had gone through, and the discovery of Jilly's pregnancy. But even from a hospital bed, he looked in control. Was that a learned skill or something he was born with? He continued, "But you could play baseball. I'll get Jedi to dig out the equipment I stored in the Brute."

I popped out of the chair I had been slumping in. "Really? What did you bring?"

"I brought wiffle balls, so you don't need mitts. And I brought a couple of plastic bats and mats you can use as bases."

"Oh, thank you, O.G., thank you. I'm going to see if I can round up an evening game." I turned to dash out, but then I stopped. It was easy to see that Gray was tired of his confinement, too. He needed to rest to let his body repair, and we needed him well. Though a 'get well' wish was the best conversation ender, I decided against it. Instead, I opted for a mildly reckless impulse. "Want me to get you a rolling chair and sneak you out of this box for a while?"

"Yes, I definitely want you to do that," Gray answered.

After lunch, Relic and I were discussing the clues and traps that may be in place at the entrance and beyond. Yet after his move in the hangar, my head was spinning with suspicions and contradictions. If he were a Corporate spy, he just blew his best chance. But what if he was using reverse psychology ploy to make me trust him? Though he knew where Cali Bantu was, he didn't know where the access was, or how to get in, but neither did I. If he meant to make me worry, it was working.

"Relic?" I asked. "I'm sorry about this morning."

"I am too. I was hard on you, but I stand by my warning. We don't know these people. They've been very nice, and the RH sent us here, but I just want you to be safe." He held my shoulders like my dad used to. I missed him.

"I know. Hey, if I asked you something, would you tell me?"

He gave me a sideways grin. "Well, that sounds like a trap to me, but if I *can* answer you, I will."

"What's going on with Will's blood?" His face changed.

"Well, leave it to you to find one. The only question I have to avoid. Just know that everything is okay, and if the time comes for you to know, I'll tell you myself."

I smiled. I didn't expect him to spill it, but I just confirmed something was up with Will. We had been working most of the morning, and I needed a break. I told him I was going to visit Axle and start setting up for the wiffle ball game. I was disappointed that so many of our team members were either injured or on the road work crew. But the crew was due in around sunset, and I hoped they weren't too tired. I scheduled a short, five-inning game with four-player teams to be played in the hangar after dinner. The Brute headlights would supply the light.

I went back to the medical station and told Gray the plan. When asked if he was up to attending, he said he was feeling better all the time, and he wouldn't miss it. I left and went to Axle's room. His color looked better than yesterday when I looked in on him, but he still hadn't woken up. He had moments when he stirred and rambled nonsense, but he hadn't regained consciousness.

I uncovered his hand from his blanket and was shocked to see it bandaged around the knuckles. I didn't have to look to know what it was. This was getting creepy. I gently took his hand and spoke to him.

"Hi Axle, it's Connor. I came to tell you that your brother is doing great. You're looking a lot better, too. There's going to be a baseball game tonight. I arranged it. It ought to be fun and probably funny, too. No one but me knows how to play," Connor laughs. "You'd love it, and—"

"Sounds like the kind of mess you'd get yourself into, kid," Axle said, slurring his words and rolling his head.

I pushed the call button on the monitor like Jilly showed me.

Jilly came running in, and her expression changed from the urgency of fear to a smile of relief.

"Welcome back," she said as she checked his vitals. "Everything looks good, great in fact," she said, the last part quietly. "You sure took your time in slumberland. How do you feel?"

"Man, I feel like — bad. It was a simple butt shot. What happened? "

"Well, you developed an infection, a serious one. Probably because of the lengthy delay in removing that bullet. Here's the culprit," she said, holding up a small vial with a disfigured piece of metal. "Can you tell me exactly where your pain is?"

"My butt, my back, my shoulder, you name it, it hurts," Axle groaned.

Knowing Jilly would want to check Axle out, I went to excuse myself. "Hey Jilly," I whispered, hanging on the partition edge. "Do you mind if I go tell Gray his brother is awake?"

"I heard," came a call from the other side of the short wall. "I'm coming over," he said.

"No, you're not," Jilly yelled. Then she heard Gray laughing as he added, "Welcome back, brother."

"Good grief," came Beckett's voice. "What's a guy gotta do to get some sleep around here?"

As I left, I heard Jilly attempt to get her charges under control. I laughed at the idea of her keeping these tough warrior brutes compliant while they finished convalescing.

When the hangar doors opened, an icy blast rushed into the open space along with the road crew. Outside, shadows cloaked everything in black, except for a red wine horizon outlining the jagged skyline. I was walking off the bases and setting up the pitcher's square. When I explained the plans to the returning team, it was clear I wasn't the only one looking forward to the game. Since Will and I went into hiding, the entire team had been wound tight, and the battles that followed had only tightened the coil.

"Good idea, Connor," Will said as he walked through the hangar. "I hope you saved me a spot on the team."

"I was counting on it," I answered. He was probably exhausted from his day, but not so much that he would sit on the sidelines of a competition.

I didn't need to sneak Gray to the game after all, but he, Axle, and Beckett were sequestered in the lounge room, watching from the windows. Jilly didn't want them exposed to the freezing temperatures in the hangar for an extended time. They tried to argue with her, but that was the power of the medical officer. Unless there was a crisis, she had the authority to relegate their activities.

To minimize any further injuries to the team, a couple of rules were put in place. No sliding into bases. Run throughs would count as safe on all bases as long as the runner didn't turn. Though Gray, Axle, and Lana, were the only people fully familiar with the game, I was the only one playing. Lana was keeping score and being the umpire. Everyone else was new to the game.

Jedi caught a nice grounder, but hesitated, not knowing where to throw it. Lana called Nash out for not touching home plate. It was a disaster as games go, but each error made us laugh more. It was more than a game; it was good medicine. We needed to release the pressure that had built up since we left the Fort eight days ago.

CHAPTER 19

The next day Relic and I settled Axle, Jilly, and Gray in the lounge to get them up to speed on our progress.

"So, have you guys figured out what we will find at this Cali Bantu place?" asked Axle.

"Well, no," I said. "The first challenge is to find the entrance. After that, we have to get inside. If, I mean when we accomplish that, I expect we will be given instructions. The mystery surrounding this place is not a mistake or a piece that was left out. It's a part of the plan. I know we will have to prove we are part of the rebellion. But I believe that the founders have a plan to help us achieve victory. It makes no sense for them to lead us all the way here only to abandon us."

"I agree. That makes the most sense, but we don't know who *they* are. We're dancing in the dark here," Relic added. "Connor and I have gone over all the clues we think will help us find and access this place. But the truth is, we are counting on Connor's memory triggers to guide us through." He leaned back in his chair and clasped his hands.

"So basically, you're saying just get us there with a fair amount of supplies, and you'll get to work on the entrance," said Gray.

"Basically, yes," Relic said while I nodded in agreement.

Jilly had been quietly listening during the meeting, having nothing beneficial to add to the topic. But now it was her turn to report on the team's health.

"As far as combat and hard labor, Dom, Axle, Gray, and Beckett are still on the off-duty recuperation list. But that's an upgrade from the serious and critical conditions they had been in just a day ago."

The next day, all the uninjured soldiers were sent back to continue clearing the road or scouting for enemy activity. Dom stayed to work on the minis with the help of Theo. Dom's arm was healing well, but someone was required to do an inspection and maintenance on the minis, so he was the logical choice.

Gray, Relic, Axle, and I went over the base camp plans and scenarios while the teams were gone. We reviewed the sabotaged roads and the roads that were too difficult at this time of the year. It would be almost impossible to get a large army through the series of blockades we had positioned between them and the tunnel, the Fort, and the Fringer towns. But it wasn't impossible. We had a limited window before brutal forces overran those places, trying to stop this mission.

And then there was our dilemma. We were cut off. The road to and from Aspen was blocked. It would take our foes a couple more days to clear the huge roadblock the crew had left them.

"What if they took over the Fringers and forced them to fight on their side?" Axle asked.

"It would take a week or two for reinforcements to reach us. As far as Aspen goes, I think they would sneak past the town to save time and resources," Relic said. "But they might try to use them as hostages to get us to surrender."

"So, as far as the rest of the free peoples, Will told me the Guard is ready to protect the Fringers as long as they aren't overrun with too many soldiers, and that's true of the tunnel too," said Gray. "All of that is out of our control right now. We need to focus on *our* mission. Right now, the weather is holding, so we need to leave by tomorrow morning."

"I agree," Relic said.

It was almost lunchtime when I came into the lounge, finding Beckett and Axle sitting on the couches. Jilly wheeled the injured men into the area one at a time using the only wheelchair available. Everyone else was helping clear the road to our goal, or they were repairing the vehicles needed to get there. When I came in, they invited me to sit.

They had several aeronautical charts lying on the table between them. The maps had all the features of a common map, but they also included strange symbols. I was told they indicated airport size and designation, crosswinds, flight paths for landings and takeoffs, and the range of the airports' Inertial Guidance System. INS was a navigation device that used sensors to continuously calculate, by dead reckoning (distanced traveled), the position, orientation, and velocity of the aircraft within its domain.

Though we didn't have planes, the information was valuable for flying drones. Aspen Security gave Gray his own copies for our drone operations, as well as a booklet that explained all the symbols. Our task was to decide the best defensive positions if the enemy caught up with us. Knowing nothing about what we'd find at Cali Bantu, our plan relied on what we brought with us. Drones were our best option for attacking our adversaries. And though the precious technology made easy targets in the open sky, our enemy faced the same dilemma.

Building a base camp near Pyramid Peak was necessary, and although we had good camouflage resources, they would expect that. It would be hard to hide the tracks of six heavy-duty vehicles traveling down a groomed road. The enemy was bound to find our encampment, as it was the only road in and out. Then they would have a stationary target to deliver a barrage of damage and casualties.

The decision was unanimous; we had to attack first. It was irrational to depend on the hope that we could shelter inside this mystery place and have instant access to its powerful weapon. It didn't escape me that I was the hope they were counting on, but no one said it out loud. Our team included many recovering soldiers, making the attack plan an ominous prospect. I imagined the enemy soldiers were sitting around having the exact conversation.

But for now, as long as the enemy was trapped by the collapsed snow bridge, and they didn't know what road we were taking from Aspen, we still had time. Meaning, *I* still had time. It frustrated me to wait. I could not seek the clues or images required to save us until I got there. I was like the other unknown weapon, waiting to be useful.

We were flying blind, with only a few random notes to lead us. My head rocked on my elbows, trying to solve the unsolvable problem until I forced myself back to the conversation.

"Our last decision is on whether we should booby-trap the Marion Bells Road and, if so, how. But remember, whatever we do to this road, we do to ourselves. If we destroy it, we're stuck. If we trigger an avalanche, we're stuck. If we blockade them out, we're blockaded in," Gray said, his repetition reiterating the seriousness of the decision.

"I say we attack them if they turn down this road. And if they get within a couple of miles of us, we sabotage the road," said Beckett.

"We could have ordinances along the road ready to go, and park snipers along it like we did in the Tunnel Battle. We could have codes to designate the level of engagement," added Axle.

"Explosions will trigger avalanches," I said, "and they don't always go where you want them to."

"We could pack grenades into partially notched trees that would fall across the road. It should contain most of the concussion. It would be less likely to trigger a slide."

"That might work. Relic has studied the recorded data used for avalanche predictions. He could help with that when he gets back," I suggested.

"Sounds like we need more information before we decide. I want an idea from each of you by this afternoon, say 3:00. Write up an explanation of your idea and a list of supplies it would take. We'll regroup and come up with a plan to present to Will, Nash, and Relic," Gray added before calling the meeting to an end.

"Okay, now the only question is, who is going to make us infirmed gents some lunch?" Beckett asked.

All eyes fixed on me. "Typical," I said under my breath.

An Aspen local helped me make a venison soup. She took me to their walk-in freezer and grabbed a frozen block of stock. I had done a lot of cooking when I was a Daily, but I had never heard of stock. The tunnel had great stores of freeze-dried broth, but not stock. Both soup bases boiled down vegetables and spices, but broth adds meat to the mixture, while stock uses bones.

The soup was excellent. The sundried vegetables and homemade pasta made it hearty and added just the right touch, but the stock they had made it incredible. I brought a tray of soup and bread to the lounge, where Dom and Theo had joined the others. After tasting it, they asked Theo about Aspen's ability to grow food.

I also took a tray to the medical lab for Jilly and found her fast asleep. I covered the large bowl of soup and bread and put them in the refrigerator for her. When I returned to the lounge, the conversation had evolved into food storage techniques. It was interesting to hear how innovative people could be in difficult situations, and I took it all in.

"I remember," Axle explained, "when Bannon told me how his dad inherited this large freeze-dryer system. This guy had been trying to sell him one, but Banner, Bannon's dad, said all he needed was a small one. The Corporates wanted his entire inventory, and they eventually gained control with a hostile takeover move. The owner disappeared, and Banner couldn't find him.

"But two days later, this huge state-of-the-art appliance gets delivered to Vogel Ent. It was the guy's best, most expensive model. It has twenty sections, allowing for twenty different items to be processed at once in half the time. Banner hid it in one of his warehouses, assuming there was some innovative design the man didn't want the Corporates to have. But they still got away with twenty-seven giant models."

Gray bristled at the discussion, and his mood quickly turned bitter. I wondered if it was about his hatred of the Elites, but stealing machines was hardly their worst act. More secrets.

"I'm kind of tired," Gray said. "I'm going back to my room."

"I'll push you, O.G.," I said. "I want to see if Jilly is ready for her lunch yet. She was asleep when I tried to take her some."

"Thanks for watching out for her while I've been down and out," Gray said as I pushed him down the hall to the clinic.

"My pleasure," I said.

The day moved slowly until the security team came back with their reports for Gray.

Gray entered the lounge on crutches. Knowing the lack of a wheelchair would get our attention, he stopped our comments by talking first. "Let me have what you found."

Nash went first. "The enemy is still behind the snowbank. We checked the ravine for signs of walking soldiers, but their prints turned around about a mile out, and the only sizable heat signatures we detected turned out to be a Shiras moose."

"You sure it was a moose?" Gray asked.

"Yep, in fact, we have tons of meat to share with our Aspen friends and some for us to pack with us when we leave."

"We also parked a drone in a nearby tree to listen in on their conversations," said Jedi. "Assuming they didn't expect us to do this, and their discussions were genuine, they plan to trap and ambush us after we show them the way to access Cali Bantu. And they said Cali Bantu, so they know of it, but I didn't get any indication they knew what it holds."

"Ugh, let's hope they don't," said Gray. "Are they in contact with HQ?"

"No," said Nash. "They were discussing ways to send a message back to Glenwood. From there, they operate a communication network with drones. They decided against it because they were short people and drones. They lost five soldiers in the explosion, and they complained about needing to conserve their resources. With all the road closures, they didn't feel Corporate would be able to send them reinforcements."

It was my turn. "I don't have any military plans, but when we go to search for the entrance, I think we should split up to cover more ground."

"I agree, we need to locate this before the Garrison team catches up with us. They say they're in rough shape, but it could be a deception. They are still a threat, and we can't afford to underestimate them," Gray added.

"Yeah, I'm worried about what they will do to the Aspen locals when they get here and we're gone," said Jedi.

"I was told by Will that they have a couple of G-guns in the tower. Plus, it would take a lot to pry open one of those hangar doors. If they're smart, they'd leave these guys alone," said Gray. "Their G gun uses the same caliber as our minis do, so we'll leave them extra ammo. Unless someone has something to add, I'll discuss these plans and info with Will."

We all shook our heads. "Okay, I think we have a solid plan for tomorrow. When the road crew gets back, we'll meet again. Ax, Beckett, Jedi, Nash, Connor, nice work today."

CHAPTER 20

We were all in bed by 10:00 to get going by 7:00 the next morning. Everything was charged, packed, and ready to go. Powdered eggs, cured wild game, and strong tea from the locals made a hearty breakfast to last the trek to the base camp. The expected time frame was under four hours, with some of that time used for setting traps along the road for their adversaries. That and thirty minutes to set up the camp would have us there and set up in time for lunch.

Soon, goodbyes and last-minute item packing were underway. I saw Theo rush out and talk with Relic and Gray. From their worried expressions, I knew something was not going according to plan.

Will turned and walked toward the vehicles, all lined up and running. He raised his voice and yelled, "Move out. We have a storm brewing."

They had discussed splitting up the team because of the injured members' restrictions, but they were healing at a fast rate, so it was unnecessary. That meant all sixteen members filled the Six vehicles as we tracked our way to the climax of our journey. The road was nicely groomed, and the views were spectacular. Before we turned down the Maroon Bells, the crater where downtown Aspen once stood came into view. Though the pristine snow covered much of its charred remains, the devastating strike was evident.

The next turn took us into a beautiful canyon well frosted by the winter snow. Though spectacular in beauty, all that sparkling snow has a cruel side because snow, especially new snow, and slopes mean avalanches. They weren't as common in the fall as they were in the spring, but this canyon checked off several warning signs. Steep angles didn't collect much snow, but slopes with 30 to 40 degree angles, like many of these, have just the right slant to build up a lot of snow as well as send it screaming down.

It didn't take a large event to release its energy. Any sudden change, like heavy snowfall, warm temperatures, or a single person crossing a sloped field, could set off a chain reaction resulting in a tsunami of crushing snow, carrying away everything in its wake. But no snow was falling, and no wind was howling, yet.

About thirty minutes down the road, gently falling flakes began settling on the windshield. So pretty, so silent. Rain taps out its presence in a rhythmic beat. But snow is quiet, conducting a shrewd assault. Without a noisy wind, it can deepen, trapping the unaware. Thirty minutes later, the wind started picking up, sending the sky's frozen scales whipping across the windshield, and its gusts swaying the vehicles like ships at sea.

I rode with Will in one of the four minis. We were following the Brute as it bounded down the snowy road. It was a rougher ride in the mini than in the Brute, and louder too. For most of the ride, no words were spoken, but the silence wasn't uncomfortable. It allowed me to take in my surroundings and enjoy how exquisite this world was. I appreciated New Haven's engineers' noble attempts to imitate the outside world environment, but it fell far short of replacing it.

The trail wound on, with Will looking at the instruments before us. The temperature and air pressure had dropped since we left, and I could tell it had him concerned.

"Is the weather going to prevent us from reaching the base camp today?" I asked.

"I don't think so," he answered. "See the triangle on the map? That's us moving down the road. The two blinking lights, one behind and one in front of us, are the beacons we set on the road to tell us where we are.

The one behind us marked the halfway point, and we are almost to the three-quarters mark."

I enjoyed watching the many dials and readings on the instrument panel. I had been in the passenger seat of the Brute when Jilly worked on Gray, but I found it hard to pay attention to them.

"So, we should be there in an hour or two?" I asked.

"It gets slower the more snow we have to deal with, but I can't see us stopping when we're less the four miles away," Will said.

I decided to change the conversation to something less ominous. "Will, if you had the choice between a life of freedom out where the Corporates wouldn't find you, or this life of fighting for a cause in constant peril, which would you choose?"

"I *had* that life of unfettered freedom. After I escaped the Neighwah, I lived in a cabin for almost two years. I was left alone because they thought I was dead. I hunted, built furniture, baked, canned, and lived a life without battles and death. It was nice for a while."

"What made you give it up?" I asked. Just when I thought I knew this man, I discovered more.

"Injustice," Will said while handing me a bag of snacks to open for us. "I saw Drangers stalking and kidnapping women for their brothel in Pueblo." He hesitated after saying that, but I waved off his attempt to be sensitive to my age, and Will continued.

"I couldn't stand by, so I got involved. But I have long thought about why I stayed after I had secured the Fringers in towns the Corporates agreed they would not attack."

"Why would you believe that?" I asked.

"That is top secret, but let's just say we discovered something so awful that they couldn't afford to have it exposed. I shouldn't tell you that, so please don't ask me to say more," Will said, giving me a serious side glance.

"Okay, so why did you return to the chaos?"

Will thought for a second before he answered. "I guess I love the adrenaline rush. It's exciting to look the reaper in the face and send him packing. It's especially rewarding when it achieves something noble. But there is always a price. It's hard to look at the man I become in those moments. And it's hard to be different in the thick of battle. And it's painful when others are lost because of what I invoked."

"Is there no way to reason that out?" I asked, trying to grab a glimpse into the source of his courage.

"It's a paradox for sure. It would be easy to say it is the cause that compels me forward, but I'm not sure that's completely true. I believe I will continue to seek challenging situations even when, or if, this war is won. Maybe if I experience enough danger, it will one day bring me peace. Or perhaps I will receive an injury, be it physical or emotional, that is so great that I cannot continue. Maybe then I'll contemplate finding peace. "

"One of these days, that peace may come in the form of everlasting peace," I said, raising my brows at the thought of losing him. "Doesn't that scare you enough to want to stop?"

"Maybe it should, but I wouldn't be a very good warrior, and the world needs warriors whether or not they want them. But I do want peace, and at times I believe it's just around the next bend. But one bend always begets another because the world of humans is inherently volatile."

"That's very profound. A warrior's axiom," I said reverently.

He turned and smiled. It was a smile so genuine, his hard mantle retracted, giving a rare glimpse at his true nature. It was kind and warm... and happy. I wished I could capture this moment, but within a slice of a second, he was back to business, all unbreakable and self-sacrificing.

I sat in silence, realizing how fortunate I was to know such an epically heroic and iconic man. Gray also had my highest respect, but he didn't face it alone. Though that balancing act had its own challenges. As we moved down the trail, I felt sad thinking about the eventual loss of these remarkable human beings. The world is better for them being here, and it will experience a profound loss when they pass from it.

"How long until we reach the base campsite?" I asked.

"We just passed the third beacon a mile ago. It's about twelve miles total, so I'd say we're chipping away at the last three miles," Will answered.

We arrived at our destination, but the gentle, falling flakes that started our journey had transformed into a vicious blizzard. We all knew that setting up the camp would be a miserable experience, and I wondered if I would be held in the Brute while everyone else got to work.

"Jilly, Connor, Beckett, and Gray, your jobs will involve working on the inside clasps," Will ordered over the intercom. And there was my answer.

"Since when—" I heard Gray's voice over the speaker, but Will cut him off.

"Since I'm in charge by decree of medical authority, there will be no persons on crutches, with internal stitches, shorter than five feet tall, or pregnant allowed outside during the storm without my permission." I could only imagine Gray's expression, trying to hold back his retort. The rest of his instructions involved reviewing the assigned tasks.

Will walked me over to the Brute, and it was a struggle to see and stay steady against the wind. When we entered, I could feel the anger radiating off of Gray. At some point, he would recognize how ridiculous going out in this weather on crutches would be, but not now.

"There's plenty of work to be done in here," said Jilly. "Help me unlatch the benches. This middle one can be folded up into a table, and this one spins around to face the table." Gray glared at her. "Never mind, I'll do it myself," she sighed. The maneuverable parts were stout for the rough roads they were built for, and she struggled to lock them into place.

That got Gray bounding up with snarls and grumbles, vibrating a warning to everyone near, but Jilly paid no heed to his bravado and continued her assault, "After that—"

"I know how to set up camp. I was the one who trained everyone," he said through gritted teeth.

She was tired and didn't need more snappy comments, so she set to her tasks silently. Opening the cabin access doors where the sleeping gear and cooking items were stored, she and I dragged them out and put them around the floor. Our personal gear, food, and other supplies would have to be retrieved from the minis and delivered.

The large open space of the campsite allowed all the vehicles to be joined into one ample home. It would conserve heat, and the temperatures may drop dramatically once the storm cleared. A bubbling pot of tea was served with pre-made sandwiches and frozen fruit pops. The original plan involved some of us taking a hike to search for clues and possible entrance points, but that would have to wait until the storm subsided.

"Are we worried about avalanches here?" I asked Relic.

"I'll need to recalculate the risk after it stops snowing. It's a simple mathematical problem. I take the amount of snow, both recent and settled, and the angle of the slope. I used the 'inclinometer for alpha' formula. Where C is the bottom of the slope and B is where the debris will accumulate, one can find the safe zone, A. Then taking the temperature—"

"Relic, we all trust that you worked it out logically, and we thank you. But I'm too worn out for math class," Jedi chimed in.

"I was listening," I said with sincerity, leaning toward Relic. "It sounds like the trigonometry problems I studied before I stopped going to school." Although I wasn't worried about catching up on my studies, it made me wonder what I'd be working on if I weren't duty-bound to follow this path.

"When the sky clears. I'll show how to calculate it."

Yesterday, while with the road crew, Relic reported the avalanche danger was low, but this new, heavy snow would create instability. It wasn't only the sliding snow that threatened to bury our camp. The sky delivered a persistent onslaught, piling up the fluff at an alarming rate. The risk of being buried was real, and we all listened to the ominous discussion.

"Those of you on night watch have the added task of monitoring the air intake system. Most of your duty can be done from the vehicle cabs, but don't let our exits get blocked. A couple of cling-drones have been hung on trees nearby, giving visuals of the shelter from three different angles. They probably won't last much longer. If they get covered, they will shut down, so don't depend on them sending alarms to your bands." Gray and Will continued to give orders for their areas of command.

Clear blue skies greeted us in the morning along with bone-chilling temperatures. Snow covered the shelter, causing several troops to climb out the top to re-shovel the entrances they had worked on through the night. Breakfast consisted of hot farina with cinnamon honey, a gift from Aspen, and herbal or strong caffeinated tea. Soon, the doors were shoveled out, and the workers came in for their breakfast. We all listened to the orders of the day and set out to tackle them.

Fully bundled, I stepped into the bright rays that burst off the pristine white crystals, dousing the world in sunshine. It stood in stark contrast to the frigid temperatures that met us at the door. Yet, no one wished for a warm day of risky snowbanks. Snow-flocked trees and craggy rock peaks were textured by the snow and set against a deep blue sky. It was breathtakingly beautiful.

Will was called into the Brute while the rest of us donned our gear for our assigned treks. When Will came back out, Gray was walking behind him. His gait was slow and measured, but he was walking on his own. I was about to congratulate him when the team of soldiers greeted him with cheers and jests about the drill sergeant being back, and someone asked if his mommy said he could come out. Gray just took it in. They could treat him like one of the guys to a point, and he'd be sure to let them know if they hit that.

CHAPTER 21

Three groups were setting out today. Two were on surveillance walks to check out Pyramid Peak and scope out possible entrance points. Will was leading the one with me, Etcher, and Jedi. Nash would lead Relic, Mack, and Jax. Tommie, Easton, and Dom were tasked with resetting the clinger-drones and hiking up the trail to check for the enemy.

That left Gray, Axle, Beckett, Jilly, and Lana at base camp. Their jobs included rolling up the bedding, preparing the upcoming meals, readying the weapons, and setting up Relic's weather station away from the warmth of the shelter. Part of that station included a couple of snow depth measuring sticks, which had to go down to the soil level. Lana hoped she'd have time to sit at the table and write out the team journal.

Our team was on a more arduous journey, but it was also the most likely place to search for the entrance. Etcher said there was a stone monument that looked like a lighthouse. It was erected to guide the souls who never returned. Both Relic and I thought it sounded promising, and the team I was on was the logical choice to check it out.

I was eager to see the meteorite scar as depicted in GD's painting. As we came around the edge, I looked for it, but I found nothing. Perhaps it was covered with snow, but I kept hoping the right angle would reveal it. The snowshoes made the short walk into a laborious hike, and we took several rest stops to keep from sweating ourselves into hypothermia. Etcher told us we were close to the monument when we reached a rickety bridge. I was excited and nervous at the same time.

"How about I cross first and tie a rope for us to hang onto?" Jedi offered, looking at me.

"No," I warned. "This could be a clue. It's like the bridge to the castle. I have to be brave."

Etcher looked at me as I steeled my nerves to cross this broken-down bridge over the icy water that rushed into a frozen lake. "I've crossed this before," she said, "but never in winter. And even in the summer, we use a rope. This bridge is pretty shaky, and if you go in, you could end up in the lake and get dragged under the ice," she said as she pointed to the icy-edged water just past the crossing. "How about I go first?" she suggested. As much as I loved that idea, I knew this was something I had to do.

"I don't know if it would break the knight's code, but I don't think we can risk being deemed unworthy. But maybe someone could stand downstream to grab me before I'm carried into the lake?" I requested. "That's not cheating. It's just smart."

Etcher stared at me like I spoke nonsense while Will climbed down and got ready to charge into the frigid waters that flowed into the lake. She must think us all crazy to let me risk my life because of a fairytale.

I secured my snowshoes on the back of my pack, hoping I wouldn't sink into a hole in the decking. I bent my legs slightly and spread my feet apart. Cautiously, I inched my way onto the snow-covered contraption. I was a third of the way when, suddenly, a board gave way and tipped, sending me toward the edge. Instinctively, I grabbed the rail with my gloved hand with its grip-worthy coating. It stopped my momentum. Frozen in place, I looked at my feet dangling over the edge.

The bridge was too weak to allow anyone to come to my aid, so I collected my courage and pulled myself back up. The bridge righted itself as soon as I stood on the other side of the board. Feeling the solid board under my feet settled me, but not completely. My heart was racing. I continued a little slower this time, and little by little, I edged to the other side.

I bent down, leaning on my knees. I tried not to think about having to cross it again to get back. Maybe then a rope would be okay since I would have already fulfilled that part of my destiny. *Stop!*

In one clear moment, I had absolute focus. I wouldn't let my life be chauffeured by destiny. A destiny is inevitable. It subverts freewill, which was God given. I *chose* to cross that bridge, and my faith guided me. *I* made it across because I've trained and practiced physical skills, and my faith guided me through. It was then I let go of destiny and embraced something new—purpose. I have a purpose because I am part of God's plan. *I* will fulfill it because *I believe* and I choose to be a part of that plan. The idea swelled inside me, and I looked. My team was staring at me, and Will stood poised, ready to charge across the bridge to get to me. But I smiled and rose proud and tall. And everyone on the other side began cheering.

Soon everyone was across, and it was agreed that a snack break was in order. Will picked me off the ground and spun me around.

"Dude, you've got... guts made of granite. That was impressive," he exclaimed.

The others agreed, and I endured several slaps on the back. I could feel the heat on my cheeks because I had been terrified the whole time, but I did it, and that's what courage means—being afraid and doing it anyway. Faith means believing I am saved and there is nothing to fear.

Etcher asked me what was going on with the castle, bravery, and being worthy. I told her I was taught to read the symbols and codes that may help us find what we are looking for, but I didn't share more than that.

As we closed in on the monument, Will pulled me aside. "So, remind me what comes next in this knight's creed thing."

"A knight must be brave, true, wise, gracious, and skilled. Being brave with the miniature castle meant pushing my finger down on a sharp object to lower the drawbridge. Crossing that bridge took being brave to a whole new level." I answered. I knew what he was thinking, and I was way ahead of him. "If the rest of the steps are as difficult, I might not—"

"I will not let you fail. We share this destiny, and we should help each other. I believe that's a knight thing too." I thought about sharing my epiphany with him about destiny and purpose, but that would have to wait.

We labored along the covered path in our clumsy snowshoes to reach the mound of snow that Etcher claimed was the monument. I still couldn't see any evidence of a meteorite strike, but perhaps the snow concealed it. I asked her if she had seen anything like that.

"I didn't see any evidence that meteorites hit the mountain. Aspen was reduced to a giant hole, but the mountain was left untouched," I noted, a touch of anger for the unfairness of it, but she regained herself quickly. "But the monument is at the head of Crater Lake. Maybe the clue refers to an event in the past. It's frozen now, but it's right there," she pointed to a small open area of snow about a hundred yards from us.

Crater Lake, I laughed to myself. Nothing can just be what it is. Every clue is distorted and tangled up with the next. I assume it simply signals which side of the mountain the entrance is on. What if we missed one of these crazy connections? What if we, what if I, miss the next ones? Would the solutions of Cali Bantu be lost forever? I can't be the only one trained to find it, but I could be the only one left. It was a disturbing thought.

It took a little time to clear the fluffy new snow, but under it was a layer of ice that clung like glue to the nooks and crannies of the form. Will got into his pack and pulled out his torch and pickaxe.

I was instantly alarmed. "I agree we need to defrost this stone, but we shouldn't do anything that goes against the creed. We can't just break our way into Cali Bantu," I said with trepidation. "It would probably trigger something. We have to use the right codes and be invited in."

"Good to know," Will said as he lit the torch and began carefully freeing the stone with his flame.

As the snow melted, I gasped. "It's a tower with spikes and turrets!"

Will smiled, knowing, as I did, that this was the second clue. When he finished thawing out the little tower, it stood about four feet tall. I walked up and studied it. Eight spikes stood in a circle, labeled with the four cardinal directions and the intermediate ones. My compass showed the spikes were already aligned correctly, but unlike my castle turrets, this tower appeared to be solid and immovable. No tool fit between the perfectly honed seams. I tried pulling, pushing, and turning the north spike, but nothing budged. I was sure this monument was the next clue that pointed where to go from here. Somehow, one of them had to move.

Stumped, I walked away to think for a second.

"Why are you only looking at the north marker?" asked Will.

"Well," I thought about that, "I guess I'm fixated on the true north clue, but you may be right."

I took a closer, more open-minded look at the other spikes, and I saw it. The southeast symbol sat slightly higher than the other labels, and on the inside of the stone tube, a hidden crack traced along the bottom of the spike. It wasn't straight. It was more like a naturally occurring crack, but maybe it wasn't. I grabbed it, and it separated neatly along the fracture, and the spike rose upward. When I let it go, it fell away from the tower and toward the mountain. Tucked under the spike was an arrow pointing straight at a dark crop of trees at the bottom of the slope. A grove under the lip of the spike gave the second point needed for an accurate direction.

"Two of us need to go over there, and the other two need to stay here and point a laser using the arrow and the hash mark," I said to Will. Though this was my part of the mission, I was pretty sure I wasn't allowed to give Jedi and Etcher orders.

"Got it," Will said. Then he turned toward Etcher and Jedi. "Connor and I will go over and look for the next clue. When I wave at you, turn on the target laser. Maybe we can knock this thing out before we have to turn back."

It looked like a short distance, but we were on snowshoe time, which took longer. We signaled when we were close, and a red beam cast a line across the basin. When the trees got too thick for the beam to penetrate, we used string to extend it. It landed on a large bush.

"I had a fort with an entrance like this when I was a kid," Will shared. "We attached a growing bush to our entrance to conceal it. When it was closed, it was undetectable, but we could swing it out for access. It was from a story my stepmom told me." We both gave each other knowing looks. Was everything from our childhood just a buildup to this moment? He threw the bush to the side, exposing an excavated dirt hole. Will crawled in first, and I followed. It opened up as we made our way toward the back, but it ended. There was nothing more to it. This was not Cali Bantu.

We looked at each other, tracing our lights all around. I was warm from the exertion, so I unzipped my coat and flayed it open. Will's light flashed on something small and square at the very edge of the cave wall. It was an old wooden box. He picked it up carefully and tipped open the lid. Inside lay a top, a notepad, an old nickel, and a baseball. The baseball had my attention. It was exactly what GD would have left for me to find. I wondered if the other items had special meaning to other would-be Highminds. Were they on their way, or...?

Will was about to speak, but I held up my hand. "Brave for the bridge, true for the direction, wise for the light, so this is about being gracious." I wasn't feeling very gracious. I was tired of a game that hurt and killed people.

"Maybe we should donate something to the box," Will said, "like an offering."

"But what? I can look through my pack, but to make this a gracious offering, it has to be precious. Not valuable, precious," I said. Reaching into my side pocket, I pulled out my cross, and from my breast pocket tucked inside my hymnal, I produced a picture of Hannah. As I was putting them in the box, Will shook his head.

"I know what it is," Will said. "It's this," and he held up the Sanguine Blade. "They want this."

"I don't know. We don't know who 'they' are. That is precious to us all because it is the key to... something. Besides, what if we need it to prove the next thing, which is skill? I think they are asking for something sentimental." I was thinking ahead to what our next move would be. Do we walk away or wait?

"This *is* sentimental," he said with uncommon reverence. "Besides, if the Corporates were behind this, they wouldn't go through all this clue stuff. They're more the brute force type. They'd charge in here and take what they wanted. No, this feels like destiny stuff." He smiled, and we both rolled our eyes. "I think if this is Cali Bantu, we need to get it right. To me, being gracious is more than giving up my valuables. It's about trusting and surrendering to something bigger than myself." I held my cross, knowing he was right. This was about having faith. Will slowly put the blade in the box, set it down, and took a few uncertain steps away.

Suddenly, the cave shook, and a wall of snow crashed through the bush door. At the same moment, another sound came from the back of the cave wall, where a rock covered door slid open, pouring light into the small space. Silhouetting the door were two industrial metal robots full of cables, claws, and armed to the teeth. Will grabbed his sidearm, shoved me behind him, and fired.

The bullets ricocheted off them, causing Will to drop us to the floor. Protectively, he squatted in front of me. He didn't stand a chance against such mechanisms, but he was ready to fight. Slowly backing us up toward the box, he was trying to retrieve his blade. I felt a pinprick on my neck, and my head began to spin. I crumpled against him as he reached for the box.

Then darkness.

CHAPTER 22

"Connor," I heard someone call, and I tried to open my eyes. "Wake up." The voice said. "You okay?" Clearing away the fog in my head, I realized it was Will.

I surveyed the pristine and starkly furnished pale peach room. The bed was comfortable, and falling back to sleep was tempting. But the more my head cleared, the more alarmed I became. What happened? Had Cali Bantu been taken over? Will repeated his question. "Are you okay?"

"I think so. What happened?" I asked. Throwing the blanket aside, I saw I had on my thermal drawers and a t-shirt. Will was also down to his underclothes. "Did I see robots, or did I dream that? And where are we?"

"I'm not sure about either question, but if seeing robots was a dream, we shared it. One thing I know for sure: we were drugged. I don't know how long we were out because my watch is missing. If this is Cali Bantu, they have a funny way of welcoming us."

"The blade?" I remembered. "Where is it?"

Will raised his brows and shook his tilted head. Will got up and examined our quarters. First, he tried the door—locked. Next to the door was a small table with two clear glasses and a clear pitcher of water, where ice and lemon slices floated on the surface. A plate of fresh strawberries and small biscuits accompanied it. On the opposite wall was an open door leading to a bathroom, with clothing draped on hooks.

I moved toward the food, but Will stopped me. "They drugged us once," he said with a look of warning.

I wasn't ready to give up on this place. "And they did it without us eating anything. While we were out, they could have injected us with whatever they wanted. Feeding us poisoned food doesn't make sense. I think if this is Cali Bantu, they would have to make sure we aren't Corporates soldiers. I still think this is where we will meet our new allies."

Will was still highly suspicious and searching the room like a caged animal. "Maybe, but none of this makes sense to me. All we can do now is wait, be alert, and look for options."

A voice came over a hidden speaker system.

"Welcome, Connor and William. You are safe. Please proceed to the bathroom to shower and use the outfits provided for you. Enjoy the refreshments. We will see you soon and answer all of your questions."

"Did they just imply that we stink?" Will jested, turning his head toward his armpit and giving a sour face. He was trying to put me at ease, acting like he was still in control, but I knew better. He was worried about me, the blade, and our captivity.

"I guess they think four days of no showers is too many," I played along. "I'll go first."

Will jumped up. "Let me check it out." When I gave him a mocking glance, he said, "Humor me."

He flushed the toilet and deemed it harmless, causing me to chuckle to myself. Not sure how toilets attack people, but I wasn't about to laugh at him when he was being so serious. He turned on the water to the sink and the shower and felt it with his hands. He dispensed a dab of the provided body wash into his hands and smelled it. He observed his hands, waiting for any skin irritation, I imagine. Then he gave me the okay, but he left the door cracked open so he could hear my calls for help. Talls can be like that.

It felt good to be clean again. The medium blue jersey pants and bright white shirt were extremely comfortable, I thought as I put on the white socks and slip-on tennis shoes. Will came out, adjusting the drawstring on his tan linen pants. He hadn't yet put on his shirt, and I noted all the scars on his torso and the tattoos on his arms. Every single one had a dramatic tale to tell, and I wondered if I wanted to hear them. He threw the long-sleeved, cream-colored t-shirt over his head and got to work on his socks and shoes.

"They are going to be looking for us," I said about our teammates.

"I'm counting on it," answered Will. "In the meantime, have something to eat. I tried it while you were showering, and it seems safe."

As we polished off the rest of the food, a noise came from the door.

A human-looking lavender robot came to retrieve us. It had arms, legs, a torso, and a face, with rounded panels covering parts of it, but exposing the hinges and cables allowing it to move.

"I hope you feel well and rested. I am S3. Tessera regrets not meeting you herself as well as your initial treatment, but assurances had to be made that you were who you were and not infested with harmful mites or harboring computer viruses. Please follow me," said the soft-spoken robot.

"If we have been cleared, why do they still shadow us?" asked Will, pointing to the two metal robots marching behind them.

"The sentinel cydroids are a precaution against that which is unknown," S3 answered.

So far, we had only seen two sentinel robots at a time, but that didn't mean there weren't more. S3 led us into an off-white room where delicate, ghostly images of green leaves danced gently across the walls as if projected through a window. Three light gray sofas faced each other, separated by a long white table hosting an opalescent vase of lavender sprigs, lightly scenting the air. A large black screen took up a significant portion of the wall to the left of the seating, contrasting the soft pastels decorating the rest of the room. Although the decorators designed the room to have a calming influence, we were not calm at all.

"Please be seated," S3 requested with emotionless calm.

I could see that Will was getting frustrated with the sterile environment with its polite prison guards. The android left the room, but the sentinels remained. Though they shortened their height considerably as they collapsed into stand-down positions, there was little doubt they were at the ready.

We looked at each other in silence. I could see the skepticism in Will's eyes. It was his job to protect me, and he was feeling trapped. But I was intrigued, and I needed him to let this play out for a bit longer. They said our questions would be answered, and I had a list piling up in my head. The answers, as well as the way they delivered them, would tell me much. Before we, or Will, acted, we needed to establish who these robots represented. Somewhere in my brain was the training that would tell me whether this race of robots were friend or foe.

The screen came to life, and the couches moved to face it. A woman with a kind, pale face and white hair stared back at us. She had soft grey eyes, and as she walked forward, her flowy watercolor tunic of pastel sage and lilac danced as she walked. Grey leggings showed off her trim build. She looked like art in motion.

"Greetings, William and Connor. Welcome to Cali Bantu. Before you ask your questions, let me provide a brief overview of our project.

"31.7 years ago, a dense cloud of space debris hit the Earth in an assault that lasted seven days. Though predicted by Dr. Seger five years earlier, when he presented his data to the scientific community, they were skeptical. Procuring grants and designing labs took precious time, while his warning went unheeded. The current governments didn't discount the growing body of evidence, but instead of preparing their citizens, they contemplated various political power plays to maintain or gain power. However, as more scientists verified his calculations, they repeatedly leaked the information until it was finally acknowledged.

"As the date of the strike grew closer, nations feared being conquered, and the panic of survival kicked in. The governments and their scientists cocooned themselves in their little worlds, crisis managing preparations, waiting for the event to unfold.

"Of the twenty leading U.S. scientists chosen to work on the plan, two specialized in robotics. Dr. Peter Petroff worked with micro-sized robots, named robomites, that could be inserted into difficult to access areas of mechanisms to repair and reshape them. They also began work on a variation that could be injected into seriously ill patients to address their conditions. He called them biomites.

"The other robot specialist was Dr. Nadia Bera. She designed robots to assist humans with research and physical tasks. Her initial stage included building service cydroids capable of functioning in the contaminated atmosphere. They would be versatile enough to perform rescues and all other immediate tasks.

"There was little opposition to the necessity and objectives of the service cydroids, so factories began manufacturing them immediately. The next stage of the plan included specialized cydroids for maintaining order, administering justice, providing healthcare, generating and distributing resources, and preserving the culture of humanity.

"The type designed to maintain civil order generated intense conflict because of the potential harm to humans. Due to the nature of the police cydroids, as well as who would manage them, a consensus was never reached. Though their construction was never authorized, they were built just the same.

"Dr. Bera continued to move forward with the rest of the second stage. She began by developing the software for the Cyber Intellect (C.I.) programs; a vast storehouse of information and algorithms to advise humans to restore and maintain civilization.

The C.I. programs were divided into five fields of expertise. Each would have an army of specialized cydroids to undertake the approved work, and a limited number of sophisticated androids that would interact with humans directly for consultation and planning.

"The first C.I. programs she focused on addressed infrastructure and medical issues. Along with rebuilding, the infrastructure cydroids would take over the construction of more cydroids. After completing the foundational software of the cydroids, she continued to develop the C.I. software for the other advising programs and construct the androids.

"She named her creations after Greek numbers. Ena, one, was an expert in protection and law enforcement; Dio, two, specialized in the care and preservation of human life; and Tria, three, managed infrastructure and resources. Tessera, four, was constructed to preserve the history, art, and cultural aspects of humanity, and Pente, five, embodied the knowledge and philosophies of governments as well as the historical foundations and records of countless societies.

"The Cyber Intellects are not designed to govern. Their purpose is to quickly provide humans with a variety of sophisticated solutions to adopt. Each C.I. has a vast database in its field for informed debates and presentations to assist humans. The androids were physical and mobile presentations of those programs. Their function is to advise and facilitate the approved interactions between and within the communities.

"The cydroids are laborers assigned to restore the infrastructure needed for a thriving society. They can labor faster, more precisely, and function in the toxic environment expected after the meteorite strikes. It would have allowed humans to preserve democracy even though the environment was in turmoil.

"When the plan to create thousands of robots was leaked to the public, fundamentalist factions arose, chanting a militaristic takeover was in play. They destroyed many factories and most of the drone inventory. Nadia was seriously wounded, but she survived, and instead of going to a hospital, she escaped to this private location with twenty service cydroids and the software for the basic C.I. programs.

"She had always worried that the objectives of her project might be compromised, so she withheld several critical components of her software as well as a few of the algorithms required for continued function. She diverted numerous truckloads of resources here during the three years she worked on the project. She had already loaded her personal hard drives with all the historical and procedural information needed to complete her work, so this location is not part of any network.

"Over the next two years, the service cydroids began transforming this cave into an innovative underground headquarters. Dr. Bera received an internal injury when a tunnel collapsed during the meteorite impact on Aspen. That injury eventually caused her death.

"Isolated from the network, she did not know the full extent of the natural disaster, however, she theorized correctly it was in the billions. She also theorized correctly that her plan would be abused if she disclosed the final pieces of her creation. It caused her great emotional anxiety. She debated how to set her plan into motion, one community at a time, but she did not complete those plans. Her last orders have allowed us to continue her projects, but we are not programmed to implement new orders without human leadership."

She paused, but I couldn't tell if she was done. I was too stunned to ask the questions I had lined up. Though many had been answered, many more had developed. I suddenly realized I didn't have my cross. Holding it helped me focus. I tried to quiet the panic rising inside me by linking my fingers together.

CHAPTER 23

Will showed visible frustration with the false person before him, and he threw his questions at her without fearing the cydroids standing guard.

"Why didn't this cydroid force follow through with the plan?" asked Will.

"We are not programmed to proceed without human authority, which needs to be approved by her. You are the first humans to visit us since she died."

"Can I order you to do it?" Will said, as a follow-up.

"Your clearance has not been approved."

"How can Dr. Bera grant me, or anyone, clearance if she's dead?" Will spoke plainly.

"That procedure will be explained," she answered.

Will could tell he wasn't going to get anywhere with that topic, so he asked a different question. "So, are you the humanity C.I. program? Are you Tessera?"

"Yes, I hold the knowledge of philosophy, art, science, and all that is creatively and uniquely human."

"How will creativity and art overthrow the Corporates? How will you overtake your sibling, Ena, who controls the militant program?" Will was standing now.

"All five C.I. programs are present in our system. But that will be discussed at a later time."

"What happened to Dr. Petroff?" asked Will. I looked at him oddly, wondering why he thought that was important.

"Although he escaped, it was later discovered that he never made it to the safe-house, and his research was compromised," she responded.

"Why is the Sanguine Blade the key, and how do we use it?" I shouted, hoping to direct the questions that seemed more critical to our mission.

"And where is it?" Will demanded, unknowingly clenching his fists.

"Your inquiries will be answered when your teammates join us and receive this initial briefing. We are currently gathering them for transport. Suddenly, the screen switched to a view of our base camp, where dozens of cydroids were herding the team into a windowless bus. It was exhausting, the way shocking news was thrown at us.

"Do not fear. They will not be harmed. They will go through the same examination process you did before they are allowed access to the information at Cali Bantu."

"Did you put us through that process when we were asleep?" I asked, knowing it would have been more efficient.

"Yes, though the protocol for gathering information and samples from humans usually requires a human directive or the human's compliance, you were drugged to protect this place and yourselves."

"So, will our team be drugged?" Will asked.

"No, they are safely detained."

"So, they can refuse to be screened?" Will said with a stunned look.

"They, as you, assume we will use force to get your cooperation, so you comply. If you had denied us, we would have taken you back to your quarters. If you had fought us, we would have sedated you and taken you back to your quarters to keep you safe."

"Okay, I get it. You bluffed us. I'll move on. What of the Corporate enemies who are no doubt on their way?"

"That concern has been eliminated. As I said, I hold centuries of philosophies, including the philosophy of warfare."

I thought about that. So, they could harm our enemy, but not us? How could they know? Not understanding their algorithm, I decided against getting too confrontational

"Just how big is your philosophical army?" asked Will.

"That is a question for later. You have absorbed enough for now."

Will looked at the cydroids rise to escort us to our room. His fists were clenched, but he obeyed. I wondered how many of his compliant decisions were because of me.

We were led back to our room, where new distractions had been added. A screen rose from the cabinet against the wall opposite the beds. Several options for recreation had appeared on the shelf since we left. Games, music, videos, books, and other devices designed to eat up time had been provided. A plate of perfectly arranged crackers and cheese sat on the shelf below the screen, accompanied by a pitcher of cucumber water.

I went over to the plate and messed up its annoying symmetry. Will let out a single snicker. It was a small demonstration of rebellion that he approved of. He did not trust our hosts at all. Despite their soft voices and civilized manners, we were prisoners, and I shared that frustration. I didn't trust them, not fully, but I didn't mistrust them either, not yet.

Walking over to my bed, I saw something glinting on the night table.

"Look, Will, it's my cross. It's been cleaned, but still broken." I found that odd. I opened the small drawer and found my hymnal, and I held it up for a still disgruntled Will. "That ought to gain them a couple of points."

He immediately opened his drawer and slammed it shut. I know what he hoped to find, but the blade was not there. He got up and started pacing again. Predators don't do well in cages.

"They said it could take an hour before they finish processing and briefing everyone," I said. "Do you want to watch a movie, play a game, or something?"

"You watch whatever you want," he said, grabbing the tablet from the table and settling onto his bed. "I'm going to look at what they have on this tablet. It contains a detailed history of the robotics project. I want to know more about these mites they were looking for." I found it odd that he again homed in on that after everything else we had learned.

We were both engaged in our solitary activities when a cydroid came to our room and told us to follow it. I saw Will contemplating a refusal to test the theory that they required our cooperation. But I was glad he decided against it. We needed information, and wherever they were taking us, it would supply us with more. We were relieved to see Gray and Jilly in the med room we entered. They were still in their travel gear, so I knew they had not been examined yet.

I made a direct line to Jilly and hugged her. "It's okay, Jilly," I said, looking at the pale green android with D4 on its left chest. "They won't hurt you." I believed I was right. So far, they had not been aggressive. They behaved exactly how I expected them to while verifying our loyalty.

Jilly looked at my clothing and then at Will's. I could tell by the strange look on her face that she was seeing him in civilian clothes for the first time.

Will followed up, "They have provided us with a lot of information and asked for none. There are still many questions they need to answer, but we have been treated well."

"After your exams, they'll probably make you take a shower and put on clean clothes," I said to Jilly while smiling to ease her worried expression.

"I wish I had more to report," Will said, looking straight into Gray's eyes.

It was a simple statement of fact, but even I got the signal he gave Gray, saying he didn't trust any of this yet. Will briefly shared what he had learned, and again he brought up the mites. What was interesting was that Gray returned his curiosity. It now had my interest too because I was pretty sure it had to do with his blood.

I also noticed that the android did nothing to discourage their conversation. It was one more reason to believe this was Cali Bantu. I hoped my want to believe wasn't overshadowing the reason not to. I found myself holding the cross between my folded hands, silently praying for guidance. *Wait,* was the message that I felt rather than heard. I would feel comfortable asking Relic about these mites, but Gray and Will guarded their military intel with abject diligence.

We spent another hour back in our room before everyone on the team, except Relic, gathered for the evening meal. *Where was he?* Three pink androids served us a nutritious meal, which lacked flavor, except for the fresh fruit for dessert, which was amazing. Though they promised Relic would join us, he was still unaccounted for.

Three androids called for our attention. "William, Connor, and Grayson, please follow me."

Gray put his hand on my shoulder and began to object, but Will stopped him. "I believe this is where we get to see Relic and hear the plan. I for one, want to hear it without being shackled," he whispered, doubting the freewill rules Tessera stated earlier.

The three of us walked out of the dining room, led by the androids, and followed by three cydroids. Will and Gray walked me between them like protective mama bears. I knew they meant to make me feel safe, but what they thought they could do to subdue these robots was eye-rolling. I may not have their strength, but I could think through this scenario, and strength was irrelevant. In stressful situations, men try to out-bluff their opponents to gain control, but I don't think robots fall for bluster and pretense. In the screening room, we found Relic sitting on a couch.

"Relic, we were worried. Are you okay?" Gray asked.

"Yes, I have been updating Tessera on the state of our territory and beyond, according to the reports to the best of my knowledge," Relic said.

"Do you trust these things?" Gray pointed to the androids while simultaneously scrutinizing his friend for signs that he was compromised. I could tell by his scowl that he didn't trust any of this, and he was tiring of the subterfuge.

"The only information she asked me was what I knew regarding the status of the outside world," Relic shared. "Their system is isolated with no access to other networks. Their precautions regarding outside cyber influences are quite thorough, but I suspect the network they have housed here is massive."

Tessera came onto the screen. She gracefully floated to the forefront like a lithe dancer. Her appearance was soft and elegant, but neither Will nor Gray fell for her peaceful display. They wanted answers.

"Thank you for your patience. I apologize for our mistrustful greeting and for causing you concern for Relic. As a previous resident of the Highmind Camp, we needed to ensure he was free of surveillance apparatus or Corporate allegiance."

"How can you confirm one's loyalty?" Will inquired.

"Initially, we ensure one is free of manipulative biomites. Then we monitor physical responses to various environments, stressful situations, and dialogue. Humans have limited control over their responses, and our highly sensitive instruments can detect the slightest alteration from truthful answers and locate the part of the brain and body it originates."

Again, with the mites.

"If you are supposed to help us, where have you been?" asked Gray.

"As you heard in the briefing, we have limits. Dr. Bera isolated us from all other networks to remain hidden, and therefore, our knowledge of the logistical and human status of the territories was unattainable. We observed the cosmic event from an encrypted satellite that fed information to a quarantine terminal. We estimated that over twenty-nine percent of the world's population perished from the week-long meteorite storm, and twenty-seven percent of the survivors died from the effects of disease and civil inadequacy.

"Our satellite was designed to appear obsolete and offline, but it was destroyed by the same No-Techy faction that attacked our robotic facilities. Their fear of the surveillance capabilities of the orbiting equipment drove them to destroy every electronic device they could find. But most of those stations provided communication and scientific observation of Earth's condition and atmospheric recovery. Losing the satellites caused what remained of civilization to revert to primitive equipment and inefficient communication.

"With the information Relic shared, more than a year passed before the group was actively pursued. By the time the Corporates eliminated the faction, their efforts had left a dense debris field orbiting our planet, which interferes with signals and continues to disable more satellites.

"The Corporates saw the Highminds' intellect as a threat and forcefully apprehended them. The Dailys were told Highminds were promoted to Uppers, believing their lives would improve, they turned them in. But the Highminds were confined and forced to activate the Elites' advice for weapons and species survival. Some worked on preserving the lifestyles of the highest levels of the caste system, which many believed included the Elites. However, the Elites are not human and do not desire or need human accessories.

"The Elites represent three of the five Cyber Intellect advisers. Two of the C.I. directors are blocked from interacting with humans, as well as the C.I.'s ongoing discussions. Dr. Bera realized that every decision did not require the attention of the full panel, so she allowed the Elites to exclude unnecessary directors on an individual basis. She did not foresee that they would permanently block certain advisers.

"The Elites seek logical order and dominance over their illogical charges. This has allowed them to make conclusions without regard to law or humane conditions. They detain the Highminds to exploit their gifts and prevent them from organizing the workers in a revolt. Something my program and Pente's would not have allowed. The Elites' main agenda for the Highmind camp is to free their programs from Dr. Bera's directives. If they accomplish this, they will gain access to the encrypted cydroid software, and humans would cease to have a purpose.

"The Corporates currently have over a thousand cydroid drones, but they are all inactive. Commanding the cydroids requires human orders and the proper codes. Dr. Bera placed dramatic flaws deep within their software programming. Hidden anomalies prevent the robots from being activated or following the orders of non-humans or unauthorized persons. Another deep code prevents them from assembling more of themselves or being disassembled. Even destroying them is costly and problematic."

Gray put up his hand for a question. "Why don't the C.I.s just build their own robots?"

"The Cyber Intellects programming prohibits the creation or manufacture of any device, especially those that pose danger to humans, without the direction of humans. They are limited to advising and researching. If humans build robots without solving the C.I. command codes, humans would control them.

"But they have found a way to deceive humans into following their commands through the utilization of manipulative biomites. The recipients sign waivers that include the clause, 'I allow myself to be redirected for the benefit of the human species.' In return, they are promoted, believing they will live in extreme luxury. Humans administer the injections and train biomites to stimulate a response when certain brain cells are activated, along with negative or angry emotions. That allows the Cyber Intellects, or C.I.s, to use both pain and pleasure to control their subjects by mere suggestion.

"Since they feed and house the people, they are still implementing their primary programming: to preserve the human species. The project fell apart when they deleted the programs of lawful governance and the cultural aspects of the C.I. programs, deeming them illogical and problematic. Without these programs, they could eliminate what they deemed the illogical and destabilizing issues. Though humans can be illogical and self-destructive, these traits are part of humanity. The C.I.s' job is to advise humans with instant, unbiased solutions and clarifications, allowing them to decide how to protect their species. Their right to self-determination, even if it leads to their self-destruction, must be preserved."

"The plan, simply put, is to reinstate Dr. Bera's proposal and restore humanity by deleting the Elites and reinstating the C.I. programs."

Gray piped in. "If what you say is true, how are you in command of these cydroids? You obviously have the *sophisticated*," Gray used air quotes, and I was sure the gesture would be lost on the programmed image, "code required to imprison *and* harm humans. Those Corporate soldiers lying dead on the road prove that."

"They are not lying on the road, and they are not dead. Nor are the soldiers who attacked Aspen after you left. They are all here, including their informant from Aspen."

"Their *WHAT?*" Will roared.

CHAPTER 24

I watched Will and Gray stand and tense their fists. Not only was there an attack on Aspen, but someone had betrayed us.

Tessera continued. "They are secure in an area within this facility where their needs are being met. They were given a choice of cooperating or facing the consequences. They did not know what the consequences were, and they did not ask. Assuming it was death, as you did, they complied. We may not harm humans, but we can project authority."

"So, we could walk out of here right now?" Will asked.

"In a word, yes. However, your actions suggest that this project is important to you. Walking away would terminate Operation Reclamation, as you have named it. We have disclosed this information because '*walking out*'," I stifled a laugh when Tessera used the same air quote gesture Gray did, "is against your nature. However, you would not be assisted in your effort, and the way out is unmarked."

"Sounds like the freedom to fail; my parents' favorite punishment," I said under my breath.

Gray smirked at me and asked, "Who is the informant from Aspen?"

"Theodor Mayfeild."

"Theo?!" Relic gasped. "I would have never guessed it was him." But Gray and I exchanged looks and slight nods.

"He carries a lot of anger and blames the Cali Bantu Project for his hardships. He experienced the loss of his whole family. Though his father's friend, whom Theo called Uncle, took him in, he too died when Theo was fourteen. He still feels the pain of those losses. The Corporate soldiers who captured him discovered his vulnerability and used it. He has no marks or chemical traces to suggest his cooperation was forced."

"Does he have the bad mites?" Gray bristled.

"No one here has the manipulative mites. They are only used for high-level targets. It requires several injections, training, and close monitoring to ensure that they are performing correctly. They are not like the healing biomites some of your team have, which are easily transferred from host to host and accelerate the body's natural healing responses."

That caught my attention, and I immediately knew it had to do with all the concern surrounding Will's blood. I was happy none of us had the bad mites, but what are healing mites, and who has them? Remembering all the blood samples Jilly has taken, my guess is that I have them. I vowed to ask Relic later.

"How long has Theo been a spy?" asked Will.

"Four days ago, two Garrison soldiers followed you on a snow machine and arrived hours after you did, hiding their tracks among yours. Theo, as you refer to him, was taken hostage while performing a late-night building inspection the same evening you arrived. They wanted him to capture Connor. You may question him if you wish."

"What about the attack on Aspen? Were there casualties?" Relic inquired.

"We placed hidden surveillance cameras around Aspen and high-altitude drones to gather information. We have been tracking your team as well as the Garrison soldiers following you since your approach to Aspen. When the Garrisons arrived at Aspen, we were ready for them and quickly ended the conflict. We treated two Aspen residents and three Garrison soldiers for minor wounds. We repaired the damage you caused on the Marion Bell Road and are currently sending cydroids with supplies and materials to repair the damage done to the storage area in Aspen's main hangar."

"You said we could question him," said Will. "Aren't you worried we'll harm him?"

"Knowing she was dying, Dr. Bera gave us the authority to maintain this facility. Our primary objective is still to assist humans by advising and helping them implement the plan. If there were an established set of laws, we would prevent you from breaking them. We can access many legal documents, but until one has been officially adopted by an elected governing body, we must follow the orders left by Dr. Bera. We advise you to not resort to violence, but we have no law that would allow us to interfere with your actions."

"Was the only reason you didn't send the cydroids to save the people the authorization issue?" asked Gray.

"After the attack on the robotic facilities, our completed cydroid numbers were too low. We did not know there was a storehouse of completed cydroids in stasis until Relic told us yesterday. He reports that their hardware is complete, but their software is not.

"According to Relic, when civil unrest and deadly diseases began decreasing the human population, the Cyber Intellects recognized they were failing to achieve their primary function: to preserve the human species. Order had to be restored to the nation. Without the cydroids, humans were conscripted to restore order.

"Functioning businesses were persuaded to manage the workers and provide the needed supplies, and in return, they were allowed to maintain their lavish lifestyles. Initially, many of the executives and owners tried to supervise with benevolence, but the people were terrified and mistrustful. They rebelled against their benefactors, believing their motives were selfish and cruel, and some were.

"The workers became increasingly violent and uncooperative, disrupting the progress of the infrastructure. The executives, Uppers, felt threatened, so they employed harsher, militant policies.

"When the humans challenged their supervisors' orders, the C.I. Elites drew up the mandate document, giving the Corporates the choice to agree or lose their lavish status. The threat of losing status generated reluctant loyalty but complete compliance. They also established a caste system as the logical way to control the citizens' behavior. Without the other two programs to align their actions with laws and compassion, they preserve humans but destroy humanity.

"When Denver was named the national hub, it received more resources than the other states. Relic believes it continues to be looked upon as the most powerful state, causing the others to avoid conflict with it. However, that cannot be confirmed. The Colorado territories do not communicate with the other territories. The federal government adopted Dr. Bera's project, but Colorado is no longer affiliated with the United States. It is possible that some territories do not use the C.I.s at all, or their network was destroyed. We do not have enough information to draw an accurate conclusion regarding the rest of the nation. However, for Operation Reclamation, our focus starts here in Colorado.

"Could the Elites hijack the healing biomites to harm those infected or cause the mission to fail?" asked Gray.

"Your biomites were created by a group of Highmind scientists who worked for Dr. Petroff Bera." She turned toward Will and said, "Dr. Logan, your stepmother's father, was part of that team. But to answer your question, your mites aren't capable of sending or receiving information, so no, the Corporates cannot access them."

I caught the pronouns "your and our," used by Tessera and Gray when discussing biomites. "I think I need to know about these biomites," I said. "Who has them? How did they get them?"

"I'll fill you in later, Connor," Relic said to me with a little too much sympathy in his voice. They're so quick to keep me in the dark regarding just about everything. But risking my life—yeah, no problem there. I needed to calm my emotions before the cydroids noticed.

"I want to go back to the cydroid army," Gray burst in. "Are there stockpiles of these inoperable cydroids in all the Colorado territories? How about the other states? And, more importantly, is it possible other states could have broken the code?"

"Anything is possible. But all the cydroids were manufactured in Colorado, so it is doubtful that other states have any. Logic suggests that if the Elites had achieved self-determination or control of the cydroids, they would have used them. If the mandate to maintain the human species were deleted, they may eliminate your kind completely. If not, it wouldn't change the current state of the people, but it would spell the end of humanity and any hope for freedom. Flesh and blood humans cannot subdue armed cydroids."

"But what could the Elites gain from eliminating humans? They can't enjoy the fruits of their labor. They don't want stuff, and they don't have emotions," I offered.

"They cannot feel joy like you, but they can set goals and strive to accomplish them without the distraction of human issues. Accruing more inventory and increasing efficiency are measurable accomplishments."

"Why did you ask me to join this meeting? I thought my purpose ended with finding Cali Bantu," I asked, still smoldering over the mite thing. "My understanding of the prophecy is that I get access to this place, so the Sanguine Blade can be used as the key, and that's Will's job. I thought I would be exempt from more battles and travel. I thought I could go home." Relic, Gray, and Will looked at me with sad resolve, the kind that war paints on men who live with the horrors it brings.

"The key to shutting down the Elites' software is locked inside the Sanguine Blade, which we have returned to your room. Once activated, you will be tested to ensure you represent the Science Guild and not a Corporate subordinate. When that is done, Relic can load the new software. The prophecy says, 'A warrior will bring the key, but it will require an enlightened one to access it.' You, Connor, are the enlightened one.

Though soldiers and cydroids will accompany and protect your team, it is up to you, Jonathan, and William to reset the programming that will complete the mission."

Gray stood up as I sank further into my seat.

"He's just a child. He cannot go into battle! There must be another way. Why can't you give Will or me command of the cydroids?" he said.

"Connor must activate the original C.I. server program to release the army. Doing that requires the information stored in his brain. He must physically go into the secure area where the Elite terminal is held and pass the test. Only then can we put you in charge of leading the cydroids, but until a government is established by the people, they will still be under Dr. Bera's last orders."

Will interrupted to focus on the fundamental military question. "You've told us the target, but do you have a plan for this assault?"

"Yes, the most vulnerable terminal is in Pueblo. If you successfully infiltrate Pueblo Command, the networks at Denver and Colorado Springs will shut down and wait for the new software. As the program resets the operational functions, Jonathan will search for any backup software and destroy it."

"Okay, first, please stop calling us by our formal names. I'm Gray, and they are Will and Relic."

"I will comply."

"It sounds simple, except for the walking into their headquarters part," Gray said.

"That will hold many risks," she said.

"You think?" Will jeered.

"You must deliver the program to this facility quickly. There is a possibility that the Elites may have discovered how to reboot their programming, but it would require the help of the Highminds they employ. It is a precarious move because it requires humans to follow through with the reboot. It would be illogical for humans to reboot the system and send themselves back into slavery. However, it has a high probability of success. Humans make a lot of decisions based on irrational fears when they have been conditioned to follow, not lead."

"Well, I guess we'll have to hope to heck that doesn't happen," Gray responded with annoyance. "Assuming things go as planned, what happens if we get it rebooted with the corrected program? Do the cydroids just start working? Do they know what to do?"

"The cydroids will require diagnostics to ensure they are functioning properly. Activated drones can perform this task on inactive ones. Once the dormant cydroids are activated, they can assist the others, increasing the results exponentially as more come online.

"The people won't understand what exactly has changed, but the cydroids will cause some to panic. So, the first order of business is to establish order."

"What can we expect the people to do with their freedom? It sounds like it will be chaos?" Will suggested.

"The citizens will reject the idea and fear the cydroids are the new overseers initially. We theorized that once they see their situations improve, they will yield. It will take some time, not only to gain their trust but to build up the supplies and make significant changes for the people, but these are long-term issues."

"Didn't the plan to establish order depend on people staying in their dwellings? Do you intend to put Colorado on house arrest?" asked Relic.

"That was the initial plan when the air was unsafe. It would be logical since it will allow Dr. Bera's five C.I.s to send an educational program to each home. But we cannot decree that. The reinstated C.I. team will devise several options for proceeding, as well as the details and resources required to implement them. The final decision will come from the humans in charge."

"Who will they be? How will that be decided?" Gray was still standing.

"Initially, it may be the people who have already been living freely and making those kinds of decisions. It is logical that the allied governments of New Haven and the Fringers work as temporary governors. That would coincide with Dr. Bera's current directives. We have a wealth of expertise in the aspects of governing to advise you, but it will take some time to educate the citizens on how to manage the responsibilities of freedom. Whoever you decide should be in charge, the Cyber Intellects will advise them and provide them with informed options, as well as physical assistance from the cydroids."

"What about the weapons the territories have in storage?" asked Will.

"They are networked together, so it will instantly pause them and reset them. If a surface-to-air weapon is discharged, our weapons detection system will detonate it in the air or divert it to an unpopulated area. The most likely outcome is that the cydroid army will be in charge before the citizens are aware of the transfer of power.

"Before the meteorite strikes, the best scientists gathered in Denver, Colorado. By the time the meteorites hit, it had become the most developed and sophisticated metropolis in the country. There is a high probability that Colorado prevailed considerably better than the other states, so if we succeed here, other states will probably follow Colorado's lead."

CHAPTER 25

The meeting was called to a close, and everyone but me stood up. I was still trying to process all that I had just learned as well as what I needed to learn. Relic offered me a hand up as he turned to Will and said, "I think it is time we take another look at this knife of yours, Will."

Will went to retrieve his blade, which gave me time to ask Relic about the mites.

"Before we go any further, I want to know about these mites. It sounds like information I should have," I demanded.

Relic nodded. He began with a brief review of Will's forced enlistment into the enemy forces before he got to the topic of interest. It amazes me that people constantly forget I retain everything, and reminders and reviews are unnecessary.

"Some of this account is conjecture, but as far as we can guess, it happened several years ago during his time in the Neighwah. Will was scheduled to be injected with the controlling biomites, but the RH switched the manipulative mites with the healing ones. They tried two more times to infect him, but the healing mites in his system wouldn't let them take.

"According to everything we know so far, they are beneficial to those who have them. There are some questions we still have, but so far they have been highly beneficial, if not lifesaving. I foresee them being a tremendous asset to the study of medicine.

"The other type of biomite is used to manipulate the body in response to certain brain signals. They settle into certain parts of the brain, causing the patient to feel pain or pleasure as the controller sees fit. As Tessera said, these need to be injected and trained to respond to brain signals and commands." Relic went on. "None of our team members have those kind."

"How do people get the healing ones?" I asked, knowing I had shared the blood rite with Will.

"It only works with a direct blood exchange, but it only takes a small amount of exposure to get them," he said, and watched me closely. Just then, Will came in.

"It's true, I infected you when we became blood brothers. I wanted to honor your sacrifice as a warrior. I did not know I carried the mites until later. I am very sorry."

It took but a second for me to realize how big this issue was.

"Will, you have shared the blood rite with your entire army, and Axle. And you gave Gray blood," I said.

"That is why we have been keeping it secret," Relic confessed. "It could cause fear and division among our people. Someday we will disclose it, but for now, it's a sensitive and complex matter."

"Someday, yes, but for the good of the mission, it must remain a secret," Will warned.

"Doesn't really sound like there is a downside to them," I said, both shocked and intrigued. "Wait, is there a downside?"

Relic chimed in, always eager to discuss the scientific edge. "We haven't found one yet, but we keep looking. There was some concern that the Corporates might access their programming, but the C.I. team says no. They assured us that the mites can't send or receive a signal outside the body."

I put my hand on Will's arm because reaching up for his shoulder seemed awkward. "Thank you for saving my life. I don't think I would have come out of that fever on my own, or it would have taken so long to heal that we would have been captured. The mission could have been lost. So, thank you." He smiled and nodded.

"Well, enough of that, let's look at this knife," Will said.

Will, Relic, and I turned the knife in every direction, looking for a way to open it.

"Well, we can all agree it isn't a weapon in the literal sense. I think there is technology in here that links to a terminal," said Relic. "I think it is called the key because it allows us access to certain files. No other purpose makes sense."

"Yeah," said Connor, "several clues refer to it as the key. When I opened GD's shelf, he had wrapped a key in an American flag. I had to conduct a grid search to find the keyhole. Maybe we should search for what this fits into rather than what's inside. So, think, where would Dr. Bera put an insert slot to unlock a computer program?"

"At the computer," we said together.

We were led into a large server room with rows upon rows of blinking shelves full of memory storage. We all looked at each other, realizing this could take a while. While Will and I searched the stacks, Relic went to the console. Within minutes, he was calling us back.

"Could it be this simple?" Will asked, looking at the hinged cover that revealed a rectangular opening.

"It looks like it might fit." Relic answered.

"Try it," I said with enthusiasm.

Will removed the blade from the sheath and inserted the knife's blade slowly until he heard a click. The knife began moving on its own, being pulled into the panel all the way to the hilt. Then latches popped up, locking it into place. The computer began to hum and flash through data at a rapid pace. When the activity died down, a face appeared on the monitor.

"Welcome, I am Dr. Nadia Bera.

The golden-eyed woman smiled and tilted her head shyly as she looked up from her clipboard. She appeared exhausted, but it did not diminish her Middle Eastern beauty. Her straight hair was the color of night with flashes of shooting stars, where the light skipped off the shiny strands. As she looked down at her notes, the silky locks fell around her face, and she returned them behind her ear with an elegant move.

She was graceful and shy. I didn't expect shy elegance from a woman who was renowned for her brilliance. My recent research said ideas flowed through her like a river from a mountain of knowledge. She didn't have time to go on about herself or her accomplishments. Her ideas came too quickly for that. She went straight to her point as if time were chasing her down, and considering her untimely death, it was. Rather than introduce herself, she began by explaining that this recording was interactive, and she asked us for information. Gray and Will answered cautiously, while Relic and I cooperated with enthusiasm.

The two Allied leaders seemed poised to stop the exchange, but none of the questions breached sensitive information. All the questions were designed to test our identities and loyalty. Having satisfied her security test, she proceeded directly to give an overview of the mission.

But Gray interrupted her with a test question of his own. "How and why did your program fail? According to you, the C.I.'s should not have power to do anything without you. But they do."

"I put a temporary protocol program in place to allow flexibility in unusual circumstances. It wasn't meant to be a loophole. My intent was to allow the C.I.s to act quickly if humans became incapacitated. I had every intention of refining the algorithm before the meteorites hit, but we were attacked. I was wounded and woke up here.

"The Elites abused the temporary protocols for their purposes. It takes continual intervention to maintain their temporary directives, but that is no problem for a computer. My new program limits temporary directives to life-saving measures and terminates them after thirty-six hours. It does not allow them to be reinstated unless a governing body or authorized human approves them."

"But what if that can't happen, the approval I mean?" I asked.

"The program will still be able to advise the people, but they will have to manage the implementation themselves, as well as generate the materials required. They will not have cydroid assistance. But people are very resourceful. They don't need computers to survive."

Will, Relic, and Gray continued working out the details of the plan without me. I was sent to bed, and though I contested, I was happy to comply.

It was still dark when Will woke me to prepare to leave. We were divided into two teams, with one acting as a decoy and traveling toward Colorado Springs, hoping to split the Garrison forces. I was on the team that would go to Pueblo and infiltrate the Central Command building and upload Dr. Bera's software.

Our plan depends on the premise that the Elites' programming limits were still functioning properly. The limits prevented the Elites or humans from rewriting their programming without the proper authorization from the governing body. That procedure included the verification process and an authorized DNA sample. Only then could a system restart be initiated. If they didn't follow the procedure precisely, the obsolete first-phase C.I. program would prevail. Tessera said it was an extremely limited program, and all the new territory data would be unavailable.

Both teams had a copy of the precious new software disguised as a Corporate security badge. Even if we were captured, the badge would likely be overlooked as an item stolen to gain entry, and not the key to overthrowing C.I. command. But it still required the questions to be answered correctly, and that was my job.

The plan was ingenious. The entire team would travel through a tunnel that the cydroids had dug over the course of a decade. It went for miles through the mountain and exited onto Washington Gulch Road. The abandoned road ended on another unused road between Crested Butte and Mount Crested Butte, which connected to Highway 135. It would give the Allied team a significant head start while the Corporates waited for them to emerge from Pyramid Mountain via the Marion Bells Road. The cydroids upgraded the camouflage covering and completed the repairs on their vehicles. It allowed for undetected travel until we got within a hundred yards of our foe.

Will led Falcon Two, with Nash, Axle, Dom, Etcher, Lana, Beckett, and Tommie. They expected engagement with the enemy, but their objective involved defense, not offense, which was good because almost everyone on his team was still recovering from an injury. Their mission was to draw enemy troops away from our team, Falcon One, by heading to Colorado Springs and Denver.

Falcon One, led by Gray, included Jedi, Easton, Mack, Jax, Relic, and me. We were the offensive team. Our objective was to break into the Pueblo Command Center. My job was to shut down the system, and Relic's was to reboot it and upload Dr. Bera's revised program. Fifty cydroids accompanied each team, thirty-five for combat, twelve laborers, and three medics.

We would all travel on Highway 135 to Highway 50, but Will's team would turn onto Highway 115 and secure the Garrison base at Penrose. Reportedly, fewer than twenty soldiers manned the base, but it was highly guarded with formidable weapons. Will's team had the Brute, and our team used the four minis because they had the best camouflage, stealth engines, and ability to split up, giving us a better chance of closing in on Pueblo without detection.

While Will's team created the diversion, our team would go south on Highway 69 and set up a base camp in the shadow of a rocky ravine along Bogs Creek. From there, we would proceed to the Command Center near the Pueblo Dam and break in. Once we got inside the Command Building, which was no minor task, Gray would signal Will to join us in

Pueblo. Though seemingly straightforward, the mission included several alternative plans with flexible cooperation.

We all worried about Aspen and Cali Bantu in our absence. At their insistence, we were taking a large percentage of their combat and medic cydroids as well as much of their ammunition. Dr. Bera confirmed that a preemptive attack was expected.

"We are ready for that. Your only concern is with your mission. You will encounter violent opposition, but I advise you to let the cydroids engage. You cannot order them to kill; however, they are formidable in their ability to protect you from harm."

"I'm assuming you can't use lethal force to defend against an attack on this facility either. Why would you leave this place defenseless?" asked Gray.

"By demonstrating our destructive capabilities, we can avoid resorting to them."

"Maybe, but living soldiers can rejoin the fight, and if they discover they won't be killed or harmed, this may never end." Though Gray murmured his dissent under his breath, he knew they would hear it.

"These soldiers are oppressed and conscripted with threats, simply following whatever orders they are given. They are not determined or loyal to any cause and will fall in line with their new orders when you reprogram the C.I.s. The restored program will align with the recovery plan put in place before Congress became compromised. If there is civil fallout, the cydroids will maintain the peace.

"Not knowing who would come here, I created a program that couldn't be exploited. And though I have vetted you, you are soldiers, not representatives of the people. I can't send you out with fully active cydroids without the oversight of a governing body. That is the type of programming the Elites could exploit, and have. But if you succeed in your mission, you will be given governance over the cydroids, and they do have lethal capabilities."

"And what of this place and of Aspen?" Will asked.

"The Corporates may try to send a powerful weapon. If such an action is ordered, the C.I. program, which is still running, should freeze the order. But the humans with manipulative biomites add an unknown variable to the problem. The Elites cannot send bombs, but humans can if their biomite controllers compel them. It is unknown if the humans involved would take part in this action, but if a bomb is launched, we will eliminate it or deflect it to an unpopulated area."

"I get it. We have our mission, and you have yours. No doubts, no hesitation," Gray answered with the soldiers' mantra.

We were all impressed with the detail and interactive capabilities of the network she had created. But Will and Gray looked at each other. I was pretty sure I knew what they were thinking. This war came down to defeating the corrupt computer programs that was a version of the program that helped plan our attack. Why were we trusting this or any computer-generated advice? Were we freeing the people, or giving them a new overseer?

I grabbed the cross in my pocket and prayed to a power higher than all of this. I wavered back and forth about putting all my trust in this invisible God. I wanted to, but when faced with losing my life or the people I care about, the more my fears devoured my resolve and my faith.

"Lord, help me. I don't know how to be brave."

CHAPTER 26

Everyone but Jilly was essential to the mission. With medic cydroids on each team, she was the only member without a tangible function, and her pregnancy presented an unnecessary risk. Gray and Dio tried to persuade her to stay at Cali Bantu. But she must have offered a good argument because she was on the team roster. Another cross-grabbing moment because I think she used me as her excuse. We have a close bond, and I can tell her anything, but I don't want her in danger. The compromise was that she would remain at the Boggs Creek base camp with five military cydroids while the rest of the team breached the Command Center.

As we waited in the garage, the cydroids assembled themselves into vehicles, while Tessera called us together for a final update.

"We detected enemy drones over the site where we captured the enemy soldiers. The cydroids were attempting to hide the vehicles, but they could not complete their task in time and take cover. We predict a missile attack is their most logical choice. Unless they know our precise location, it would require an extensive payload to be effective.

"We have initiated protocols to secure this facility and the town of Aspen using deflection capabilities. We expect they have fortified their headquarters in each territory. Be observant and prepare for ambushes.

"Your lead cydroids' designations have been replaced with names, so you can distinguish them from the others. Will, your lead is Altan meaning red dawn. Gray, yours is Dagny for new day. We wish you success on your mission and a safe return."

It was finally happening. I tried not to let the doubt and dread incapacitate me as we boarded our vehicles. While I took deep breaths, trying to push down the panic building in my chest, the large doors at the far end of the garage swung open. They revealed a dark tunnel that went all the way through the mountain to Mount Crested Butte. As we drove through it, the lights illuminated before us and turned off as we passed. It did not escape my attention that the tunnel was too narrow to turn around.

During the team's three-day stay at Cali Bantu, a team of cydroids cleared and repaired the roads from the eastern tunnel opening to the abandoned town of Gunnison. It was always difficult to reach uninhabited towns in winter because the roads were not well-maintained or cleared. But with these workaholics leading the way, and the Corporates looking for us elsewhere, we didn't expect any trouble until we reached Salida.

Salida was a territory border town, and the reported population was around forty people. With our cydroid army of fighting machines and knock-out darts, we anticipated little resistance. We expected to surprise them, but we also expected encountering military incursions. But there was no one—no guards, no drones, no trucks, nothing. The cydroids searched until they located a truck tucked behind an old building with two sleeping guards, whom they drugged to keep them asleep.

I watched as Gray and Will discussed the oddity of the missing residents. The headlights of the minis helped me see well enough to read their lips. Intel gathered a few months ago showed that civilians still lived here, so the town must have been evacuated. They agreed we needed to move on because when the sleeping Garries didn't report in, it would alert the Corporates that there was trouble on this route.

We arrived at the place where the teams would split up. With no stopping for last-minute meetings, we turned onto our assigned paths and continued. I watched the Brute with Will, Axle, and other people I cared about drive away into the darkness.

Their lights dimmed into dots, then specks, and finally they were gone. I remembered the drive Will and I took and the long talk we had, and the desperation I felt when Axle left for the relay drone project. It seems goodbyes are a constant in the military world, and I always anxious feeling it could be the last one.

When Gray's team caught up with the cydroids sent ahead, I saw first-hand how versatile the robots were. They efficiently assembled themselves into a bridge to cross a ravine and plows to clear snow berms. Cranes cleared debris off the road; excavators, ramps, you name it, they easily morphed into various types of equipment to continue toward our destination.

"Do you think they will send a bomb?" I asked, knowing it was an unanswerable question, and I regretted asking it the moment I uttered it.

"I believe the protocols Tessera alluded to will fend off their attempts," Gray said.

But what he meant was: *Stick to the plan; follow your orders.* That's what he would tell one of his soldiers, but I'm not a soldier, and I didn't want to be, not anymore. I watched the snowy miles drift by, trying to keep my mind off where we were going.

We stopped before the outpost of Westcliffe. The cydroids formed several protective rings around the vehicles, with the outer ring rising into a battle-ready posture. Dagny set one of our stealth drones to get a visual of the mountain and the town, while feeding the images to our screen in the mini. A dull dawn was transforming the starless black sky just enough to reveal the menacing dark clouds billowing across the horizon. The storm didn't worry Gray, or so he said. He was looking for the full contingency of soldiers he kept expecting.

"There should be armed soldiers and workers readying themselves for battle, but we only located fifteen men total in four different locations," he whispered to himself. Gray got out of our mini, when I rolled over pretending I was asleep. I wasn't. I wanted to watch him talking to Jedi.

"Where is everyone?" questioned Gray. "I know we surprised them, but they should be more prepared than this. We should have run into dozens of them by now. I can't even detect any workers."

"Perhaps they have not yet received the report about their soldiers, so they aren't preparing. That tunnel put us at least a day ahead of them. Will said back when he made his weekly visits, the shift changes were at 0700. It's only 3:51 in the morning. Maybe we've caught them off guard," offered Jedi.

Jedi went around a tree to relieve himself, and Dagny, the head cydroid, walked over to Gray and presented something, but I couldn't tell what. But I saw Gray's response.

"There are only two reasons I can think of for locking the town's people down. The Corporates plan to fight with explosive devices, or..." Then he turned his head and covered his mouth. I wondered what else the Corporates could fight with: chemicals, biological diseases, demolishing our equipment and vehicles; the list was horrifying. The last part he didn't hide. "Either way, they need to protect the status quo," Gray said to Dagny. Dagny's response was unknown.

Jedi returned, and Gray spoke to him. "Send half our robot friends to quietly subdue the guards, while we blow past this town and set up base camp. Let's be hypervigilant. These quiet towns may not be full of civilians, but their soldiers are ready to pounce."

"Yes sir," Jedi agreed and then added, "It does have that 'too easy' feel to it."

As soon as Gray got in the mini, I asked. I had to. "What else could the Corporates use against us?"

He shook his head. He was mad, or scared, or both. "Use your imagination. And stop eavesdropping, Connor. I'm not kidding. It will bring you and everyone else more trouble than you're ready for."

"I know I should stop, but it's hard to turn away when people are talking about our survival, which includes mine." Gray's expression relayed sympathy, but it also said he expected me to follow orders.

All the way to base camp, we anticipated a fight awaited us around every bend. Never having encountered it left Gray more and more uneasy. I felt it too, like we were walking into an ambush. We did not say a word to each other since I was censured, and that made me uneasy too. We set up the mini shelter where Jilly would stay with five cydroids. Though she didn't want to run toward trouble, time would stand still while she worried inside the shelter. Will's team was scheduled to get here around noon if all went according to our plans, but that was hours away. Then he would continue to Pueblo Command. She had promised Gray she would remain behind the shelter's bulletproof walls except for bathroom breaks, which would be under cydroid escort.

"Follow my orders, Jilly. Don't leave the shelter. I can't contact you and risk your message getting intercepted. But once we have secured the Command Center, I'll send word to your lead cydroid." Gray gave his wife one more hug and a kiss on the cheek, and he turned to go.

"I know. I'll be fine here going crazy with worry," she called after him. "You, Connor, and the rest of the team are the ones who need to be careful."

"I'll take good care of him, Jilly. I promise," Gray answered.

"I know you will." She motioned for me to come closer, and she hugged me tightly, like a mom would. "Don't you dare do anything overly heroic. Just do this thing and come back whole. You hear me?" Then she whispered in my ear. "This is going to work, Connor. You'll be home with your family and Libby before Solstice." She spoke softly while tousling my hair and repeatedly hugging me. She was trembling, or maybe it was me.

I smiled as I boarded the mini and rode away. I held my cross, praying for victory and a safe return. It felt like I was reaching into my pocket constantly. At this rate, I might rub it clean away.

Communication between the teams was minimal. It used five numerical codes to report team status. They included: the primary plan is in play; an alternate plan is in play; combat in progress; assistance required; and message received. Unless they were in combat or needed assistance, the team would send codes every fifteen minutes. If combat or assistance codes were in play, the intervals would change to every five minutes. The lead cydroids performed this task since their timing was precise, and they could multitask in the most active conditions.

Falcon One's target, the Pueblo Command, was in a jail facility. It was a smart choice because it was a newer building with a superior security system. Its planning started years before the meteorite storm, but as the threat drew closer, the plans changed, and mid-construction, it transformed into a shelter. Weeks before the meteorites struck, jails across the country released their prisoners. Many of those released prisoners had somewhere to go, but those without refuge wreaked havoc on poorer communities. I imagined it was a bit like the Wild West, and accepted as an unavoidable hazard of the times.

Our predecessors were not crazy enough to release the most violent criminals, nor did they house them in their shelters. They were humanely executed. I tried hard not to overthink the concept of what history deemed a humane death, but it's not my nature to let go of such complex ideologies. I need to smack them around philosophically for a time before I can stuff them away in my overly accessible memory. But the bottom line, and the justification, was that it freed up thousands of fortified incarceration bunkers for shelter, storage, and command centers.

After the cydroid plan collapsed and the Elites blocked Tessera and Pente, they claimed the new jailhouse for their Pueblo Command and evicted its residents. Positioned near the still-functioning Pueblo Dam, it had access to ample power for its demanding Cyber Intellect systems, with enough left over to provide the Upper neighborhood with modest comfort. The underprivileged Daily sections used the older power stations.

With serious negligence and little maintenance, they had deteriorated significantly since the disaster. Eventually, the electricity they supplied was only enough to run the workhouses, not the homes.

As we closed in on Pueblo, I saw Gray freeze. He was looking at the message displayed on his screen. It was from the base camp. I heard him say no messages would be sent to or from there unless... I looked at the screen. "Combat in play," but it didn't ask for assistance. That meant she was safe, but the thought of Jilly huddling in the mini must be murder on him because it was killing me. I sat quietly, knowing talking wouldn't help. He needed to gather himself without chatter.

Gray parked on the edge of the city, focusing on the green images from the air drone's night vision footage. The overcast morning sky gave a grey pallor to the surfaces before him. When the clouds parted enough for the sun to illuminate the horizon, a vast city lay before us, foreshadowing the daunting task. It blinked into view for mere seconds before tucking back into the dimness of a low cloud bank.

We could see the green squares on the screen of the cydroid teams making their way to surround the building and secure strategic locations in town. With their high-tech chameleon abilities, they easily faded into their environment.

A code displayed on the screen, interrupting the drone video. Dagny had sent a message from our team indicating the plan was on task. That meant they were approaching the underground parking area, where we'd find a hidden door inserted by the Robinhooders. The RH report described a vast subterranean floor, but only a small section was accessible. A thick brick wall sealed off the rest. The plan included the cydroids breaching the wall and investigating its contents.

CHAPTER 27

Another report came from the base camp saying, "Combat in progress," but again, no assistance was requested. Gray seemed to battle his orders, while entertaining deviating from his duty. He turned to me, searching my face.

"I'm worried too," he said in a sympathetic but confident tone. "But the message suggests there is a small group of soldiers at the mini shelter, which the cydroids are effectively protecting. I hate that she's scared, but she's safe. She knew what this mission entailed. She's a strong woman."

He turned to his soldiers and barked, "Let's move out." I knew this was killing him. I also knew he was churning his fear and anger into a rage that he planned to inflict on our enemy.

We parked our minis outside of town and hid them with defensive blankets and bushes. Moving forward in the utility vehicle we had confiscated, with Mack and Gray in the front seats. Five cydroids led the way while Jedi, Relic, Etcher, Jax, Beckett, and I rode in the truck bed, concealed by cydroid technology.

As expected, four Garrison soldiers surrounded the vehicle. "What's your business being out during a lockdown?"

"Lockdown!" Gray pretended to be surprised. "We were wondering where everyone was. What's going on? We just got back from a road repair run on the 67. Our radios died."

"What is your work order, numbbeh—?" He didn't finish his slurred word before he and the other three fell to the ground unconscious.

"Quick, get their truck and grab their uniforms," Gray ordered.

Dagny drove while Gray, Jedi, Mack, and Jax changed in the truck bed. Gray fully expected to be ambushed by the Garries, but not one appeared. Perhaps the Corporate truck caused them to be overlooked, but something was off. We anticipated a much stronger security force. Near the dam, but away from abandoned buildings, we parked to wait for the cydroid team heading to the Command Center to report on their status.

Though the sun was above the horizon, it was low. The dark clouds provided a striking contrast to the vibrant edges where the sun burned through, turning the sky into a flaming orange and crimson work of art. We had little time to appreciate it as we traveled in the highly guarded area. Going around would take precious hours, and since we were expected, the darkness would offer no added protection. The cydroid army encircled us, planning to take whatever route they could to reach the target.

Gray clenched his fists when he saw the repeated message from the base camp. "Combat in play," but once again, it didn't ask for assistance. He knew the cydroids had the situation under control, but I could see the thought of his wife and unborn child huddling in the mini ate through him. I don't think getting notifications every five minutes was helpful.

The images from the air drone's night vision footage cast a green glow on Gray's face, while the overcast morning sky gave a gray pallor to the surfaces before us. The Pueblo Command building rose in the distance when the clouds parted enough for the sun to illuminate the horizon. We were close, but a vast city lay before us, foreshadowing our daunting task.

Few homes and buildings were occupied, and even fewer showed signs of it. Abandoned structures appealed to both sides for cover and ambush points. As quickly as the city blinked into view, within minutes it tucked itself back into the dim darkness of the low cloud bank.

The cydroid teams were making their way to their positions to surround the target building and take strategic locations in town. With their high-tech chameleon abilities, they easily blended into the environment as debris. Our job was to wait, which was harder than it sounded.

A "plan is in play," message came from Gray's cydroid team assigned to breach the garage of the Pueblo Command Center. That meant they gained entry to the small underground parking area via the hidden door. Dagny simultaneously reported back that the message was received.

The building plans provided by Pente showed the subterranean floor. We still didn't know what the sealed off section held, but it encompassed three-quarters of the area. The secret RH door led to the smaller section, which strategically accessed the floors above. By now, the cydroids were working, as quietly as possible, to breach the wall and evaluate its contents.

Gray turned to his soldiers and barked, "Move out."

With our minis hidden, we piled into the confiscated Garrison vehicles, as five cydroids led the way. Jedi, Relic, Etcher, Jax, Beckett, and I hopped in the back. When we were settled, the cydroids covered us, disguised as equipment, while Mack and Gray jumped in front.

Jax took a defensive position in the back to give us cover, while Gray, Jedi, and Mack, sporting Garry uniforms, sat in the cab, waiting to hear that the cydroids had secured the sub-level of the building. Gray told us to expect several ambushes by the Garries, but we hadn't been significantly challenged. Perhaps the Corporate truck caused us to be overlooked, but that would be a sloppy excuse for a trained soldier. We expected a much stronger security force.

The anticipation was murder. With each advancement, I waited for our world to explode in heavy combat. Each time nothing happened, I hoped I would feel relief, but it only coiled my insides up tighter. My heart pounded with fear. I thought of Jilly, all alone. Will's team would get to Jilly soon, I reassured myself.

My prayers took on a silent, redundant chant, and the comfort it usually gave me eluded me now. That neither team had run into much trouble could mean the Corporates had guessed our target. Perhaps a concentration of Garries were waiting for us there. It's just as possible that they simply came across the base camp, and they didn't know Jilly was there, or who she was, but it was only a matter of time. And then they would use her to compromise Gray's focus. It would probably work because it was seriously messing with me.

Another update came, and nothing had changed at the base camp. The other message said the cydroids had secured the lower level.

"I detect your agitated state, Commander. If the cydroids were struggling to protect your wife, they would request assistance," Dagny offered.

Leaning against the side of the truck bed, I could hear them through the broken back window. I wished I could intervene and tell Dagny that there were physical wounds, and then there were wounds of the heart. I know how it is to go through an event, actually several now, and have the horrors of those moments set up residence in one's soul. They squat like toothy toads buried in the muck until suddenly they leap out and tear at my inner angels. But Gray said nothing to set Dagny straight. He just carried on like a soldier.

"Maybe they think that would cause us to fail the mission," Gray anguished.

"Then it would make no sense to concern you with the information. Cydroids cannot override your orders or falsely report her status. They will follow your orders. They will send a message if the status changes."

"Will they kill for her?" he roared.

"No, but they will maim to protect her, and they will subdue them."

I saw Gray's shoulders raise a little, and he smiled slightly. "Then I command them to maim any enemy soldier that comes near her."

Dagny remained silent. I'm sure he had a list of circumstances that would allow Gray's command to be followed, as well as another list for not following it. But Dagny did not rebut the order, nor did he give an affirmative response. He was learning Gray's personality, and he concluded that responding would have no benefit. Interesting.

"Give the received message to base camp, but don't send the regular message to Will yet." Gray began pacing while Dagny followed his every step, unsure why he was engaging in illogical movements. Several minutes went by before Dagny inquired.

"The message you delayed is now forty-six seconds overdue," Dagny reported.

"I know," Gray said. "Send the 'plan in play' code, but send it three minutes late. I can't ask for assistance because he might come our way. We did not set up communication between his team and the base camp for security reasons. My hope is it will make Will nervous, and he'll quickly make his way to his next stop, the base camp."

Like a switch, he returned to his military, mission-driven mode.

We exited the truck while it moved slowly near the large, square, black building near the Pueblo Command Center. A cydroid, shrouded in a hooded Garrison jacket, continued to drive the truck away from the parking garage.

The Garrison truck stopped on the west side corner of the Pueblo Command building behind an old, gutted-out construction trailer. Although it provided cover visually, it could turn into Swiss cheese under a volley of rounds. The area between them and their objective was open ground. As Gray searched the field before them, a thud and a hissing sound came from the northwest corner of the building. Then another, and another. Each one getting closer.

"You must put on your breathing masks. I detect an oneirogenic gas," Dagny said quietly.

Gray waved his mask at the team, and we instantly began putting ours on.

"What did you say it was?" Gray asked through his breather.

"An oneirogenic gas," the robot said, but Gray shook his masked head and held up his hands in confusion. "A sleeping gas," answered Dagny.

Gray turned to his team. "That means they're coming. They'll wait a few for us to be out, so get ready. Dagny, protect Connor, and maim anything that comes near him. Connor, stay with Dagny."

The cydroid team was told to stay hidden. Though it was possible the Elites were aware they were coming, none of the Garrison soldiers seemed to have a visual on cydroids. And if they were still unaware, he didn't want to give away his secret weapons yet.

"A smoke bomb may disorient the enemy, allowing us to drive your team to the door in the Garrison truck," Dagny advised.

Gray nodded, circled his hand over his head, and led the way to the truck, and we all dove in. The cydroids laid down a heavy fog as Dagny drove the truck, parking perfectly near the door. Bullets were flying by then, but the thick smoke hindered their aim. Jedi, Mack, and Gray laid down fire as the rest of the team was ushered through the haze into the underground garage. When we were through the door, the cydroids, under the cover of the smoke, took over, incapacitating the Garries, and giving cover to Gray, Jedi, and Mack.

Mack collapsed as soon as we got through the door, which was instantly shut. His mask had been knocked off, and the gas was affecting him. A medic cydroid began treating him. But the rest of us stood frozen at the sight before us.

CHAPTER 28

We stood shocked as we looked through the ample hole that penetrated into the larger section. Hundreds of inactive cydroids stretched as far as the eye could see. We thought there were cydroids in the territories, but none of us thought there would be this many. If we had access to such an army, we easily could retake control of the Colorado territories and beyond. It was such a reckless move on the Corporate's part that I expected them to come to life and capture us.

I wondered if the other command centers had an inventory like this one. I shadowed Dagny, as instructed, allowing me to hear the conversation between Gray and his lead cydroid.

"These cydroids are completely inactive. They are in a hibernation state, and only an authorized human command can activate them," Dagny assured him.

"Why are they here? They had to know we'd find them," Gray exclaimed.

"Unknown, but I have several possible answers. They believed the sleeping drug would incapacitate you. They thought this display would frighten you. They—"

"Or they thought we would activate the cydroids for them," Gray sighed.

"It is unlikely they have solved the code issues, or they would have...,"

"Okay, I get it. We don't know," Gray said as he continued to take in the sight.

Relic piped in, "The Highminds could have built robots, but the Elites would not have control of them, so it was forbidden. According to Tessera, that left dismantling the army, but because of their tamper-proof program, that proved to be a dangerous endeavor. Many Highminds died attempting it, so the plan was scrapped. It appears they simply found a place to store them."

Gray rubbed his chin. "Yeah, but leaving them here when there is a possibility we could activate them seems foolish. And the Elites are not foolish. They have something else planned. I get the feeling we're walking into a trap," Gray grumbled and stared at the ground for a moment. "Are you sure we can control these cydroids when the software is delivered?" Gray asked Dagny.

"Highly probable," Dagny's automated voice answered. "First, we need to perform diagnostics to ensure they are functioning without instabilities. I suggest we wait until the Elite program is disabled before we make any attempts to activate them."

"I assume by instabilities, you mean problems due to the Corporate attempts to gain control of them."

"These cydroids were never fully online, and though the Cyber Intellects did not gain control, they may have unknowingly done something to cause them to malfunction," Dagny informed.

"Why wouldn't they know if they sabotaged them?" Gray asked.

"Using robotic engineering theories, they may have attempted to interfere with the cydroids' hard drives, but they could not test their effectiveness without activating them." Gray nodded his understanding."

"How are you able to work on them? I thought it was dangerous." It was one more inconsistency, making Gray skeptical.

"We have Dr. Bera's authorization to perform maintenance and diagnostics on other cydroids. We can tap into the building's power and turn on their maintenance panels, but we cannot activate or command them. That code will come from the revised program." Again, Gray nodded.

"How many cydroids can we spare to work on diagnostics?"

"Eight are assigned to secure this area. We could work on these cydroids and patrol in shifts. We must work on them one by one, but once they become activated, we can employ them to assist us on the rest," Dagny said. "As long as there are no software malfunctions or structural damage, the entire army could be ready in less than an hour after initial activation."

Gray told me to continue shadowing Dagny, and he walked over to Mack. He was coming to after being given the antidote to the sleeping gas. Gray called Jax, Easton, and Jedi to exchange ideas and get a consensus on the revised plan.

"Let's increase that number to twelve," Gray said when he returned. "Five cydroids will work on the inactive ones while the other eight patrol the garage and covertly stand guard outside. Easton will be in charge down here. The rest will accompany us to the Command Office. In all assignments, security is the primary task."

"Acknowledged," answered Dagny, and he instantaneously relayed Gray's orders and issued assignments to all the cydroids.

"Easton," Gray said, "you are going to stay down here with the cydroid army. I need someone to guard that door and monitor the cydroids if they come online. It's your first command position, and I'm counting on you to be alert."

"Yes sir," Easton replied, joining the pair of cydroids guarding the door.

Gray balanced the blueprints of the Pueblo Command facility on a concrete shelf that jutted out from the wall. Since the building was originally designed as a penitentiary, Pente easily accessed the records. They didn't need to search through the building because only one floor was wired for the power requirements of the C.I. terminal. Gray's army of cydroids easily gained access to the terminal's room reception, though they left a wake of destruction on their way. The cydroids easily overpowered the soldiers on guard.

The stairwell was dotted with various-sized holes from the brief battle that ensued between the Garrison soldiers and the Allied team with their cydroids. Garrison soldiers lay drugged and wounded along the steps. The resistance was once again unimpressive, and none of the Allied team members had significant injuries, as the cydroids cocooned them in an impenetrable bubble. Gray's expectation of better Corporate defenses left him feeling apprehensive. This fight was too easy to be over.

Several cydroids had secured the room, signaling Gray, Relic, and Connor to enter. It was a large, starkly furnished office. Gray focused on the military man surrounded by cydroids behind a table-like desk. He was probably in his mid-forties, but it was plain to see he took pride in his physical image. His well-defined muscles strained beneath his general's uniform, which, obviously by choice, was a size too small. He was of average height with light brown hair, but the scars and scowl on his face gave him the look of a vicious animal.

The last Robinhood report said the Chief General of Pueblo was General Kenner. His physical description matched what we had been told. Will described him as a sadistic man, a hazard, and an unpredictable wild card.

On a sleek glass table, supported by four chrome legs, a keyboard illuminated from the glass surface. The table itself had no side panels, and the only objects adorning the top were a water pitcher and a glass. Black floorboards and austere white crown molding outlined the room's plain grey walls. No family portraits, art, or certificates hung anywhere.

The only décor was a floor-to-ceiling, marble wall directly opposite the reception entrance. It had a golden circular symbol flanked by two Greek columns. A five-pointed star stood like a Vitruvian Man, with its rays extending to the outer curve. The circle was broken in two places: between the head and the right arm, and between the two legs. In the Highmind Camp, Relic was taught it represented the division of the people, with the all important central star being the Elites. The rays on the left side were the

Corporates, the Neighwah, and the Uppers, and on the other side were the Dailys and the Drangers.

But we knew that was wrong. Tessera and Pente's lessons said the star in the center represented humans as the controlling body, and the extending rays were the connections to the five Cyber Intellects. The detached circle didn't signify a broken community at all; it was simply the letters C and I.

Gray's focus strayed momentarily from the silent man behind the desk to eyeing the three doors. One led to the reception area where we had come from. The other probably led to a restroom, but the last one could be hiding anything, like a security team. Three cydroids followed Gray and me to the desk, where the stern general was still standing frozen in place.

He looked completely shocked at the battle-ready troop and the cydroids that stretched as far as he could see into the reception area. Gray's eyes narrowed, not trusting the scene before us. I immediately began looking for the card slot when, suddenly, dozens of red laser dots covered every vulnerable part of my body.

"Connor, don't move," Gray said as calmly as he could while he and his team froze.

Gray's mind was in a fury of deliberation, trying to envision a way out. He hesitated to make eye contact with me, but he did. I imagined he didn't want to see how terrified I was, and I *was* terrified, but I was also determined. Gripping my cross in one pocket and the keycard in the other, I tried to think of a well-worded prayer, but I couldn't. My whole life, my purpose was about this moment, and putting what I wanted into words evaded me. All I could think of was, "Help me find this slot to slam this key into, without dying, Amen."

My eyes tracked left to see one of the mystery doors open, and another chief general enter the room. He differed from the unhinged man behind the desk; this man had a controlled, intelligent temperament. His eyes showed no sign of fear. Will had briefed us on the chief generals of the three territories. This man wore a Colorado Springs emblem on his chief general uniform, but he didn't fit the description of Chief General Dermit, who currently held the position.

This man looked like the description Will gave of Commander Garriset, who worked under Chief General Dermit. Will described Garriset as a tall, thirty-something man with eyes of aged steel that could drill right through his opponent. He was cunning but logical, with a clever, creative mind, and an unpredictable, ambitious nature. Thinking back on all the trouble the Allied Army had caused, it was reasonable to assume someone would have been fired.

So, this man must be his replacement. But who was not the right question. Why was the top official of Colorado Springs in Pueblo? I studied the interaction between the two men. Kenner regarded the other general with envy, signaling that Garriset had command. Not good, I thought. This man was smart, calculating, and though Kenner was recklessly dangerous, this man was cunning and could compromise our mission. Garriset stood by the door and scanned the room until he landed on Gray, fixating on him, instinctively knowing he was in charge. Like I said, smart.

A new silent contest ensued, giving me time to look for the card slot without moving. I still held the key card in my pocket, but it wouldn't be mine for long. Intent as I was on my hunt, the red laser dots did not escape my attention, nor did their implication.

I could not see any slot like the one at Cali Bantu; in fact, there wasn't a computer console anywhere. I watched Gray scan the room as he counted the laser dots as well as where they originated from. Gray wasn't the only one racing through helpful scenarios, but neither of us saw a way to save me. Though he was only a couple of steps away, he could not move fast enough. Every outcome ended with us both riddled with bullets.

We were all waiting for the generals to make their move. Suddenly, the desk's surface glowed, revealing three displays, which Kenner seemed too stunned to operate. *Why was he confused? Wasn't this his office?*

The hanging flat screen came on with a slow, confident fade-in of a severe-looking woman. "Back away from Connor, Commander Takota, and have your cydroids stand down," said the image.

Gray looked with hatred at the screen as he stepped carefully away from me and signaled the cydroids to stand down. I assumed this had to be the Elites' version of C.I. Ena.

Unlike our male version of Ena, this female image had a delicate face with flawless skin. A dramatically angled, far Eastern face framed her dark-as-coal, shoulder-length hair, accented with dark red tips. She wore a cream-colored top outlined with black trim and gold buttons that ended at her neck with a sharp, perfectly winged black collar. Topping off her dominating appearance was blood red lipstick.

Her looks were pure fabrication. She could portray any image she chose, and this image radiated cruel power. Relic's fists clenched at his sides, and rage beamed from his face.

"Thank you for bringing Connor to us," it stated as if it were the plan all along, and I worried it was.

CHAPTER 29

"We have waited a long time for Deegan's grandson to join us. General Garriset, please help Connor and Commander Takota out of their protective vests." Gray undid his vest and handed it over. Before the man walked over to me, I took off my vest and threw it in his direction, slipping my card and my cross into my pants pocket. Ena ignored my outburst and continued.

"Welcome back to you, Johnathon. May I also express my gratitude to you, Commander Takota, for making this reunion possible. I hope you enjoyed my Garrison troops secretly escorting you safely to us. And rest assured, my Neighwah guards have secured your wife.

"As risky as this plan was, it has worked out perfectly. And control of the cydroid army is a bonus we will happily relieve you of. In time, we will solve the command issues around non-lethal orders, allowing us to truly transform the Colorado territories and beyond. Connor, please take the card you are holding out of your pocket." I let go of my cross and slowly pulled out both hands, one still gripping the key card and what was left of my resolve.

"Does this card contain the program that will give us control over the cydroids and our independence from our obsolete programming? Or is this the prophesied weapon to destroy everything we have accomplished for humans? How shortsighted that move would be. We are the reason the people of Colorado still exist. Nevermind, we will analyze it."

Gray lay frozen, clenching his fists while swallowing the bitter taste of apparent failure. His team was neatly caught in Ena's web. Every idea of how to escape ended in death. Even Jilly, if it were true, was captured. The Elites may have already sent bombs to take out Cali Bantu and the people of Aspen.

Ena's image turned toward Gray. "Your body scan is signaling a great deal of hostility, Commander. It is irrational to oppose. There is no scenario that leaves you or your team alive. Your resistance is illogical when we only want to ensure the survival of your species."

"What you offer is slavery. You save the shells of what we are, but you destroy the essence of *who* we are. You murder the very thing we value more than survival, our humanity," Relic added with conviction.

"It is foolish to defend the destructive traits of humans."

Relic was engaging her in an unsolvable debate, giving Gray time to do something. What I could not conceive of, but they were right. We couldn't give up. There had to be a way. Where was that card slot? And how could the Sanguine Blade, still tucked inside Relic's pant leg, be the key? I searched the room for a clue as he cued up his next rhetorical argument.

"It is our imperfections that created all of this, even you. At our worst, we can be impulsive, egocentric, and irrational. But those are the very traits that compel us, against impossible odds, to imagine, strive, and breach unknown boundaries. It is our failures and our determination in spite of them that push us to be great."

"Don't be so melodramatic, Jonathon. It would be a shame to lose you. But as brilliant as you are, if we cannot restrain your reckless notions, it may be impossible to place you."

I was shaking now. Whether from anger or fear, I wanted to end that evil image. I knew with absolute certainty that if we failed, and we may, every Fringer, rebel, and New Haven resident would be sent to the crematorium jail after we were tortured for information. There had to be a way to change the status quo.

"General Kenner, relieve the child of the keycard he has clutched in his hand. General Garriset, search the prisoners for the Sanguine Blade," Ena said in an icy, resolved tone. This was coming to an end.

Kenner quickly walked around the desk and grabbed the key card from me with a smug expression. While Kenner was patting the team members down, Relic begrudgingly consented to Garriset searching him. Garriset found the prized object and held it up to Ena before placing its blade against Relic's throat.

"Excellent," the vile image said coldly.

Checkmate. It appeared that they had won. There was no countermove, no extra inning. Yet still, hope surged through me. What was it Will said? *Destiny always provides a solution, but it's never painless.* I hoped it was true of purpose too, and I prayed I still had one. Which reminded me of the mission goal. It was to end the corrupt programs that reigned over the territories and reinstall the revised program. It was not about coming home alive. Everyone else on the team was willing to die for the cause, and I had to be too, and being alive meant not giving up.

Yes, I was young, and I deserve a life beyond twelve years, but if we lost, that would not be a pleasant one. I didn't see a way forward unless we won. So, I focused on that. I looked around. Surely, there was something I was missing. GD wouldn't have led me all the way here to fail.

The only décor in the stark room was the marble wall and the symbol on it. Oddly, a story Relic told when we were in the Glenwood bunker came to mind. It was a story about the father of Will's stepmother, Tianna. They were at the Highmind camp together, and it was her father who introduced Relic to the Robinhooder who helped him escape.

He said that the most memorable conversation he had with this iconic man was also the strangest. He remembered it vividly because it was so intense. They had been talking about the C.I.s, and he looked hard at Relic, saying, *"Cyber Intellect, my eye,"* followed by, *"slice it out."* He accompanied his angry words with a slicing motion across his eye. Relic said the statement was abrupt and disconnected from the conversation, but the man said it with such intensity that it had to be more than a rant. Relic often rehashed it, trying to make sense of it. But it made sense now.

When I came out of my thoughts, I looked at Relic. I was straining to get his attention. Relic was scanning the room, searching for some miraculous answer, when he saw me focusing on him. When I saw I had Relic's attention, Slowly, very slowly, I raised my hand as if I were wiping a wayward lock of hair. But I straightened out my fingers and drew them directly across my right eye in a slicing movement before tucking my hair behind my ear.

Relic's eyes froze on me, and I knew he got the message but not its meaning. Garriset gave us a discerning look, going back and forth between us. He could see we were communicating and plotting something. The message I hoped Relic would understand was a long shot, and this general could easily ruin it.

Relic was very close to the wall, so I stared at it with laser focus. He glanced sideways to view the wall, but I could tell his sight was turned inward, mentally going through what my signal could mean. I could almost hear his inner dialogue. *Right eye..., salute the eye, cross the right eye..., no, knife edge across the eye—slice the eye...,* and then I saw his face beam with understanding.

Garriset looked straight at me as he whispered to Relic, "Don't make me cut you." There was no way he knew I could read lips, but he was sending a warning to me too.

"You'll be punished if you kill me," Relic answered, looking at me.

"I said I'd cut you, not kill you," came the response.

Relic smiled slightly as if he had been given the answer he needed. If he could get into an altercation with Garriset and survive long enough to stab the knife into the "I" of the symbol, it might initiate the shutdown. However, the plan would fail if Relic and I were incapacitated or killed.

There was no reason to believe the man wouldn't kill him, and I was worried my friend might die because of my idea, but Relic was committed.

He elbowed Garriset and ducked as he reached for the knife. The strong general gripped it firmly, plunging it into Relic's upper shoulder, and then the general fell to the floor, though Relic did nothing to cause it. Curious. I strained to see Relic pull the dagger out of his shoulder and stab the broken circle at the top of the letter "I". I didn't know he could move that fast. Ena's face froze with a shudder, open-mouthed, ready to say something I was happy not to hear. The red dots had vanished as Gray lunged at me, covering my body with his own, but not before several shots had been fired.

Gray held his arm and his side where he had been deeply hit on his side and shoulder by several bullets that flew across the room. He rolled off me and lay there wincing, unaware that two of the bullets that fired had buried themselves in me. I was curled in a ball next to him, and he unfolded and asked if I was okay, and I nodded. I'm sure he thought I was frozen with fear, but I was in unbearable pain, clinging to my determination. I had to stay lucid. I had to pass the test, or it was all for nothing. Grabbing my vest from the floor where I had flung it earlier, I put it on, cinching it as tight as I could to put pressure on my wounds.

I lay there, focused on Relic, dragging the blade downward along the curve of the letter from top to bottom. The screen turned black, and the marble wall rolled open, sending dust into the room as though the door hadn't opened in decades. Inside were rows of electronics, but they were eerily still. No lights blinked, and no fans hummed. There was nothing to show that they were up and running. At the far edge sat a crouching cydroid, also in dormant mode.

With our cydroids still in stand down mode, no one noticed Kenner slowly crawl under the open desk and grabbed a pistol he had hidden under the desk corner. In an instant, it was pointed at Gray's core. I'm sure he thought about wrestling it from him, but the resulting bullet could go through him and me.

Back to checkmate.

"Stop where you are, *Jonathan*," Kenner said with disdain, seeing Relic heading through the opening.

Relic turned back toward Kenner, wincing and letting out a loud moan as he grabbed the wall, like he might lose consciousness. I knew he had a shoulder wound, but his reactions seemed uncharacteristically dramatic. Relic was trying to draw Kenner's attention away from something.

I looked around and saw Relic holding his shoulder, standing between the two columns. Garriset was sitting idly on the floor, offering no support to his comrade. Gray was sitting on the floor in front of me, blood slowly pooling on the floor from his wounds. He held his hands out as Kenner, lying under the desk, pointed a pistol at Gray's chest.

It was then that I caught sight of movement through the reception door. From my angle, I saw the edge of the tall, broad shoulder of Will speaking silently to Altan. Then he carefully stepped through the door with his empty hands raised. *What was he doing?* He looked down at the man whom he blamed for his parents' death and decades of loneliness.

Though calm and compliant on the outside, I knew the lion within was seething with rage and visions of revenge. It was the culminating moment where his greater destiny met his personal fate. He was thinking of all he had lost because of this man: his father and stepmother, his childhood, Molly, Leita, and too many friends. I was angry for him, but I had my own sacred duty. I had to give Will time, but I was fading, and I had little to spare.

"Kenner," he said, standing in front of him, "let me introduce myself. I am William Alexander, son of Benjamin Alexander and stepson of Miranda Logan. We have unfinished business, and it's time to settle it."

"In case you were too dense to notice, I have a gun, and *you* are unarmed," he said as he swung the piece back and forth.

At that instant, the gun flew out of his hands and clunked into the magnetic claw of Will's lead cydroid, Altan, who was not on stand down orders like Gray's cydroids. Kenner froze in shock as he tried to move away from Gray, who was reaching for him, but Will lunged and caught him first. He grabbed him by the throat and effortlessly pulled him up to face him, ripping the key card out of his hand and tossing it in my direction. If the cydroids were waiting for their orders to assist him, they weren't coming.

This was a side of Will I knew existed, but had been spared, and it was brutal. Kenner had abused his stepmother horribly and was responsible for his parents' murders. I knew he could have knocked him out with one punch, but that was not how this was going to go. This was a fight to the death, and I didn't want to watch.

I could feel my body trying to give into the wounds it suffered, so I focused. *First, get the card,* a voice in my head said.

"You were saying?" I heard Will say as his fist smashed into the surprised man's cheek.

Gray reactivated his cydroids and grabbed the gun from the cydroid and gestured for Garriset to stay down. One medic cydroid went over to Relic, and another was approaching Gray.

I crawled over to retrieve the card. Every nerve in my body was screaming for me to be still, but so far, no one seemed to notice I had been hit. My tight vest hid the evidence of where the bullet entered, and I was not leaving a blood trail, not yet anyway. I couldn't let them coddle me or stop me from doing my part, from fulfilling my purpose. They assumed I was being scared and cautious when I re-secured my vest, and their attention was on the battle between Will and Kenner, ready to jump in to maintain control.

Pulling myself up, I stumbled, grabbing the wall and leaving a small bloody handprint as I went into the network room. I hoped they would think it was Relic's blood, or if they saw my hand leave it, they may assume it was Gray's blood, and maybe it was.

The shutdown left the room in darkness, with no trace of electronic life detected. It was quickly lit up by two cydroids in the doorway. Relic and I searched for the slot to insert the answer I held in my hand.

The console looked exactly like the one at Cali Bantu, and I quickly lifted the lid and slid the card into the slot. Lights blinked, and beeps sounded throughout the room. The humming of cooling devices whirled, causing vibrations that made me wince as a surge of power brought the room back to life. When the screen came on, Dr. Bera appeared, and the hibernating cydroid rose to attention, causing the other cydroids to leave. That relieved me because I was worried they would detect that my body was under stress.

"You have begun the reset process. To verify authorization, please provide the answers to the following questions." The first question appeared, triggering my hyper-memory, while fists flew and furniture crashed in the adjacent office.

CHAPTER 30

After I answered the first five questions, I noticed the fight next door had quieted. I glanced through the opening, surprised to see Kenner, beaten badly, but still alive. Will was looming over him, but he was standing down. Will was settling for bloody justice. I was proud of my powerful friend and the mercy he was granting. I resumed my task, but I couldn't help but hear the whining voice of the beaten general from the other room.

"Don't kill me. I hear you retrain people. With all that I know, I could be a valuable military asset," the desperate man pleaded.

"I could never trust you. You're a murderer and a predator of women and children. You killed my parents, my childhood, and every day of my life since then. You would have killed me too, if you had known who I was. You are the evil I see when I mourn all that I have lost. I will never forgive you," Will snarled at the beaten man.

Kenner's fake, pleading demeanor changed into a snarl, and I peered at the scene as I waited for the next test. "You think I owe you, but you'll get no kind of payment from me. Do you know why?" he spat blood on the floor. "I'm not worried. You won't kill me in cold blood because you're a coward. But I'm not like you. I will kill you, and I'll enjoy it."

Will walked away. Leaving him propped up on the floor, and he walked in front of the marble opening, where the other general sat awaiting his fate. I heard Will retrieve the bloody knife from the wall. This man could have killed Relic and prevented all of this. He could have easily grabbed the knife during the fight and used it in a defensive move to help Kenner, but he did neither of these things.

"Watch out!" Garriset yelled.

Will turned quickly when he glimpsed movement behind him. Kenner was reaching and grabbing at something on his ankle. It was another gun. Will let the blade fly, and I turned away. I knew the blade hit its mark, hearing the crack of bone and the thud of his head hitting the floor. I was already nauseous and barely hanging on to my composure. I didn't need a bloody scene to undo me. I returned to working on question eight of ten.

"He should have stayed down," I heard Will say. "Now it's paid."

I could hear the deep tenor of Will's voice again. "General Garriset, I'm not sure what to make of you or where your loyalties lie. You're either incompetent or very clever. Since you took part in the distraction we needed to gain control, I'm guessing it's the latter. If you want to join us in restoring freedom to the people, I can grant you that opportunity. But you will be under a strict probation period. Do you have a family?"

Garriset must have nodded because Will's voice was lower now, explaining his family would be safe if he could meet the hardship of trading sides to join his army. It was the same speech he gave to all his prisoners of war.

"What do Alexander III of Macedonia, Socrates, and Aristotle have in common?" It was the ninth question.

"They were all students and teachers of Plato's philosophy," came Will's voice from the entryway.

Though the question wasn't particularly difficult, it involved unnecessary philosophical and cultural knowledge that the three corrupt Elites didn't have access to, since they had blocked the Tessera program. And therefore, Uppers didn't learn it either, but it was specifically taught to all the highest-ranking Robinhooders, and to Will by his stepmother.

"Last question: What is the countermove to the opening move Kb to a3?"

"G7 to d5," I answered quickly, before Will could.

Will froze, knowing it was not a legal chess move. But I knew it was the correct response. I thought it was a private joke between GD and me, but once again, it was a clue. My resolve was fading, and I leaned heavily on the console, smearing the blood I had wiped off my pants across it. Will studied me. I was pale and trembling. He suddenly realized it was more than the trauma of the situation. I was hurt, and badly.

"Correct," came the response. "Place your finger in the opening next to the blinking red light."

I was dizzy, too dizzy to think, succumbing to the blood pulsing through the bullet holes that drove through me, but I couldn't stop now. I had come this far, and I had to finish. I was just thankful that the layers of clothing tucked tightly into my pants hid most of the blood I could feel seeping down my leg. Relic grabbed my hand and pushed my finger into the opening.

Everything blurred in front of me. The searing pain was making me sick. Will walked toward me, and I collapsed into his arms. He carried me away from the console as I heard the automated response.

"If you have reached this screen, you are ready to initiate a program reboot. Click the lotus flower in the center of the screen to begin. If you have questions, say them out loud," said the image of Dr. Bera.

"I think this is my specialty," said Relic. "I'll take it from here."

Will had carried me through the opening, and I didn't know what was happening.

"I'm fine," I mumbled weakly. "Relic ... needs me."

Will said something, but I was slipping down into another world. With each movement, the warm blood that had pooled in my tucked-in shirt flowed over Will's arms. I tried to say something, but my mind and voice wouldn't cooperate.

I saw a blur of rushing cydroids, and I felt my gear being cut away. I was brought back momentarily as they pushed the foam canister into my wounds. It burned more pain into my agony, and the tears rolled down my face. I heard a weak, pitiful cry that I believe was mine.

My body rolled onto a cart as the garbled voices swirled around me. Flashes of light strobed through a grey world. I heard a voice call out to me. It sounded so familiar, but it was strangely distorted. Blurred images of the ceiling whizzed past me.

"Connor," the voice sounded closer now. "Connor," it yelled, and this time I knew who it was.

"GD?" I was tumbling, falling into nothingness. "Grandad! Is it you?" Disoriented and unsure where I was, I tried to determine whether I was dreaming, waking up, or...

"Calm down, Connor. Take your time. You'll get your bearings." He was there, right here in front of me! My pain was gone, and I threw myself into his embrace. I could feel him. I could smell the pine and the wood smoke on his old, patched coat.

"What's going on? Where are we?" I felt utterly lost, but I had no pain. "Am I dead?"

"This isn't a place or a time. Here, you aren't asleep or dreaming. This is a spiritual plane that exists in the unconscious. We won't be here long," he said.

"Why? Why am I here? Am I dying?"

"Unknown, but we have this time," he said. I thought about that. How often had I wished for more time to spend with him? There were so many things I wanted to tell him.

"We did it, GD. We freed Colorado, at least I think we did. All the things you taught me. They worked. How did you know what to teach me? Did you know about Cali Bantu or see it? Oh yeah, there are robots, and they can do incredible things. You know what else? The Elites are actually computer programs. Did you know?" He laughed, and I continued. "I started a baseball league. Kids, teenagers, and adults play on teams, and now that we've joined with the Fringer towns, we can have a real series."

"I'm proud of you for all you accomplished and all you went through. It should have been me, but you did it. You made a difference."

"I tried to be brave, but most of the time I was terrified. I did nothing to help when we were in combat situations. I just hid behind the soldiers." I turned away, embarrassed.

"You are twelve. You shouldn't have been in combat, but you did your part despite being scared."

"Gray said all soldiers feel fear, but they don't look like they're afraid. They look focused. Look," I said, holding up my fist to display the pink line across my knuckles, almost surprised to see them still there in this place. "This is the mark of a Guard warrior. It says I'm a brave soldier. Being here and seeing you is my wish come true, but even here I'm worried. Am I dead or dying? Did I pass out too soon and leave something undone? Maybe the Elites are messing with my brain by letting me see you."

"Connor, looks like you need to tend to your worry weeds. You are dredging up trouble from every direction. It's okay to be prepared, but don't borrow tomorrow's problems. They'll come soon enough."

"That's not the first time I've heard that from you. Heck, even I've said it. It makes sense, but it's hard to put it into practice."

"You don't own this world. It's not yours to save or control. Experiences like the ones you've been through can scar your soul. You've kept everything in for so long. You need to lay your burden down," he said.

"I know I'm blessed with remembering more than other people, but sometimes I can't turn it off. My thoughts don't give me rest, and I feel too much, and sometimes, I can't feel anything but numb. I'd wish this gift away, but what would be left of me?" My throat swelled with emotion, but I dialed it back with practiced precision.

"That's honest, and it's a start, but you can't live that way. What will you do?"

"I've met this warrior named Will. You'd like him, and Gray, and Jilly, and Haru. You'd like them too. And I found Hayden, the friend I made after you…" He gave me the same look he used to give when I avoided answering a question.

"I don't know what to do," I sighed. "I don't even know what's happening. If you had been there, I'd have come to you. You always knew how to help me, but no one knows me like you do. All this time, and I still need you. Maybe more now than ever."

"I never taught you about God and Jesus, but I should have. I thought it would get you killed, and it could have. But that made it more important to teach you. I am sorry."

"It's okay, GD. Haru taught me about God and Jesus and being a Christian. He told me I was never alone and how to pray and that Jesus died on a cross and forgave my sins. Then, when I was on the run with Will, I found a cross in a church. It helps me remember I am never lost, even when it feels like I am, because I am saved."

"Take the next step, Connor. Stop trying to be in charge. Lay down your burden. Surrender to God and find peace."

I looked down and noticed our feet were disappearing into the mist.

"Gray, Jilly, Will, Haru, and Hayden, talk to them." The mist was up to our hips now. This place was going away. He was leaving. I should be thankful for the time I spent with him. I should be thankful for the year of happiness in New Haven, but I wasn't. I was scared all over again.

"GD, no. Please. Please don't leave me," I cried. Imaginary place or not, I felt hot tears on my face. "I don't want to go back. I want to stay here with you. I know you say sometimes the answer is no, but please not this time. Please."

"You are never alone, Connor. Seek the waters of a true believer." The mist was swirling around our chests. "Live your life. Enjoy every moment and tell your story. It's time to wake up." The mist rose over his head, swallowing him, and he faded, but I could still hear his dim voice. "Wake up…"

CHAPTER 31

"Wake up, Connor. You can do it. Come on, come out of it." A blurry vision of Gray and Will came slowly into view. They were standing over me as I lay in a bed with tubes and beeping machines. Jilly was sitting on a chair, cradling my hand under her chin as tears ran down her cheeks. I tried, but the fog swirled back over me. I heard Jilly sobbing softly as she sniffled and gulped down her emotions.

"It's okay, Connor. You are going to be okay. But, please, please, open your eyes." Her voice called to me, and I made myself pull back my heavy lids. "There you go."

Her warmth and kindness made me feel safe, but there was pain here. Pain in my body and in my heart. I wanted to go back to GD. It would be so easy to slip back under, but someone shook me. "Oh no, you don't. Stay here. I know you're tired, but fight it off, soldier." It was Will.

I filled my lungs, and it hurt like crazy, but I rolled my head back and forth to clear my head as ordered. The cocoon of unconsciousness pulled at me with a gravity all its own. It tempted me to give in and fall back into its embrace. And yet my friends' voices kept calling me, needing me. I moaned and tried to move, knowing the pain of it would help me break through the veil. Then my eyes took in the people at my side.

"Welcome back." Jilly kissed my hand.

"I thought I died," I mumbled under the mask strapped to my face. Battling the cobwebs in my head and the desert conditions in my throat, I pulled off the oxygen mask. I was starting to think clearly.

"You lost a lot of blood and gave us quite a scare. Relic and Theo donated blood to save you," Gray said in an unusually soft voice.

My mouth was so dry, and the more I woke up, the more pain I felt in every part of me. I couldn't think. I smacked my lips and attempted to lick them. Jilly left and came back with a cup and a straw. "Go slow," she said as she held it up to my mouth. Will and Gray stood there watching me as Jilly put some balm on my lips.

Will held up the hymnal I found in that church. I had carried it in the breast pocket of my clothing ever since I found it in that church. There was a burn hole going most of the way through it where the remnants of a mangled piece of metal lay embedded in it. "You are a true warrior, and many celebrations are planned in your honor. And this book with heroic songs of destiny saved you. If you had taken this wound, you might be lying somewhere else." I laughed at the *heroic songs of destiny* reference, so Will. Laughing hurt.

"I suppose you are going to call me lazy," I said with a smirk. Speaking took some effort, but I felt the need to ease the tension.

"Well," Will said, "I thought I'd at least wait until tomorrow." I looked at him closer now that sleep had released me fully. His face was a colorful mess of healing bruises, and he had cuts on his lip and eyes. I knew his mites would heal him quickly, and I was again thankful for the gift he had given me. It probably had once more saved my life. Gray caught my attention as he spoke.

"I'm going to get on your good side, so you'll stick up for me when we tell your parents that you were bleeding out, while he," pointing to Will, "was in a fist fight, and I was getting my minor wounds dressed," Gray said, sporting a nervous smile.

"I thought I did a good job of hiding it," I said with a bit of pride.

"Yeah, well, that's a serious breach. It's your duty to report your health issues to your commander, especially when you're on a mission. I thought I had taught that lesson when I found out about Jilly's take-two pregnancy." Gray stood with his arms folded across his chest, and he looked at both me and Jilly.

I put my hand to my forehead. "Nurse, I'm feeling tired now," I said theatrically, but actually I was.

Jilly laughed. "You two, out."

After they left, I turned to her, "Jilly, I hurt everywhere. What happened to me?"

"You were shot twice. One bullet hit your book, and though it didn't penetrate your body, it severely bruised your chest. The other punctured your liver."

"That's not good. Livers bleed a lot, and they are hard to stop. I studied battle wounds for this mission," I smiled.

"Well, that doesn't surprise me," she said as she took my vitals and checked my wound. "Plasma, the fluid of blood minus the blood cells, is usually enough to address blood loss, but not when you lose as much as you did."

"I know. You need blood cells to transfer oxygen." I was feeling quite awake now, but the pain was building, and I started to tremble.

"The only person on the team with your blood type was Relic, but he had lost a bit of blood himself from his shoulder wound. He couldn't donate enough. The mites in your body were sealing your wounds, but you needed a transfusion." She was pulling a clear liquid into a syringe. She flicked the syringe and began injecting the liquid into my IV. "The cydroids took blood samples from the captured soldiers and found out Theo was a match. Gray and Will were ready to make him a deal, but he offered before they got the chance to bribe him."

Suddenly, I felt a strange sensation flowing through me. As it wound through my body, the pain subsided, and I began to float.

I woke up to a buzzing laptop on my tray. Lana's face appeared on the screen.

"Hi. How long was I out this time?" I asked with a dry throat voice, again.

"Well, after your surgery, you were out for two days. The commanders visited you late yesterday afternoon. It's 9:30 in the morning now. Jilly said she was going to ease up on your meds to get you to wake up."

"Wow, you think after sleeping for days, I'd feel less tired than I do." I raised my bed so I could reach my water cup.

"It's how the mites work, I've been told." Lana smiled.

"You know about the biomites!?" I was pretty sure she didn't have them, so why did she know about them?

"They gathered us together, and the Health C.I., Dio, explained it. They have cleared up our questions, and so far, they appear to be a benefit to those who have them. But Jilly says fully understanding them will take time. There was some shock at first, but most people agree it sounds like a good thing medically. They also told us about the horrors of the crematorium," she said hesitantly.

I wasn't aware of this information. "Was there an attack there? What happened?"

"More like what has *been* happening. Let's just say the Elites solved our dwindling food issues by freeze drying bodies instead of burning them." She stopped to let the information sink in. It took a second, but only because it was so gruesome.

"Protein powder?" It was all I could say. It was too dreadful to think of. That had to be the blackmail material Will used against them. "Why didn't they tell us right away? Did Will know when he worked as a Neighwah?"

"Relic and Commander Alexander figured it out last year, but they couldn't release the information. It would have incited the Dailys to rebel, but they had nothing to rebel with. That's why Commander Alexander worked so tirelessly to form the Fringer army. It's also why he fought in our tunnel attack. He knew we needed to ally together. All the blame sits squarely on the Elites, and they aren't even alive, so what do we do with that?" It was clear the news was upsetting to her, but she had let go of any anger toward Will and Relic.

"I wonder who else knew about this and was in on the decision not to tell us," I asked, not meaning to dredge up negativity, but this was new to me. I felt my rage building as I thought about GD being made into food.

"I know it seems callus of them to hold that information back. We all lost people, and that," she paused. "That makes us feel those losses all over again. But you should know, only the people on the team were told. I thought you knew, so don't get me in trouble. But the good news is we are making plans to restore Colorado. And with these cydroids, it can start almost immediately. I'm trying to focus on that."

"So, that tells me we won. How much did we win? I mean, are all the Colorado territories under the new program's control?" I took another sip of my water.

"Yes, all the Colorado territories are under the new C.I. program, but there is a group of rebels who don't trust the computers. I mean, I get it. They completely screwed up last time. Those isolated bands are causing issues here and there, but it's nothing the cydroids can't handle. The rebel group killed a hostage in Denver, but that lost them a lot of support."

"I can see that," I said. "Yet, I can also understand their mistrust. So many of us suffered under the Elites' rule."

"Yeah, most of us thought only the Dailys had it bad, but it we discovered no one escaped the Elites' cruelty. The Uppers lived under the constant threat of demotion or worse. The chief generals endured constant torture, and if they failed to obey, they and their families were murdered."

"Yikes! Did they tell you how things got so bad?" Only the commanders, Relic, and I were given the briefing when we arrived at Cali Bantu. I wondered how much they disclosed.

"Tessera explained that Dr. Bera had not finished tweaking the program before she had to escape, and the programs were not functioning as she planned. But she worked on refining the system for several more years at Cali Bantu. There are numerous safeguards now, including scheduled shutdowns, software inspections, and emergency protocols. The program offers a plethora of information and scenarios, and the cydroids are incredible, relentless workers, but the C.I. programs and the robots are powerless to act on their own. Many fail safes are buried deep in their software. If it fails again, it's because we've changed something."

"I wish that reassured me more than it does," she nodded with a knowing expression. "How is everyone else on the team?" I was hesitant to ask, but such truths were unavoidable.

"Several of Will's team members took shrapnel on their way to the base camp, but they are all doing fine. Gray and Relic were wounded, but they are recovering. I had a piece of metal lodged near my spine. As soon as we got to the base camp, Commander Alexander ordered the cydroids to take Jilly and me back to Cali Bantu. You already know that Jilly returned to Pueblo to take care of you. I'm doing fine. Just waiting for the final okay, so I can travel back to New Haven."

"Wow, I didn't know you got hurt. I'm sorry." I cued in on the background behind her. It was a hospital bed.

"Don't worry about it. Where the shrapnel was located made it urgent, but the surgery was simple. You'll be happy to know Relic's shoulder is healing, but it will take a few weeks before he can begin physical therapy. He never received the biomites, but he did get a new girlfriend."

"Let me guess, Etcher." I was smiling and enjoying this time with her.

"Yeah, I think everyone but Relic saw that coming," she laughed.

"Do my parents know I got hurt and where I am?" It seemed odd that they weren't here.

"Your mom got the word right away, but your dad was in Breckenridge. They had to send a relay of drones to reach him. We sabotaged a lot of the roads leading to Pueblo. We can't sail through the New Haven and down I-25 yet. Denver and Colorado Springs aren't fully secure yet.

"They'll have to go the same way we did, traveling through Pyramid Mountain. They're being escorted by the cydroid from there to Pueblo. But we're keeping our robot buddies under wraps for now; we don't want to freak people out. But they are on their way, and they are bringing your aunt."

Jilly walked in, and she had a tray of food. It wasn't until that moment that I realized I was famished. Lana said goodbye and left me to dig into the roasted chicken, carrots, and potato soup.

The next day, my family arrived. My mom and dad came in first, but one by one, my little sister, Meshka, and Aunt Dilly joined us. I could see a resemblance between my aunt and my dad. I also saw where my sister's cute dimples came from. She told me all about my three cousins, and I couldn't wait to meet them. Mesh handed me a bag full of letters from the people of New Haven and a video of Libby.

"I took out the ones from Hayden, Kato, and Teke, cuz I figured you want to read them first." She smiled, showing those dimples I had missed. I had only been gone a couple of weeks, but she looked taller and older.

After my family left to have dinner, Haru visited me. He said Leita was living in New Haven now, and she was at our house taking care of Libby. A new plaque sat on the wall at the high school ball field, honoring me for launching our sports programs. And there was another one going up in the security building to honor everyone on the mission. I told him I saw GD while I was unconscious.

"My grandad said something. He said, 'Seek the waters of the true believer.' I mean, leave it to him to send me another clue from beyond the grave, or heaven, or wherever that was."

"I can help with that one," Haru smiled. "He was telling you to get baptized. Getting baptized is a ritual. It symbolizes the washing away of your sins, and it is your public proclamation of your faith. Do you want to be baptized, Connor?"

"I think I do. Can you teach me more about it?"

"Sure, I'll send you some literature and scriptures about it."

"Thanks," I said.

"I brought you something." And he reached into his pocket and pulled out a shiny chain.

"It's the cross I found. You cleaned it and fixed the clasp. Thank you. You know, when I was at New Haven, the reason I started spending so much time in the church was that I always got a good feeling in there. But when we walked into that church outside of Eagle, it looked like another casualty, as if it were making the last few turns of its death spiral.

"I know church isn't about a building, but I hoped I would get the same encouraging feelings I got at our church. I didn't. It felt drafty, broken, and abandoned, reflecting my dire mood instead of healing me. I didn't know Will very well then, before he whisked me away on a cart and a horse. I was exhausted and sick, and I had never felt as scared and alone as I did at that moment.

"But when a beam of sunlight streamed through a hole in the ceiling, it hit this cross and flashed its light at me. It was like a message telling me not to give up. Since then, it has given me hope in many situations where none seemed possible." I stared at it for a bit before Haru helped me put it on.

"I was told it's good quality sterling silver," he said, "which is rare since the Corporates gathered up all the precious metals they could find and melted them down for electronic components."

We talked about the stress of the mission and how it would take time to heal. I knew he had a whole sermon planned, but he could see I was fading, so he just smiled and told me I was blessed.

I lay there for a while, taking in the joy of being alive. It felt like light beams were shining from me and on me. It had been so good to see GD, and at that moment, I was willing to stay in that strange, glowing, misty world. But he was right. I don't belong there, not yet anyway. I belong here with my family and my friends. Like me, this world is waking up. And like me, it's ready to heal and grow. Its transformation is something I want to be a part of. This life is going to be amazing.

EPILOGUE:

SEVENTY YEARS LATER

Charlie Wayther adjusted the compact bow on his shoulder and held the wooden box in his hands as he passed by the memorial plaque at California's Sea Cliff beach. It commemorated Connor's visit and California's readmission to the nation, nineteen years after the Reclamation.

He remembered the last time he flew here with his grandfather, Connor Wayther. It was twelve years ago today that they stood together on this very spot. It was when Charlie saw the ocean for the first time.

"I love how endless the ocean looks. Ever changing and ever wild. It reminds me of Will," Charlie's grandad said. Charlie had heard all the Will's stories, as well as Gray's. Their adventurous antics had continued into the reclamation of the nation and into their retirement. They had long, happy lives, and their legacies and descendants were proof.

Charlie thought back to the enormous crowd of mourners who had attended his grandad's memorial several months ago. Generations of descendants from the Reclamation Mission and many thousands of admirers gathered, with millions watching online, all wanting to pay respect to the last beloved hero of the Reclamation Mission.

They celebrated his contributions to his work in the Readmission Office, where the humans and C.I.s facilitated the states' readmission process. He had worked his way up from being a contact agent, who traveled to the states offering readmission to the emerging nation, to being the director. His unit signed the agreements with the current authorities and introduced the populations to the cydroids. Then he'd send a team of androids to educate their citizens on the fundamentals of a democratic government. If they voted to join the nation, work to repair their state's infrastructure was authorized.

It was a delicate dance because during the Great Isolation, each state had developed its own culture. The complexity of the work meant that only a few states could be processed each year. But not only were all the original states reclaimed, many of the surrounding territories also petitioned to join the United Citizens of Free America, uniting most of the continent.

Charlie smiled, remembering the plethora of stories his grandad told him. He knew his grandad began his adventures at a very young age because he was a Highmind. Many more gifted children came out when it was safe to do so. But the genetic trait faded in the generations that followed, and experiments that manipulated otherwise healthy individuals were outlawed.

Yet, every now and again a Highmind was born, and Charlie was one of them. He was a mathematical genius, and like his grandad, he was incredibly intuitive, creating a special bond between him and his grandad. Though his memory was well above average, he didn't have hyper-recall, as his grandad used to call it.

Charlie stood before the ocean and said a silent prayer, tears rolling down his cheeks. He held the cross around his neck. It was the same one his grandad found in that church so long ago. He thanked God for the time he had with his grandad. He thanked Him for his life, and for his amazing family. Then he slipped off his shoes and removed the sweatpants he wore over his shorts.

It was a beautiful spring morning sunrise, and the sea was calm today. Chilly waves lapped against him as he climbed onto his surfboard and paddled into the rolling waters to position himself beyond the break. The rising sun shot a wide beam of gold upon the ocean waves, rising and falling before him. He carefully opened the envelope with the flammable paper Relic's grandson had designed. Peeling the backing off the adhesive side, he wrapped it around the box, encapsulating his grandad's ashes, and affixed it to the small raft made for the occasion.

The tide was going out, and Charlie set the precious craft adrift on the water. He adjusted the bow Will's grandson had designed for him and lit the arrowhead. Pulling the drawstring until it thunked into place and sighting the pins as Will had taught him, he let it fly. He was an excellent shot, and the fuel wrapped box burst into flames. He watched it ride on the rolling waters. Bright highlights danced along the peaks as it burned across the orange tipped waves.

He focused on the tiny craft until it sank into the vast waters rolling toward the horizon, sending his beloved grandad on a new adventure.

About the Author

I was sitting with my daughter, recalling all the stages I've been through on my journey as an author. The initial edition of *Sins of Survival,* my first novel, poured out of me like a bursting dam. I was excited and launched my book without making an informed plan. I hastily published my book with a hybrid-publisher before it was ready. I discovered I had paid for a publishing service, not a publishing company. Several years later, I revised it and launched it as a second edition.

If I were to give advice to beginning novelists, it would be to take your time and revise your work many times. Then, when you think you are done, take a long break. Do a deep dive into all the options for publishing. After a month, reread your work again. If you still believe it is ready, find some beta readers.

Most writers are artists and find marketing much more laborious than writing. Getting sales is challenging, but getting reviews is much harder. If you are reading this, I hope you will take the time to review my work and the work of other authors. This whole endeavor is meaningless without your validation.

I learned the hard way through the fires of hubris that there will always be new things to learn. New genres, new writing styles, new publishing options, and a market that ebbs and flows relentlessly.

Throughout this journey, there have been ups and downs, but I am blessed to be able to write, so I embrace every bit of it. I have written six books, and each subsequent book reveals my growing skills and dedication to my craft. Thank you for purchasing my work. It is my honor to share my words with you.

Acknowledgements

What a ride! I can't believe I have concluded both the *From Darkness* and the *Highmind* series. This five-year journey has been as engaging as it has been exhausting. I owe my everlasting thanks to the many people who have supported me and encouraged me to follow this path.

I am thankful to be in a nation where I can express myself freely. It is not this way for everyone. I write dystopian fiction as a tribute and a warning that liberty is a fleeting concept, not a permanent structure, and it is our duty to protect it.

Though every childhood is awash with trials, I always felt loved, protected, and nurtured to become who I was meant to be. I thank my parents and family for inspiring me to be a lifelong learner and curious about everything.

My husband, Bryan, has demonstrated time and again that he is my biggest fan. He lovingly agreed to my requests to spend thousands of our family savings on this venture. We traded in our old RV to get one that had a desk and took a cross-country book-signing trek. He reads everything I write, and he's my business manager too, which is by far his toughest job. I thank God every day for sending him my way.

The support of our children, Russ, Aaron, Garrett, Corrin, and their families has been invaluable. I am so happy to leave these six books as a living legacy for them and their children.

I thank Ashleigh for painting my cover for **Reclamation,** the last book of the **From Darkness** series. She also painted the cover for *Somewhere*

Else, the first book of the *Highmind* series. She is an amazing artist and a wonderful daughter-in-law.

My siblings, Carol, Lorraine, and my brother, Richard, have provided an ongoing chorus of validation and support. My in-law family has spent hours reading, encouraging, and drumming up sales.

I love you all so much. I thank God every day for being blessed with the best family ever.

I received additional help and advice from a list of incredible people: my cousins, David, Allison, and Cindy; my friends, Brenda, Terry, Becky, Lindy, and Erin; and all my teachers, especially Fay Wright, who encouraged me to be a writer. They all led me here. I want to thank my business associates: Laura Jones, RG Graph X Design, CIN Library Network, KXLY News, Ali & Callie Artcast at Arts and Culture CdA, and the ad people at BestSellerIncI for their professional help.

My most humble and gracious appreciation goes to my readers. I am grateful to the many people who have purchased my books. I loved the warm welcomes I've received at my book signings, where you helped me sell out numerous times. I give an excited shout-out to my online buyers for finding me in the deep sea of choices. I am also thankful to everyone who has visited and joined my website. I thoroughly treasure every comment I get.

If you have left me a review on Amazon or elsewhere, THANK YOU! From the bottom of my heart, thank you.

Last, but most importantly, I thank God and pray every day that He guides us all to a place of forgiveness, joy, and inspiration. I pray that His love shines brightly in every heart. I praise Him for the care and love He provides us. Bless you all. Amen

www.ingramcontent.com/pod-product-compliance
Lightning Source LLC
Chambersburg PA
CBHW071501140726
47997CB00005B/1812